McShannon's Heart
By: Jennie Marsland
ISBN: 978-1-927134-43-6

CW00340975

Bluewood Publishing Ltd
Christchurch, 8441, New Zealand
www.bluewoodpublishing.com

Also by Jennie Marsland

McShannon's Chance

For these and other exciting books, please visit:

www.BluewoodPublishing.com

# McShannon's Heart

# by

# Jennie Marsland

## *Dedication*

To my parents, who gave me roots and wings.

# CHAPTER 1

Morgan County, Georgia, 1861

"In My Father's house are many mansions. If it were not so, I would have told you…"

Rochelle McShannon closed her eyes, but she couldn't shut out the minister's words or the scent of the freshly turned earth waiting to fill her mother's grave. She couldn't connect the thought of death with a beautiful March morning like this, cloudless and bright, with new green everywhere and the wind carrying the fragrance of Morgan County's rich soil, ploughed and waiting for seed.

*But not our fields. Not this year, maybe never again.*

The spring sun warmed the black wool of her dress, sending trickles of perspiration down her back. She slipped her gloved hand into her twin brother's, felt his fingers close tightly around hers and knew he was struggling for control, too. Through the rest of the service, Chelle clung to Trey's hand, gathering her strength for the task of receiving condolences.

Most of the county was there. Sidonie McShannon had been popular with her neighbors, from the Sinclairs and the other large planters down to the hardscrabble farmers. It wasn't in her nature to look down on anyone, and she'd been good at smoothing the feathers that the less than tactful little Yorkshireman she'd married tended to ruffle. She'd possessed an easy grace that Chelle had long ago given up trying to emulate. She was too much like her father.

After Reverend Mader's final prayer the family stepped away from the grave, into the shade of a spreading pine. Their neighbors formed a line to pay their respects. Justin and Cathy Sinclair, Trey's closest friends, came first with their parents. Justin's hazel eyes usually held a gleam that meant he and Trey

1

were up to no good, but now they darkened with sadness as he gave Chelle a gentle hug.

"Twig, you look tired. Why don't you and Trey come over tomorrow afternoon for a while?"

Hearing the nickname Justin had given her at seven brought fresh tears to Chelle's eyes. She blinked them back and whispered, "Thank you. Perhaps we will, if Dad is feeling better."

She glanced at her father as Justin's parents offered their sympathies. "Bless you, Colin. Our thoughts are with you and the children." He responded with a silent handshake. He'd been moving like a machine since his wife's death, all of his usual ebullient energy gone. Chelle couldn't shake her fear that his heart had failed along with her mother's, and wouldn't recover.

Justin moved on to take her brother's hand. Trey spoke quietly to his friend. Bruises discolored his face, reminders of his fight with Nate Munroe the week before. His dark eyes burned with as much anger as grief, anger Chelle knew and shared.

*Thank God the Munroes had the sense to stay home today.*

With each day's news bringing war closer, tempers flared easily. The local boys had formed a cavalry troop in the winter and elected Justin Sinclair captain, but Trey hadn't joined them. Most people accepted Sidonie's illness as a reason, knowing Trey was needed more than ever on the farm to spare his father, but not the Munroes. The fight with Nate had been a long time coming.

As people filed past her Chelle cast covert glances down the line, looking for the one person she most wanted to see, the one neighbor whose comfort she craved. Rory McAfee had been in the church. He couldn't have left without speaking to her.

No. There he was, standing with his parents, talking to Reverend Mader. Fresh courage welled up in her at the sight of

Rory's strong-featured, clever face, a face Chelle had been seeing in her dreams for months.

With his usual negligent grace, he bowed to the minister and joined the receiving line, with his parents behind him. Chelle followed the progress of his dark head as he moved along. It seemed to take forever for him to reach her, but the heat that raced up her arm when he took her hand still caught her by surprise.

"Rory."

Her heart skipped a beat, then gave a painful little bound. Rory had been able to do that to Chelle since the first time he'd kissed her, last summer. He could make her skin burn with a look. Their attraction would have been the worst-kept secret in Morgan County if the coming conflict hadn't taken precedence.

At first glance Rory looked studious, but that was only until you noticed the gleam of deviltry in his dark gray eyes. In his perfectly-cut black suit and white ruffled shirt he looked like what he was, the son of one of the county's large planters, but the proper clothes and manners didn't hide the strength of his lean body or the recklessness beneath the civilized veneer, a hint of danger Chelle loved so much it frightened her. It took all her self-control to lower her gaze and listen demurely while he spoke, his breath tickling her ear.

"Chelle, your mother was a great lady in every way that matters. I'm so sorry for your loss."

Unable to speak, she squeezed Rory's hand and nodded. When she'd spoken to his parents and they moved off toward the line of buggies parked at the end of the churchyard, Chelle took a deep breath to steady herself. She couldn't betray her feelings until she'd talked to Rory and told him her family's plans. What happened then would depend on whether or not he loved her as he said he did, loved her enough to wait for her for years. Thinking of it hurt so much she could scarcely breathe.

It seemed like an age before the ritual ended, the churchyard emptied and the sexton's men began filling in the grave. Chelle's father stood frozen beside Trey, dwarfed by his son's lanky six-foot frame. They looked nothing alike. Chelle had inherited the McShannon blonde hair and sapphire blue eyes, but Trey was all Surette, dark-haired with eyes the color of blackstrap molasses.

"Dad, let's go home." He put an arm around his father's shoulders, gently turned him around and led him away. Before following them, Chelle lingered to toss the three miniature red roses she carried, picked from her mother's favorite potted bush, into the grave.

"Goodbye, Maman. I love you." The words sounded so inadequate. In spite of her long illness, it didn't seem possible that Maman could really be gone. Chelle turned away and didn't look back as she ran to catch up with her family.

A mile's drive took them to the farm. The buds on the azaleas Sidonie had planted in the front yard were swelling in the mild spring air. The house hadn't lost its air of repose or its charm of simple, clean lines, ivy over white-painted shingles and ample windows, but the heart of it was gone.

While her father and Trey took care of the horses Chelle set about making a lunch, hoping she could get her father to eat something. She moved around the kitchen with practiced ease. The house had been her responsibility for nearly a year.

"I'm *glad* Maman's gone," she'd said last night, when the last visitors were gone and her mother lay alone in the front room, a bouquet of ivy and cedar in her hands. The flowers she'd loved weren't blooming this early in the season. Chelle wondered if she would ever love ivy and cedar again. "I wouldn't wish her another day of lying in that bed, and I wouldn't wish any of us another day of seeing her there. She's free, and...we're free now, too. I hate myself for feeling that way, but I do."

She was young enough to wonder if her father would be shocked, but he just gave her a tight, sad smile. "Of course you feel like that, lass. Your mother wouldn't have it any other way."

Her mother's presence still lingered in the sunlit, yellow-painted kitchen, Chelle's favorite room in the house. Lace curtains blew in at the open window. The pine table with its gracefully turned legs sat on a dark green rug in the middle of the room, with the tall china cabinet in the corner behind it, filled with the family's floral-patterned cream ware. Red geraniums lined the windowsill. Ordinary as they were, Sidonie had loved the splash of color.

Chelle had the pot of soup Mrs. Hughes had dropped off that morning hot by the time her father and Trey came in. Her father rested his elbows on the table, something Chelle had rarely seen him do. Even at meals, he never sat completely still. He talked with his hands, as often as not with a knife or fork forgotten in one of them. It had been her mother who brought calm to the house. Sidonie's Cajun background gave her animation, but her own reserved nature restrained it. Trey had the same kind of contained energy.

Right now he sat rigid in his chair, his thoughts far away. As Chelle put the bowls of soup down, her fingers brushed the initials carved in the table's edge in front of her brother.

"Dad, do you remember the licking you gave Trey when he did this?"

Trey snapped out of his trance and looked down at the crudely formed letters. "I sure do. I was old enough to know better."

His father's eyes lit up for a moment. "Aye, you were nine." He glanced out the window, toying with his napkin, his gaze unseeing. "And Chelle, do you remember the licking you got that same summer for daring your brother to walk across the barn rafters with his eyes closed?"

"I certainly do. And that after he fell in a pile of straw and hardly got a bruise."

Her father tasted his soup, his eyes still on the window. On his memories. *Like beads on a string,* Chelle thought, *only now the string's broken.* He brought himself back to the moment with a sigh.

"Trey, we'd better start making plans. With the news we're getting, I'd say there's no time to waste. George Sinclair will buy the cattle, and we'll take the horses North with us." The cattle could be sold locally, but Chelle knew her father and brother wouldn't allow their prized Thoroughbreds to end up in the army. Their dream of a breeding operation would have to be put aside for now, but they wouldn't risk the lives of Trey's stallion, Flying Cloud, and Colin's three mares. "All that's left is to pack up the things we're giving away, cover everything we're leaving and board up the house and barn." He put down his spoon and held Trey's gaze. "Lad, are you sure you won't come with us?"

"Dad, we were through this again last night." Trey shrugged out of his suit jacket and ran his fingers through his unruly hair. "I don't want Chelle here any more than you do, not with what's coming. You have to go, but you know there'll be no real future for me in England. There won't be one for me here, either—not if I don't go with the rest of the boys." The anger Chelle had seen in the churchyard flashed in her brother's eyes again. "And I can't. It's suicide and I won't be a part of it. Win or lose, I won't be able to stay here. If I'm going to have to go West, I might as well start sooner as later. I'll have Cloud, and I'll get a couple of mares when I can." Anger dulled to sadness as Trey looked around the room. "We can sell this place when the war's over. The land will still be here, whatever happens."

Chelle knew he was right. Uncle Jack in Yorkshire could make room for her and her father, but he had a son of his own, with a wife and baby. There would be no room for Trey, but still, she hadn't been able to help hoping he'd come with them in the end. Now she'd be losing him, too.

*Unless I marry Rory. Then Dad and I would stay here until the war ended and Rory came home, and...*Chelle silenced the selfish thought. If she married Rory now, her father would give up his plans to return to his old home to heal, and Trey would feel that he had no choice but to join the troop and fight for a cause he didn't believe in. She couldn't be responsible for that. If Rory proposed, as she was sure he meant to, they would have to wait until the war was over.

Her father broke into her thoughts. "I'll see to the legal arrangements tomorrow. I'll sign the place over to you, lad. Whatever you get for it later will be yours to help you along. It would have been yours one day, anyway." He looked at his children with tired eyes. "I never thought this day would come so soon…not so soon. But we'll keep putting one foot in front of the other. It's all we can do."

He'd barely touched his soup. Chelle got up and put her arm around him. It felt so strange to be offering him comfort. She wasn't ready for their roles to be reversed.

"We'll manage. Dad, why don't you go upstairs and try to get some sleep?" After he left the table, she cleared his dishes away, returned to her seat and faced her brother. They'd always supported each other and watched one another's backs. She'd never needed him more than she did now.

"Trey, there's something I need to tell you."

Trey crossed his arms on the table and put on his big-brother expression. "Is it about you and Rory McAfee? I saw the way you looked at him this morning. So they're true, then, the whispers I've been hearing all spring? Justin tried to tell me, but I wouldn't listen to him."

She should have known better than to be surprised. Chelle knew she and Rory had caused some gossip, but Trey had been so busy with spring work on the farm and so distracted by torn loyalties, he'd had little time for her and her doings. He looked as if he didn't know what to make of her now.

"I don't know what you've heard. A lot of malicious gossip from Clara Hughes, probably, but it's true that Rory and I love each other. We have for months, but I didn't think it was the right time to say so, with Mother sick. I told her two weeks ago. I—I think he's going to propose, so I thought you should know."

Trey's mouth set in a stern line, giving him a fleeting resemblance to his father. "Then Rory had better show his face here and talk to Dad, before I go and pay a call on him. Do you want to marry him?"

Chelle felt herself blushing. "Yes, I do. Is that so surprising?"

Trey sighed and let his mouth relax into a grudging smile. Chelle knew how he felt. She felt the same—as if they'd both grown up overnight. "No, I suppose not. Rory's decent enough, and he isn't a womanizer, but I don't like the thought of your name being dragged through the mud over—"

"Over some dances and a few kisses…well, more than a few, maybe, but nothing has happened between us that didn't happen between you and Cathy Sinclair, or you and Clara, though what you see in that little cat is beyond me."

"You know I broke off with Clara in February. You're right. She is a little cat." Trey slumped in his chair. "It's not as if I haven't been giving folks enough to talk about myself. Chelle, you know Mother would have been pleased if I'd joined the troop. I still could. Dad would understand."

Chelle's heart squeezed as she looked at him. Trey had been doing a man's work on the farm for years now, but at eighteen his lean frame hadn't finished filling out yet and his face still showed traces of young curves. It hurt Chelle more to think of him fighting than it did Rory, who was three years older and looked it.

"Yes, Mother would have been proud. She believed in the Confederacy, but you know she didn't want to see you go to war. As for Dad, he'd understand if you joined the troop and so would I, but not if you do it for us." She reached for his hand. "Trey, Dad really wants to go home. I think he needs to. And as much as I want to marry Rory, Dad comes first."

Trey lowered his gaze and sighed. "What do you suppose Rory will think when he finds out I'm going West?"

Chelle squeezed his fingers lightly to make him look up. "He won't understand, but he doesn't have to. You have to live with yourself, Trey, not with Rory. Now let's not talk about it anymore. Today has been hard enough already. And after all, there's still a chance it won't come to war."

Trey studied her face for a moment. His expression lightened a bit at what he saw there. "A damned slim one, but you're right. We've got enough to worry about as it is."

# CHAPTER 2

Chelle turned down her lamp, pulled her quilts close against the chill of the spring night and closed her eyes, hoping sleep would come quickly. Her head buzzed with the stress of the four days since the funeral. Sorting through her mother's things, receiving good-bye calls from neighbors, packing, seeing the sadness on her father's and brother's faces as they prepared to leave the farm they both loved, had left her exhausted and empty.

She hadn't seen or heard from Rory since the funeral. The whole county knew by now that she would be leaving. His parents had paid a brief good-bye call, and it had seemed to Chelle that Mrs. McAfee was a shade cooler than usual. Could she have heard something? Was Rory simply being cautious?

The silent house seemed to reproach her, as if it knew it was about to be abandoned. Chelle turned on her side and curled up, trying to block out her sadness. Drifting on the edge of sleep, she heard a small sound like rain being driven against glass by a strong wind. But it wasn't raining. Then she heard it again. Holding her quilt around her, she rose to her knees on the bed just as a few pieces of gravel hit her window. She looked down at the lawn and saw Rory crouching by one of the azaleas, grinning up at her.

*The fool.* They needed to talk, but this wasn't the way. If her father or Trey heard him there would be the devil to pay, but it would be ten times worse if he'd been seen by anyone on the road. Clutching her quilt around her, Chelle scrambled out of bed, opened the window and beckoned him closer.

"For heaven's sake, Rory, what are you doing here? Go home before you wake the whole house."

He showed her another handful of gravel. "I'm not leaving 'til I talk to you."

She rolled her eyes, but she knew he meant it. She wasn't going to get rid of him easily. "All right, all right, I'm coming out."

Skin tingling with apprehension and another kind of tension she couldn't name, Chelle drew the curtains and pulled off her nightgown. She grabbed the first dress in her wardrobe, of navy cotton, and fumbled with the buttons. The stairs creaked under her bare feet, but no one heard her. After a breathless wait at the bottom Chelle breathed a sigh of relief, slipped outside and eased the front door shut behind her.

The cool moonlight cast crisp shadows in the empty yard, silent except for the rustling of the ivy over the door. Good, he'd had the sense to hide. Chelle knew she should be ashamed of herself, knew she was flirting with disaster, but something stronger than common sense drove her. This might be the last time she'd see Rory before leaving, and they needed to settle things between them. She wasn't afraid of him. She knew nothing would happen that she didn't want to happen. It didn't occur to her to be afraid of herself.

The ground stinging cold under her bare feet, Chelle started down the lane, looking for Rory in the shadows. When a hand covered her mouth and a strong arm wrapped around her waist, she wrenched away.

"Rory, I swear, the next time you scare me like that I'll kick you as hard as I can."

He lost his grin, but mischief still lurked in his eyes. "Sorry. I just can't resist." Rory captured her hand and held it warmly in both of his. "How's your father doing?"

Chelle shook her head. Between nerves and his nearness, it took her a moment to find her voice. "He's about the same. Rory, have you lost your senses? If Dad or Trey sees us—"

He released her hand and slipped his arm around her. "They haven't, and anyway, they wouldn't kill me."

Chelle couldn't stay as angry as she knew she should, not with Rory's arm around her. He felt so solid, so comforting. If only she could stop time, right now, and never have to leave him.

"Don't be too sure of that. Trey's in a foul mood these days. It'll be bad if they see us, but worse if Mrs. Palmer saw you turn in here."

"Mrs. Palmer? At this hour?"

"You know she stays awake half the night. Your mother would hate me for the rest of her days if she heard about this from that busybody. Where's your horse? If you put him in the barn, our stallion will raise the roof."

The devil-may-care gleam came back to Rory's eyes as he squeezed her. "He's in behind your chicken house. Cloud won't catch scent of him from there, and Mrs. Palmer's lights were out. Stop worrying, Chelle, no one saw me."

Chelle pulled away from him and glanced down the lane. She caught a glimpse of moonlight on the dark front window of the Palmer place. Rory was probably right, but she wasn't about to take any chances.

"Come with me. We can be seen from the road here."

She took his hand and led him in behind the house, following a path down to the creek that ran behind the McShannons' cow pasture. A lopsided moon hung above them, giving the dew on the grass a chilly sparkle and turning the slow-moving creek to shimmering ripples. Near the bank they came to a sorry-looking structure, made of old boards and branches, leaning against a pair of poplars.

"Come in here."

A wicked grin spread across Rory's face. "Were you expecting me?"

Chelle dropped his hand. "Idiot, this has been here for years. Trey and I and the Sinclairs used to play down here all the time. I fixed it up a bit one day this winter. I guess I was in a sentimental mood. No one will see us here."

She ducked under the low roof, with Rory right behind her. A mossy log served as a seat inside. Rory sat and pulled her onto his lap.

"I hope you're in a sentimental mood tonight."

Chelle wanted to hold on to her irritation, but it vanished, blown away by Rory's familiar spicy scent, the feel of his arms around her. She reached for his mouth and it fused to hers, harder and more demanding than ever before. This had been building between them for months. She couldn't deny him, whatever tomorrow might bring.

He shifted to taste her throat, finding the sensitive spot at the angle of her jaw. "Marry me, Chelle. I'll speak to my family and your father tomorrow. It'll work out for the best, I promise. I love you."

She heard him through a haze of passion, but a shred of reason still remained to her. It told her this was wrong. She couldn't do this to her father and Trey.

She couldn't do this to herself.

Barely able to breathe, she squirmed off Rory's lap. He swore under his breath as she took a step back and fought to find her voice. Her legs shook, ready to melt for him. She grabbed the edge of the lean-to for support, showering herself with old rust-colored pine needles.

"Rory, we can't."

His face flushed with frustration, Rory ran his hands through his hair. "You're right." He gave Chelle a ragged smile. "I just can't keep my head around you."

Pulse still racing, knees still weak, Chelle took a few deep breaths. When Rory held out his hand, she hesitated for a moment, afraid to trust herself. Finally she took it and sat beside him.

"If it weren't for this damned war—oh, for heaven's sake, you look like your mother when you lift your eyebrows like that. After what we just did, what's a swear word? And it's the right one in this case."

The old teasing gleam came back to Rory's eyes for a moment. "I'm just surprised. I've never heard you swear before."

"It isn't a habit of mine."

Rory sighed and lifted his hand to her cheek. "Chelle, I can't walk away from this fight. You know that."

"I know, and I understand, but I still think you're wrong." Chelle took his other hand and interlaced her fingers with his, struggling for words. "Rory, things are never going to be the same here again, war or no war. Why fight? Do you realize how badly outnumbered you'll be? It's a battle that can't be won."

"Can't be won? We have to win. We'll be shown no mercy if we don't." He kissed her palm. "Chelle, I want to marry you now. I want to have at least some time with you before I have to go. If your father still wants to go to England, then you can go with him and stay until I come home."

Her breath caught in her throat. This was exactly what she'd dreamed of, but would he still feel that way after she said what she had to say? Chelle said a silent prayer before she spoke.

"Rory, your parents are as strong for the Confederacy as you are, but my father isn't, and neither is Trey. He told us today he isn't going to join the troop. He's going out West. I know your mother will think me beneath you, but how will she feel about me when Trey doesn't fight?"

Rory dropped Chelle's hand, his voice an angry growl. "I don't understand him or you. If we lose, we lose everything. I know Trey has no use for Nate Munroe, but I'd fight beside the devil himself to protect my home, and Trey loves your place. I also know Justin asked him to be his first lieutenant. His best friend. If Trey can't stand by him, who can he stand by? After what he did to Nate last week, I wouldn't have pegged him for a coward."

Anger swept away the remnants of passion. Chelle stood and faced Rory with her fists clenched.

"Don't ever say that about Trey in my hearing again. You know as well as I do that he isn't a coward. He's leaving because he believes the war will be suicide. I won't apologize for my brother to you, your parents or anyone else, and I won't force you to choose between me and them."

Rory rose, eyes smoldering. Chelle realized she'd never seen him really angry. It took all her will not to turn and run. His words came out cold and cruel.

"Then you're the one who'll have to choose. If we marry and Trey goes West, he won't be part of our family. He won't be welcome in our home, and you won't write to him. There's a reason why marriage vows include forsaking all others, Chelle." He stepped out of the lean-to and stopped, framed in pale moonlight. "If you really love me, you'll do as I ask."

Before she could reply, he was gone. Chelle stumbled backwards, collapsed on the log and buried her face in her hands.

*He didn't mean it. He's angry. Give him time.*

She tried to think past her hurt, to see through Rory's eyes. He was willing to risk his life for something she felt was wrong. She was asking him to accept that, to accept her with a stigma that would alienate his parents and reflect on him, his children, his grandchildren. In a small, tightly-knit community like Morgan County, there would be no escaping the bitterness.

*Forsaking all others.* Rory was right. People made that vow for a reason. If she wanted to belong to him, why couldn't she pay the price? She loved him, didn't she?

Didn't she?

*Yes, but do I love him enough?*

Perhaps she wasn't capable of a strong love, one that could withstand challenges. Perhaps she wasn't worth waiting for.

Chelle had never known what real shame was, until now. She wished she could shrivel up and disappear, but deep inside a small voice insisted that Rory could have been kinder. He could have tried harder to put himself in her place, though he had no siblings, let alone a twin. Casting Trey off would be like casting off a part of herself.

There was no time. A week from today, she'd be leaving. She couldn't talk to Trey or her father about this. She couldn't add to her father's grief, and if she told Trey in his present mood that she'd sneaked out at night to meet Rory there'd likely be a fight—or worse, he'd join the troop for her sake. Who could she turn to? Most of her girlfriends would be as scornful as Rory when they found out that Trey was turning his back on the war. She'd have to make this decision alone.

After a few minutes, Chelle gave up trying to make sense of her whirling thoughts, stole back to the house and crept upstairs to her room. She had to wait for her hands to stop shaking before she could light the lamp and get into her nightgown. She could still taste Rory's kisses, still feel his hands on her. She hung her dress in the closet, sat on the bed and willed her heart to stop pounding.

*Even if Maman were here, I could never tell her this.* Chelle knew her parents had eloped. Her mother had found the courage to defy her Catholic family and marry a Protestant, a newly-come British immigrant. Unlike her daughter, she hadn't been afraid to follow her heart.

Sidonie's favorite silk-embroidered shawl lay on the chair beside the bed. Chelle shared her mother's love of needlework. She picked up the length of soft, cream-colored wool and stretched out on her back, hugging the fabric to her chest.

*"Maman,* what's the matter with me? If I lose Rory, I'll regret it for the rest of my life. I love him so much."

She closed her eyes and pictured her mother smiling at her, a smile full of understanding.

*"Ma petite,* real love doesn't die that easily."

Chelle held on to the vision, to the love in her mother's voice. Exhaustion taking over, she closed her eyes and let sleep claim her.

The building was full of clean, spare light. Was it a church? A school? She didn't know. She'd never been in such a place before. Chelle stood at the top of a staircase, at the end of a long hall lined with doors. Doors that compelled her, drew her in. She took a few steps, grasped the handle of the first door, felt the cool metal in her hand. Turned it and pulled.

The voices of children at play rang through the churchyard, Chelle's among them, carrying on the hot summer breeze. Then she heard Reverend Mader's voice, slow and thoughtful as always. *When I was a child I spoke as a child, I understood as a child, I thought as a child.* But she was a child no longer. With sadness weighing on her, Chelle closed the door.

She wandered further down the corridor and opened another. Hooves raised clouds of dust on the road in front the Palmer place. Justin and Rory and Nate Munroe, all the local boys were riding home in the twilight after the troop's weekly drill. Trey wasn't with them. Laughter mingled with the clatter of the horses, but Rory's face looked grim and set, his eyes troubled. Had she done that to him? No. She could never hurt Rory.

Chelle turned away. The corridor seemed even brighter now, with light streaming through the window at the far end. She reached for another door.

Her mother sat in her favorite chair in the front room at home, haloed in a soft glow of lamplight. She wore her familiar wine-colored cotton, the dress Chelle liked best because it brought out the dusky color in Sidonie's cheeks and the deep brown of her eyes.

"Maman. Oh, Maman, where have you been? I need you so much."

"I'll always be here for you, darling. Trust me, and trust your heart."

The door closed of its own accord. The light was blinding now, but somehow not painful. Chelle stood at the end of the corridor, before the window. Then there was no window, only blue sky. She was flying, soaring on bird's wings, free to go where she wished. But before she could decide where to go, darkness settled around her again.

She woke at dawn, still clutching the shawl. It smelled faintly of her mother's jasmine perfume, making the dream seem even more vivid and real.

*Trust me, and trust your heart.*

With perfect certainty, Chelle knew her only choice was not to choose at all. She pulled her writing case from her nightstand and found her pen.

*Dear Rory,*

*Please try to understand. I love you, but I can't marry you on the terms you've given me. What chance would we have for happiness? Let's wait for each other until the war is over. We'll be able to see things differently then. If we're meant to be together, it will happen.*

*Dad says that when the fighting starts, the first thing the Union will do is blockade Southern ports. Writing might not be possible, but I won't stop thinking of you while I'm away. Cathy and Justin have my uncle's address in Yorkshire, and I'm going to give them this note to give to you.*

*We're leaving next Thursday. Please don't let me go without saying goodbye. I can't bear the thought of parting with you on bad terms. Until I see you,*

*As ever*
*Chelle*

\* \* \* \*

Seagulls skimmed the harbor, their harsh voices at odds with their grace as they dipped and swirled, free as the sea breeze that carried them. Chelle took in a breath laden with the scents of salt water, tar and refuse, pungent and unfamiliar.

If the worth of a thing could be measured by the price paid for it, then freedom was precious indeed.

She'd never seen anything like New York before. She stood on the pier with her father and Trey, watching as sailors and stevedores went about their jobs, their shouts rising above the voices of other passengers saying their own farewells to family and friends. The city loomed in the background, its tall buildings creating a wall of brick and stone as cold and unforgiving as the light of the gray April morning. The scene didn't seem real.

Rory had let her go without saying goodbye. Not a word, not a note.

Through the blur of shifts and changes as they made their way North, Chelle had refused to look back. If what she and Rory had felt for each other was love, it wasn't worth regretting. Truth was truth, even if it broke her heart.

She felt miserably selfish. Everywhere along their route, people had been sober and preoccupied, preparing for what was all but certain to come. What right did she have to waste tears on a man who hadn't wanted her, when the whole country was holding its collective breath, waiting for the first shot to be fired? If Rory could have seen the factories, the thousands of people in the New York streets, perhaps he would have understood why she couldn't stay with him. The war was over before it had even begun. What would become of home, of the peaceful landscape she loved?

The McShannons had been exploring the ship, putting off the moment of parting, but the time had come when Trey had to go ashore. When they couldn't delay any longer, Chelle threw her arms around her brother. She looked into his eyes and knew that this was tearing him apart, too.

He'd be traveling West, alone, through country that could be as dangerous as any battlefield. Her childhood playmate, her best friend. Trey might be capable and strong, but in so many ways, he was still a boy. Chelle didn't want to make this harder for him, but she couldn't let him go. She hugged him closer and laid her head on his shoulder.

"Trey, come with us, at least until the war is over. You can always come back then. Please. If we can't get you on this ship, we'll wait for another one."

"It's for the best this way, Chelle." He lifted her chin and ruffled her hair. She felt him take a deep breath as he fought to control his voice. "It wouldn't be any easier to leave you and Dad after the war, and what about Cloud? He's waiting for me in that stable in Washington, remember? I'd have to sell him and that would take some time, even if I could do it, which I can't. Maman wouldn't want to see us going on like this."

Somehow, Chelle steeled herself and stepped back. She couldn't show less courage than Trey. "You've been the best brother a girl could have. Be careful. Write as soon as you get settled."

"I will. You look after yourself too. Don't worry about me, I'll be fine. And so will you." Trey hadn't spoken to her about Rory, but his silent sympathy had done wonders to help Chelle through the days since leaving home. He forced a grin. "Someday you'll be able to visit the finest breeding farm west of Kentucky. Give my regards to Uncle Jack and Aunt Caroline."

Her vision blurring with tears, Chelle watched as Trey turned and wrapped his arms around his father. "Goodbye, Dad. The two of you take care of each other. I'll write as soon as I can. You'd better get aboard."

"Aye." Colin put his hands on his son's shoulders and looked up at him with suspicious moisture in his eyes. "I'm proud of you, lad. Always have been. Remember that, and remember you're your mother's son. Goodbye."

Trey stepped away with a bleak, young smile. He looked like he couldn't speak, and Chelle knew she couldn't. How many years would pass before she saw him again? She followed her father back across the gangway. As the ship started out of the harbor, Chelle pulled her mother's shawl closer around her, stood at the rail and watched her brother's figure dwindle to a lonely gray dot at the end of the pier. The life she'd always known disappeared with him, and at the moment she didn't think she had it in her to build a new one.

# CHAPTER 3

One Month Later

Chelle looked around from the seat of Uncle Jack's cart as they drove past the woolen mill at the top of the hill and down through the village of Mallonby. The huddle of stone buildings followed the curve of the river Mallon, slate roofs glistening black from the shower that had just passed by. The sun was breaking through the clouds now, checkering the distant dales with patches of light and dark. Out there, a tracery of stone walls patterned the green. Grazing sheep showed as moving dots on the landscape. The river wound across it all, a shimmering ribbon in the sunlight.

A raw wind blew down from the open country. It didn't feel like spring. Chelle moved closer to her father and felt his arm go around her. For the first time since her mother's death, he looked something like his old self.

"I never thought I'd see this place again. What do you think of it, lass?"

Chelle huddled deeper into her jacket and shivered. She hadn't been warm since they'd left New York. They'd landed in Liverpool in a cold drizzle, then made their way North by train over a gray, sodden landscape to York, where Uncle Jack had met them. She was beginning to wonder if the sun ever shone here.

At home, the days would be bright and warm. Her mother's azaleas would be in bloom and so would the white French lilac, perfuming the air around the empty house. Chelle pushed the thought away with another shiver.

"I'll tell you when spring comes."

Her father hugged her closer. "You're your mother's daughter, Chelle. She thought it was cold in Morgan County.

21

This *is* spring. When the wind eases up in a few weeks, it'll be summer. When it turns wet and windy again, that'll be autumn. And in the winter it snows. You've never seen snow like that before." He pointed to the church coming into view as they rounded a bend. "Your grandparents are buried there, lass. I'll show you on Sunday. And over there, that's where I went to school when Mam could make me, which wasn't all that often. By the time I was twelve, I was off to the racetracks."

Uncle Jack snorted. "Aye. Too scrawny to be of much use around the forge, and too lazy to go to school."

Colin just laughed at the affectionate contempt in his brother's voice. "You've got me pegged, but I always came back here when I could. And there's the store. The Binghams still have it, don't they, Jack?"

"Aye, they do."

"And there's the Split Crow. It looks the same."

Jack looked sideways as they passed the pub with its cracked, peeling sign depicting a double-headed crow. "Aye, it hasn't changed. Harry Tate still runs it. I'm sure he'll remember you."

Most of the square stone houses were set in neighborly fashion close to the road. To Chelle, used to wood and whitewashed brick, they looked gloomy and uninviting. As they passed one small cottage, she made eye contact with a girl sitting on the doorstep. She looked to be about Chelle's age, perhaps a little younger, with a head of riotous sandy brown curls, a pert freckled face and a sullen look in her light blue eyes. Obviously pregnant, she sat with her legs tucked to one side under her gray drugget skirt, hands folded on her belly. The girl watched Chelle defiantly until she lowered her eyes..

"Who is that, Uncle?"

"That's Kendra Fulton." Jack's heavy blond brows pulled together in a frown. As big and bulky as his brother was slight and wiry, he could certainly look formidable when he chose. Chelle drew the most likely conclusion from her uncle's curt tone and didn't ask any more questions. There was no need.

Her father had told her that Jack's wife Caroline was the local midwife, so she'd probably see Kendra again.

Jack McShannon's home stood where the village proper merged with farm country. The river flowed past behind it, shaded by a short copse of trees. The house resembled all the others they'd driven by, squat and solid and, to Chelle's eyes, a little grim. Behind a wooden fence, she caught a glimpse of the stable and a whiff of smoke from the forge fire.

Jack's family waited for them inside. Aunt Caroline, a high-colored brunette, met them as they stepped into the kitchen, a surprisingly cheerful space in spite of its small windows. Copper pots and pans hung from the ceiling and a rug braided from bright rags warmed the worn oak floor. A coal fire glowed in the fireplace. A gray tabby cat left the lumpy high-backed sofa to brush around Chelle's ankles. She obliged it with a tickle behind the ears. The room smelled of fresh baking and the bundles of dried herbs hanging by the window.

Caroline stood smiling beside Jack, dwarfed by his bulk. Chelle's cousin and his wife got up from the table to join them. Brian had his father's build and his mother's coloring. His wife Jean held their dark-haired baby son in her arms.

"Now then, Rochelle, come in and welcome." Caroline enveloped Chelle in a hug, then turned to her brother-in-law. "Colin, it's been a long time. You've not changed much."

Colin swept off his cap and flashed a rakish grin. "You're a poor liar, Caroline. We're all twenty years older."

Laughing, Caroline hugged him in turn. "It's good to have you back, even at a time like this. Jack's got plenty of work for you."

Brian came forward and extended a hand. "Pleased to meet you, Uncle. And you, Rochelle." A teasing grin played across his face before he pecked her on the cheek. "The village lads will be pleased to meet you too, I'll warrant."

Jean's amber eyes lit up with a shy smile. She tossed her pale golden-brown hair and pinched Brian's arm.

"Don't mind him, Rochelle. Come along and bring your things. I'll show you your room."

Two carpetbags in hand, Chelle followed Jean through a doorway off the kitchen and up a tightly winding, narrow flight of stairs. The little white-plastered bedroom barely had space for a bed, a square bedside table and a wardrobe in one corner. Chelle dropped her bags on the bed and sat next to them.

The yellow cotton warp bedspread added a welcome splash of color to the spare, clean room, but the most attractive thing was the view of the dales from the window. Chelle had to admit that from what she'd seen so far, Yorkshire was beautiful in a wild, rugged way.

Jean opened the wardrobe doors. "There should be enough room for your dresses in here."

"Yes, plenty." Chelle fought off a spasm of longing for her room at home. "I didn't bring a lot with me."

Jean sat beside her on the bed and put a hand on her knee. Perhaps three years older than Chelle, her gaze softened with sympathy. "I'm sorry about your mother. This must all be very hard for you. So the war has already started, the papers say."

"Yes." Fort Sumter had been taken two days after Chelle and her father sailed from New York. By the time their ship had completed its stops at Boston and Halifax, the mail packet carrying the news had been several days ahead of them on its way to England. She turned away from Jean, pulled clothes from her bag and laid them on the bed. *Rory, has it started for you yet? Are you still safe? Do you have any regrets?* She smothered her own before they could show on her face. The pain was still raw whenever she thought of Rory.

With her son balanced on her hip, Jean picked up two of Chelle's dresses and hung them in the wardrobe. "These are pretty, though they'll be a little light for a while yet. You're lucky you got out in time."

"I know. You might wonder why I'm not wearing mourning, but Mother told me before she died that she wanted me to dress as I always did. She said we're only young once, and she wanted me to enjoy it. I made those dresses myself. Mother liked sewing, and so do I."

Jean wrinkled her nose as she sat again, shifting the baby in her arms. "I'm afraid I don't, but they really are lovely."

Chelle reached out to take one of the little boy's hands. His chubby fingers curled around one of hers. "This little mannie is adorable. He's a big boy for eight months. He's going to be built like his father and grandfather. He looks like Brian."

"Yes, you do, don't you, Peter?" Jean tickled her son's chin. He giggled, and another baby voice mimicked him from across the hall. Chelle look up in surprise.

"Do you have another child?"

Jean got up and handed Peter to Chelle. "Not exactly. Would you hold him for me, please?"

Jean left the room and returned with another baby in her arms, a little girl about the same age as Peter, with big gray eyes and a mop of fine auburn curls. "This is Greer Rainnie. She was born a week after Peter, and her mother died, poor mite, so I'm nursing her. Her father has a farm a mile out of the village, toward the fell."

Jean unbuttoned her dress and put Greer to her breast. Holding Peter on her lap, Chelle laid a hand on the little girl's back.

"What a shame."

"Aye, all the more so since she might as well have lost both parents." Jean shifted Greer to her other breast and brushed the baby's silky hair back from her forehead. "Her father doesn't want anything to do with her. He pays us to keep her now, and we don't know what his plans are for her once she's weaned. He can't seem to bear the sight of her."

Greer's eyelids drooped as she fell into a drowse, delicate dark lashes brushing her cheeks. A pang of longing made Chelle hold Peter closer. She'd never had much to do with babies, but little motherless Greer tugged at her heartstrings in a way she'd never experienced before.

"It's his loss, then. She's beautiful."

25

"Aye, she is. Her mother was pretty. The Rainnies – Martin and Eleanor - had been married for a year and a half when Greer was born. Martin hasn't any other family."

"So Greer has no relatives who might take her?"

Jean's fresh-colored face set in a frown. "Well, Eleanor's parents live in Carston. I suppose they might take Greer when the time comes, though I can't say I like the idea. They're getting on to be raising a baby, and they're rather set in their ways. Not that Martin would be much better, as things are. He's become a bit rough since Eleanor passed on. It's a pity for Greer that she has her mother's eyes. I think that's what he can't stand. Otherwise, the child is his spit and image. There's Caroline calling. Lunch must be ready."

For the rest of the day, as she got acquainted with the family and listened to her father and Jack rehash old family stories, Chelle couldn't get Greer's story off her mind. When she went to bed, she lay listening to the small sounds coming from the room across the hall as Jean settled the babies for the night.

Chelle thought of Ellen Bascomb at home, Clara Hughes' older sister. Ellen had been married to Luke Bascomb for less than a year when she'd died giving birth last winter, two days before her nineteenth birthday. Her baby had died less than a week later.

Chelle had flirted mildly with Luke at one time, before his engagement. His blond good looks and easy humor had attracted more than one girl, but before leaving home, she'd heard Justin say that one of his biggest challenges in leading the troop was keeping Luke from inflicting casualties before the enemy could. He'd become surly and aggressive, but she knew that he hadn't left his son's side in the few days the baby lived.

Martin Rainnie suffered badly by comparison, but a heartless man wouldn't grieve so deeply for his wife. Chelle tried to picture a man with little Greer's coloring, a masculine version of her square jaw, and bitter eyes – what color were they? Before she could form an image of Greer's father in her mind, she fell asleep.

## CHAPTER 4

After her long journey and her night in a strange bed, Chelle woke full of aches and kinks. Once the breakfast dishes were done, she decided to limber herself up with a long walk. The view she'd seen from her bedroom window beckoned.

She set off along the road that led out of the village into farm country. The leaf buds were just beginning to swell, and the fell reared up before her, swathed in tender green. The rough wind coming down from the high country pulled strands of hair from Chelle's braid and whipped them around her face. She re-tied her thick blue cloak and walked faster to warm herself. An early morning shower had given way to sunshine, and the breeze didn't nip as keenly as it had the previous day.

The village disappeared behind a low hill. Chelle found herself in the middle of a sunny expanse of short, rough grass, intermingled with darker patches of heather. Rocks showed through the thin soil here and there. The air was alive with birdsong and the slightly sour smell of awakening earth.

The track crossed the river at a shallow ford, with stepping stones conveniently placed for crossing. On the other side, it soon dwindled to a walking trail. Chelle strolled along, feeling like she was walking on the roof of the world, until she reached the point where she could see over the end of the fell. Her breath caught from more than exertion.

She'd never seen anything like it. Chelle felt herself shrink to nothingness as she took it in. She sat high above miles of moorland that extended as far as she could see, empty except for the occasional farmhouse and sheep in the stone-walled pastures. A village similar to Mallonby showed in the middle of it all, a huddle of dark buildings dwarfed by distance.

This was where her father had grown up. Chelle's mind still clung to the familiar landscape she'd left behind, but underneath that homesick longing she responded to her new surroundings so strongly tears came to her eyes. She could only describe what she felt as a sense of homecoming.

She sat still with the feeling for half an hour, until she started to cramp with cold. A queer feeling of regret came over her as she started back along the track. Since leaving home, she'd envied Trey moving into untamed country. Now, she'd found a bit of it for herself.

In no hurry to get home, Chelle followed an alluring side path that looked as if it led around the jutting bulk of the fell to the open plain below. She followed the sound of sheep bleating, came to the top of a rise and found a flock grazing below her. One ewe stood alone near a patch of brambles, nosing at something hidden inside.

A weak bleat told her what the 'something' must be. She hurried down the slope and, as she expected, found a young lamb caught by its fleece in the bramble's thorns, nearly exhausted from struggling.

"You've got yourself in a fine mess, haven't you?" Chelle didn't relish the thought of getting her hands in among those thorns, but she didn't see much help for it. After a quick glance around, she wrapped one hand in her cloak and started pulling the branches away from the lamb's fleece.

In spite of the protection, the thorns reached through to her skin. The lamb didn't help. Not as exhausted as Chelle had thought, as soon as she freed it from one clinging branch it struggled and got caught by another. By the time she lifted it out of the bush, she'd earned a couple of nasty scratches and mislaid her temper.

As she bent to set the lamb on its feet, a dog's bark startled her. Still crouching, Chelle spun around and faced a grizzled black and white Border Collie, standing a few feet away with its teeth bared and hackles raised. Luckily, the dog's owner stood close by. Her heart in her throat, Chelle released the lamb and slowly raised her gaze from a pair of heavy boots to eyes the color of a stormy sea.

"Come, Gyp." The dog returned to the man's side at the curt command. Hands in his pockets, he watched Chelle straighten up. She felt herself blushing under his cool stare.

He'd be as tall as Trey, perhaps an inch or two taller, but with his bulk he didn't look it. He reminded her of Charlie Bascomb at home, broad in the shoulders, thick in the legs and torso, but the resemblance stopped with his build. Charlie was quiet and easy-going, always wearing a smile, but there was nothing approachable about this man with his lowering brows, grim mouth and slightly freckled face. His features, along with his rusty hair, told Chelle who he must be.

"Hello. I'm Chelle McShannon. You must be Martin Rainnie."

The Collie stood braced beside his master, the fur still standing up on the back of his neck. Mr. Rainnie looked no more welcoming. He spoke as curtly as he had to his dog.

"Aye. What are you doin' out here?"

It seemed Jean had done the man a favor by saying little about him, or perhaps Dales farmers were usually rude. Chelle lifted her chin and showed him her bleeding hand.

"That's obvious enough, isn't it? That lamb's fleece was caught in this bush. I freed it."

Mr. Rainnie looked her up and down with those cold gray-green eyes, then softened his tone and made an effort to curb his broad Yorkshire. Perhaps he'd recalled that his daughter was living with her family.

"So you're Jack's niece. I didn't know you'd arrived yet."

"We arrived yesterday." Chelle fished a clean handkerchief from her skirt pocket and wrapped it around her scratched hand while she fumbled for something to say. "I've been out for a walk to the end of the fell. The view is lovely."

His tenacious-looking mouth twisted in a sardonic grin as he stepped closer. "Aye, but it's not very sustainin'. Not much but sheep will grow up here. This is Carswen fell, and the village down below is Carston."

Chelle took in his well-worn clothes and large, work-roughened hands. Martin Rainnie's face showed the effects of wind and weather, but she thought the lines around his mouth and eyes came from bitterness. He looked like he could do with more sleep and less of the whiskey she smelled on him. With the breeze plucking at the sleeves of his faded canvas jacket, he seemed as much a natural part of the landscape as the sheep and the moorland grass, and just as rugged.

"I thought as much. Dad mentioned it, so I came out for a walk to see it for myself. I was on my way back when I decided to follow this trail and heard the lamb."

He shrugged and stuck his hands back in his pockets. "You could have spared yourself the trouble. This is my flock, and I check on 'em every day. You'd best get home and look to those scratches." With that, he strode past her toward the sheep, his dog at his heels.

Chelle watched him go, his shoulders high, his broad back stiff with annoyance. Because she'd rescued one of his silly sheep? She turned on her heel and started back toward the village, muttering under her breath.

"I'm sorry for your daughter, Mr. Rainnie. As for me, the next time I find one of your animals in trouble, I'll be leaving it alone."

When she entered the forge yard, she found her father working by himself. Chelle slipped into the house and tended to her hand, then came back out to talk to him. He set aside the hinge he was repairing, wiped his hands on a rag and sat on the kitchen step.

"Did you enjoy your walk, lass?"

"Yes, most of it. Where are Uncle Jack and Brian?"

"Off doing a job on one of the farms."

Chelle sat beside him. In spite of weeks spent traveling, she thought her father already looked less tired than when they left home. Coming back here had been good for him. It was worth it to her for that alone.

"I walked out to the end of the fell. It's beautiful."

31

It did her heart good to see him smile. "I'm glad you think so. I loved our land at home, Chelle, for the sake of your mother and you children. But here – I love this place just for itself."

"I think I will too, Dad. There's something about it that almost makes me feel like I've seen it before."

Colin's blue eyes turned thoughtful. "Perhaps you have. My mother would have believed that."

With all the stories he'd told about his family, Chelle had never heard him say such a thing before. It made her shiver.

"Why?"

"Well, Mam was one of those people who seemed to know things before she was told. Jack and I knew better than to even think about lying to her. She said her mother had the Sight, and I think she might have had a touch of it herself. Maybe you do, too, and that's why things here seem familiar."

Chelle sidled a little closer to him, grateful for his warmth. The dales might be lovely to look at, but spring in the North of England certainly took getting used to, as did the idea of having what her father called 'the Sight.' Another shiver ran through her at the memory of her dream the night she'd quarreled with Rory. It still seemed so clear and real.

"Really? I can't remember anything ever happening to make you think that."

Colin shrugged. "Nor can I. Anyhow, I'm glad you appreciate the place, lass." He took her hand and squeezed it. "You and Trey, you're quite a mixture, you know. Scottish and Irish and French. All movers."

Chelle gave him a quick, amused sideways glance. "Like you?"

"Aye, it's in the blood, though circumstance has played its part, too. My father's family came here from Scotland after the Highland clearances, with nothing but the clothes on their back and the tools of their trade. Mam's people came to Yorkshire from Armagh after her father got involved in the troubles in Ireland. And Sidonie's people ended up in Louisiana after they were expelled from their homes in Nova Scotia. Now you and I have been chased back here again." He held Chelle's gaze, and she saw grief pass in his eyes like a cloud across a clear sky. Jaw set, he shook it off. "Wherever they landed our people always survived, and so will we. I'm content. My only regret is that I never brought your mother here. I wish she could have seen it."

"So do I." Chelle knew her mother would have loved it here, except for the climate. The place would have appealed to her poetic streak. "She wouldn't have appreciated the weather, though."

"That's for sure and certain." Her father glanced at her scratched hand. "What happened to you?"

"I found a lamb caught in a bramble bush. Then Martin Rainnie found me. He scratched almost as hard as the brambles. I don't envy poor little Greer her father."

"You look like you'll survive. I remember Martin as a young lad. He would have been six or seven when I left. I'd taken a fall in a race and was home for a few weeks that summer, and I'd see him now and again in the village. He used to loiter around Connor Larkin's harness shop and listen to Connor play the fiddle, and then he started teachin' Martin his notes."

Chelle tried to picture a fiddle in Martin Rainnie's big hands and failed. "Really? I can't imagine him having any interest in music. He didn't seem like the kind of man who'd have much use for anything that impractical."

"He did back then, any road. I remember Connor saying what a quick learner Martin was." Her father shook his head. "I don't know whether he kept it up or not, but he had talent. Jack says he's been hard on himself since losing his wife."

"Jean said the same thing. He could certainly stand to learn some manners. He was so standoffish and rude he made me feel guilty for rescuing his silly sheep."

Colin stood and gave her a teasing grin. "Ruffled your feathers, did he? Don't be too hard on him, lass. He's got his troubles. Now I'd best get back to work before Jack and Brian get home and find me idling."

Back in the kitchen, Aunt Caroline was in the middle of dinner preparations while Jean sat at the table, trying to soothe her fussy son. Greer lay asleep in the family cradle nearby. Chelle looked down at her and saw the resemblance to Mr. Rainnie stamped on her little face.

How could he turn his back on Greer when she was so obviously his own flesh and blood? Unable to fathom it, Chelle put on an apron and started peeling potatoes for Caroline.

\* \* \* \*

Martin Rainnie leaned into the cow's side and felt his irritation drain away as his hands took up the familiar, calming rhythm of milking. He wasn't sure why, but the McShannon girl had set his teeth on edge. Probably just because he'd come upon her without warning.

She had the look of her family, for sure and certain, but her slender, shapely height was her own. Her father would likely have a time with her. Headstrong, Martin guessed, with a fine-featured prettiness that would turn the lads' heads.

He'd seen more than a strong will in those sapphire eyes. The girl was unhappy, which wasn't surprising. The whole village knew Colin McShannon had decided to come home after losing his wife. Martin had even heard some idle speculation as to what Colin's daughter would be like. New young, single women didn't move into the district every day.

Now that he'd seen her, Martin had to admit that gossip hadn't come close to the reality, though she wasn't his type. He'd always preferred dark girls, like Eleanor, with her ebony hair and sweet gray eyes, her body generously curved where the McShannon lass was tall and lissome…Martin closed his eyes, remembered the feel of Eleanor's curves under his hands. Then his gut clenched at the memory of her labor, her screams, her blood. The same memories that assailed him whenever he thought of Greer.

Eleanor's daughter deserved better. She deserved to be raised by people who could look at her without flinching. Right now, she got everything she needed from the McShannons, but she'd be weaned by summer's end. Before then, Martin would have to find a place for Greer to grow up. A place where she'd get the affection he couldn't give her.

Martin knew people gossiped about him turning his back on his daughter, but if he wasn't going to raise her it was best he stay away. The less confusion in the child's life, the better.

*And in your own.* Martin ignored the taunting whispers of his conscience, finished milking and took the full pails to the cellar. As he poured the rich, creamy milk into enamel pans to separate, Gyp came to the door and looked hopefully down the stairs.

"Aye, lad, I'll save some for you." He left a cup of milk in the bottom of one pail, returned to the byre and poured it into two dented tin bowls, one for the cats and the other for the dog. The cats would clean up after Gyp if he left any behind, but Martin had never seen the old lad take more than his share.

He ran a hand over the dogs' back as he drank his milk. Time to be bringing on a young Collie while Gyp could still help train it, but after nine years of working together, Martin hated the thought.

"I don't like to think of you growin' old, Gyp. We'll wait another year, perhaps."

Martin worked his way through the rest of the barn chores, then turned his thoughts toward supper. The house faced the byre across the cobbled yard, both structures built of the unyielding local stone that made light of two hundred years of weather. The years hadn't left much more of a mark inside. Eleanor had liked the place as it was, and Martin felt no need to change the familiar surroundings of his youth. He washed his hands, lit the lamp and kindled a coal fire in the range. Once it was hot, he pulled a few smoked sausage links from a hook in the rafters, tossed them into a skillet and put some potatoes on to boil.

The first floor of the house consisted of one large room, with the range, pantry and table at one end and the hearth at the other, taking up the whole wall. Martin lit a fire there, too and ate his supper beside it, sitting in the threadbare armchair that knew all his kinks. Afterwards he moved to the table and tried to read the newspaper he'd picked up at the store that morning, but found he couldn't concentrate. His gaze wandered to the fiddle and bow hanging on a peg near the door.

He hadn't played since losing Eleanor, hadn't wanted to. It reminded him too much of the dances where he used to play, of the swirl of Eleanor's long dark hair as he spun her around, of all that life no longer held. But tonight, for some reason, his fingers itched for it.

Martin took the fiddle down, returned to his chair by the hearth and plucked the strings. They were badly out of tune, but hadn't lost their vibrancy. He coaxed them back to their proper pitches and drew the bow across them. They sang in response.

Disconnected notes formed an improvised melody that gathered pace until it swept along like the wind off the fell, full of anger and frustration. It stabbed at Martin's heart until he had to stop playing. Fighting for self-control, he hung the fiddle and bow back on their peg.

He took a bottle and a glass from the pantry cupboard. He'd acquired a taste for Scotch during the few months he'd spent in London years ago. This wasn't the finest, but it was more than good enough for a plain farmer like him, and it would help him sleep for a few hours. He poured a generous shot and downed it quickly, wanting the burn to erase the pain his foolishness had dredged up.

When it didn't, a black rage swept over him, sudden and familiar. "Damn it, you should have known better!" The next thing he knew, he'd hurled his glass across the room to shatter against the door of the pantry cupboard.

"Bloody good on you, stupid sod. You're pathetic." Cursing, he swept up the fragments, blew out the lamp and went to bed.

## CHAPTER 5

On her first Sunday in Yorkshire, Chelle sat beside her father in the dark, drafty stone church, remembering how many times they'd sweltered in the heat through services at home. The Mallonby parson's sermon was shorter and more to the point than Reverend Mader's rather rambling affairs, but before it ended she fell into watching the people around her instead of focusing on the service.

Most Mallonby people worked at the textile mill. They stood out from the farming families and business owners because of their pale complexions and general air of exhaustion. The hard, adult faces of the children reminded Chelle of some of the hardscrabble farmers' children at home. Innocence was a luxury they couldn't afford. She noticed one girl of fourteen or fifteen with her thumb and two fingers missing from her right hand, winced and looked away before she could be caught staring.

She didn't see Martin Rainnie or Kendra Fulton. Chelle supposed Kendra wouldn't feel very welcome, and she doubted if the chip on Mr. Rainnie's shoulder would fit through a church door.

After the service Jack and his family headed home, while her father took Chelle to the far end of the churchyard to see her grandparents' graves, which he had never seen himself. One lichen-encrusted white slab stood between them.

*Robert McShannon, died May 4, 1850. Eileen, beloved wife, died Nov. 6, 1851.* Her father squatted down and pulled a newly sprouted thistle away from the granite.

"You would have liked them, Chelle. Mam loved to dance as much as you do, and Dad...Jack's Dad alive again, except for his gambling streak. I'm the one who inherited that."

Their neighbors in Morgan County would have agreed. He'd bested them all at poker at one time or another. Chelle knew a lucky streak at the racetrack had given her father the money to emigrate, though he'd never told her the whole story. She suspected there was a reason for that.

"I'm sure I would have. I almost feel like I did know them. You made sure of that."

"I tried to, lass."

The last of the congregation were just leaving the church. A group of boys passed the cemetery, their broad Yorkshire intelligible enough for Chelle to catch the punch line of a very crude joke. She blushed, and her father glared at the boys until they quickened their pace.

"They're a rough crowd, the mill hands, but they have to be."

Chelle recalled the old young faces she'd seen in church. "I suppose so."

"Aye. They don't take them in at seven like they did when I was young, but there's plenty that start at eleven or twelve. Twelve hours a day, stinking heat and grease and a din fit for hell, for a pittance of a wage. Well, like I told George Sinclair once, the South doesn't have a corner on slavery."

As they were leaving the cemetery, a small iron-fenced plot caught Chelle's attention. It contained seven graves, all of children between twelve and fifteen, with different surnames. Her father stopped beside her.

"They had accidents at the mill. I thank God I've a trade."

"I thank God you have one, too. Who owns the mill?"

"It changed hands about ten years ago. Jack told me the owner's name last night…Phillip Westlake. He lives just across from the mill."

Chelle remembered the house, a once-modest brick Georgian made imposing by graceful additions on either side. Mr. Westlake lived well off Mallonby's labor, but how could he live with himself?

Her father read her thoughts. "The mill here's no worse than most of them, lass. Now, with the cotton supply from home cut off by the Union blockade, there'll be places a lot worse off than Mallonby."

"I know." Chelle looked back at the mill hands' plot as they left the cemetery. Later, when she sat down to Aunt Caroline's Sunday dinner, she counted her blessings doubly – that Mallonby's mill hands made woolens, not cottons, and that she wasn't one of them.

* * * *

The chill winds died down, as Colin said they would. Chelle welcomed the change. At home, the seasons slid into each other seamlessly; here, the distinctions were sharper.

The dales began to bloom, enticing Chelle out for long walks. She still ached with grief for her mother, but when she sat alone in the fragrant stillness of some hollow in the grass, listening to the hum of life around her, the ache lost its bitterness. She'd done enough grieving over the past year. Now she was healing. It shamed her, but she couldn't deny it.

It still hurt to think of Rory, but Chelle valued the bit of worldly wisdom he'd taught her. She might not know what love was, but at least now she knew what it wasn't. If she sometimes felt as if it didn't exist at all, no one had ever told her wisdom came easily.

Her father was healing, too. Jack didn't always have enough work for him, so he'd cast his net a little further and found work with one or two of the local landholders who owned racing Thoroughbreds. There was nothing he enjoyed more than working with fast horses.

He was away the morning Chelle washed her hair and went out to sit on the kitchen step with Greer while it dried. With the baby settled comfortably on her lap, she gratefully closed her eyes and turned her face up to the warm sun. Spring had arrived at last.

The jangle of trace chains brought her back to earth. She opened her eyes to see Martin Rainnie leading two Clydesdale mares into the yard, his Collie trotting beside him. She saw him stiffen as he noticed his daughter in her arms, then he walked by her without a word and tied his horses to the hitching post. Jack and Brian came out of the stable to greet him.

"Now then, Martin."

"Mornin', Jack, Brian. These two need doin' again."

In spite of his gruffness and his broad Yorkshire, there was something pleasing in Mr. Rainnie's voice. Deep, but not too deep, its tone varied in a way that made Chelle think perhaps he really was musical. Jack gave one of the mares a friendly slap on the neck, loosed her from the hitching post and backed her into the middle of the yard.

"Aye. You first then, Tessa."

Brian stoked the forge and blew the fire to white heat with the bellows while Jack pulled the shoes from Tessa's plate-sized hooves. Mr. Rainnie held the mare's halter and kept his back to Chelle. She couldn't help thinking that he resembled his horses. Massive but in proportion, without the quickness and agility of a man with Rory's lighter build, but graceful in his own way. Like her father and brother, Chelle had always preferred Thoroughbreds, but she didn't doubt that a lot of women would find Mr. Rainnie attractive.

The dog seemed to remember her. Tail wagging shyly, he took a couple of steps toward her, then trotted up when Chelle held out her hand.

"Hello, Gyp. You trust me when I'm not near your sheep, do you?" He sniffed her fingers, then settled down on the cobbles at her feet. Mr. Rainnie made a restless movement, but he didn't call Gyp back.

Brian broke the silence. "Have you started shearing yet, Martin?"

"Nay, not yet. Next week, likely, if I can get help. That mightn't be easy this year. I ran into John Watson, Westlake's agent, this morning at the store, and he told me Westlake's dropping his price for wool. Market's all upset because of the mess overseas, he says. It's hard to pay shearers when the fleece is worth a pittance."

Brian took a red-hot shoe and pressed it briefly to the mare's hoof. The reek of burning horn filled the air as Jack began trimming the hoof, using the blackened imprint as a guide.

"It wouldn't surprise me if that sharper has got himself into some kind of a scrape with his business concerns in London, a scrape as needs cash to get out of."

Mr. Rainnie shrugged. "Perhaps. I'm thinkin' that he's gettin' on, and his daughter would no doubt rather be in London. His wife's spent all her time there for years, any road. He hasn't any sons, so he may be gettin' ready to close up shop here." His eyes flickered toward Chelle, the merest tell-tale glance before he looked away again. "Westlake knows most of us farmers can't afford to look elsewhere for buyers, so he can drop his price if he pleases. Well, I won't starve with the farm to feed me, whether he buys my fleeces or not."

The men talked sheep and crops while they shod Tessa and the other mare, Neely. When she thought Greer had been in the sun long enough, Chelle took her inside. Not once had Mr. Rainnie glanced her way if he could help it, but she felt his gaze on her back as she went in.

Perhaps he wasn't quite as indifferent to Greer as he seemed. Or had he been watching *her*? If so, she'd just as soon he turned his eyes elsewhere. At his best Mr. Rainnie would not have been Chelle's type, and now, he was what old Hiram Dawson at home would have called "plain hell". She shook off the feeling of those green eyes on her, took Greer to Jean and started for the village to run an errand for her aunt.

A waft of fragrance welcomed her when she stepped into the Binghams' shop – a blend of mint, spices, soap and tobacco that reminded her of the mercantile at home. Here, candy jars lined the front window to entice passersby, while a row of bags and barrels along the back wall held the usual staples. Behind the counter, Mrs. Bingham looked up from her newspaper.

"Now then, Miss McShannon, what can I do for you?" Mallonby people hadn't quite decided how to speak to Chelle yet. They weren't sure where she fit in their social order, but most of them chose to be polite.

"Aunt Caroline needs some sugar. Five pounds, please."

As she paid for her purchase Kendra Fulton walked in, followed by two men Chelle had never seen. One looked to be about Brian's age, good-looking in his way, if you liked an arrogant swagger, auburn hair and hazel eyes. The other was much older. Mrs. Bingham leaned on the counter, pursed her lips and glared at Kendra.

"Mam wants a dozen eggs, please, Mrs. Bingham."

Mrs. Bingham waited until Kendra handed over her money, slapped her change on the counter without speaking and stepped out back to get the eggs. The young man who'd come in behind Kendra stood there with a blatantly suggestive smirk on his face. Chelle felt her own face burning. Without saying a word, he made her fingers itch to slap him.

The other man picked up a newspaper and studied it while he waited his turn. When Mrs. Bingham returned Kendra took her eggs, glanced sideways at the younger man and hurried out, forgetting her change. He reached to pick it up, but Chelle covered it with her hand.

"Don't trouble yourself. I'll return it to her. I know where she lives."

The smirk didn't leave his face. "As you wish, Miss." Chelle threw him a scornful look as she picked up the coins, gave the older man another glare, took her sugar and walked out.

She overtook Kendra just before she reached her cottage. The girl turned with a start when Chelle tapped her shoulder.

"Miss Fulton, you forgot your change."

43

"Oh…thank you." Kendra's face was still glowing, partly from hurry and partly, Chelle guessed, from the behavior of the lout in the store. "I don't know you."

"Rochelle McShannon, Jack's niece. He told me your name is Kendra. I saw you on my first day here, three weeks ago."

"Aye, I remember." The color in Kendra's cheeks deepened. Chelle thought she was probably recalling her less than friendly reaction when they'd seen each other the first time. "The American. I'd heard you'd arrived."

"Yes. Here you are."

Kendra dropped her change in her skirt pocket, nodded and turned to leave, but Chelle put a hand on her arm.

"Kendra, I wondered, who was that young man in the store?"

Kendra rolled her eyes. "Drew Markham. Why?"

"I thought he could stand to learn some manners. The way he looked at you, I thought that older man might have said something."

Kendra shook back her loose, rebellious curls. "If Drew had looked at you that way, he would have. It doesn't matter. I must go in. Thank you again."

She hurried into the cottage. Chelle headed home and passed Aunt Caroline on the way in, weeding the vegetable garden. In the kitchen, Jean called to Chelle as she put the sugar in the pantry.

"Thank you. I used up the last of what we had in this jam."

Jean stood at the range, stirring a pot of bubbling strawberries. Chelle put on an apron and joined her.

"That looks almost done."

Jean nodded and pushed her damp hair back from her face. "It is, and just in time. The babies will be waking up any minute." She moved the jam pot to a trivet on the table. "Will you bring the jars?" Chelle moved the pot of boiling water containing the jars to another trivet and started lifting them out with tongs.

"Jean, do you know Drew Markham?"

Jean's amber eyes flashed scorn. "Aye, of course I know him. Where did you run across him?"

"At the store. He was giving Kendra Fulton a difficult time."

Jean huffed and ladled jam into the first jar. "Drew is a clerk in the mill office. He thinks that makes him a catch, but the truth is no decent girl in Mallonby wants aught to do wi' him, in spite of his father's farm."

Chelle dropped a sealer lid on the counter in surprise. "If his father has a farm, what is Drew doing in the mill?"

"Well, you'd have to know the family." Jean spoke without looking up as she filled jars. "Drew is John Markham's son by his second wife. He has an older son, Richard, by his first. Richard's mother died when he was seven. From what I've heard John didn't get on well with Drew's mother – she's been gone seven or eight years now - and he's never gotten on well with Drew, either. Nor has Richard. So, once Drew finished school, he got himself hired on at the mill. He started out on the floor, showed himself clever and willing to work, and caught the manager's eye. A year or so ago, he got promoted to the office. He lives on his own in one of the mill houses now. He isn't stupid, but he's a regular horse's ass and always has been."

Chelle giggled. Jean hung her ladle on the jam pot wiped her hands on her apron and rolled her eyes. "When he's not at work, that's how he behaves. Drew was still on the mill floor when Kendra started there, and he took a bit of a fancy to her I think, though he did naught about it then. She was only fifteen, and they're pretty strict about morals. Then, after she was fired, he started 'courting' her, if that's what you call it when a man pesters a girl and she tells him to go hang. Not that he had any notion of marriage, I'll warrant. He wouldn't saddle himself with someone else's child."

"I didn't know Kendra worked at the mill."

Jean nodded as they began covering the jars. "Aye, and so did David Phelps, her baby's father. They were both let go when word got out that she was pregnant. David went to his uncle in York to work in his warehouse, and he asked Kendra to go with 'im, so we've heard, but she wouldn't. I don't know why. So folk are doubly hard on her, and Drew takes advantage of it."

That explained why Kendra didn't look like a mill hand. Chelle's respect for her rose a few notches. Right or wrong, Kendra hadn't chosen the easy way out.

"She has courage, I'll give her that."

"Aye. It's made things difficult for her Mam, losing Kendra's wages, but so far they've managed. Her father died years ago. Kendra does washing and mending for parson's family, and a few others who aren't as narrow-minded as most. Her mother works at the mill, too. It's a mercy they didn't let her go as well."

Chelle put the lid on the last jar and screwed on the rim. "I intend to be Kendra's friend, if she'll let me."

Jean paused in the middle of wiping drips of jam from the table. "She could use a friend, that's for sure and certain, but be prepared to be tarred with the same brush if you befriend her."

Chelle tilted her chin. "I suppose you're right, but that's a chance I'm willing to take."

## *CHAPTER 6*

Martin glanced out the window and nearly dropped the plate he was drying. A buggy was pulling into the twilit yard, with Hugh and Margaret Paxton on the seat, as rigid and unbowed as they'd been at Eleanor's funeral.

Martin had only seen them once or twice since then. They'd visited rarely enough while their daughter was alive. He'd never really felt acquainted with Eleanor's parents, but he knew them well enough to surmise that this was more than a social call. With a tense knot forming in his stomach, he answered the door.

"Hugh. Margaret. Come in."

Eleanor's father nodded and stepped inside, with his wife behind him like a drab gray shadow. Hugh Paxton looked like the church elder he was, tall and spare, with a thin-lipped mouth and small, pale blue eyes that didn't warm when he smiled. Eleanor had inherited her generous curves from her mother, but Margaret's generosity ended with her figure. She and Hugh were well-matched. Martin had never been able to fathom how they'd produced a daughter like Eleanor, with her easy laughter and love of music and dancing.

"Now then, Martin." Hugh cleared his throat, an unconscious habit of his. "We're glad to find you in. We'd an errand to run at the Mallonby store and we decided to stop in on our way home. We've been meanin' to call for some time."

"You've something particular on your mind, then, I'll warrant." Martin gestured toward the sofa facing the hearth. "Come and sit down."

Margaret's gaze darted around the room as she perched on the sofa next to Hugh. Martin kept the place clean after a fashion, but not as Eleanor had. Her mother made it plain that she noticed, without saying a word. Hugh cleared his throat again.

"You're right, Martin, we do have summat in particular to discuss. Greer's nine months old now, so you'll be lookin' for a place for her soon. We've been talkin' it over, and we've decided we're willing to take her ourselves rather than see her go to strangers."

Martin barely managed to keep from showing his surprise. As far as he knew, Greer's grandparents had never visited her at the McShannons', and they'd certainly never broached the subject of raising her before.

Eleanor hadn't said much about her childhood, but Martin couldn't recall seeing her parents show her any real affection, anything more than a nod of approval. When he and Eleanor were courting, they'd taken little interest in getting to know him. He had a good farm and a respectable reputation, and that was enough to satisfy them. They'd shown little emotion at the wedding, and no more at Eleanor's funeral. Somehow, Martin found words, and somehow they came out more or less politely.

"I can't pretend I'm not surprised, Hugh. You've never mentioned this before, but Greer is your granddaughter. I thank you for your offer, and I'll consider it. Have you been to see her, then?"

Margaret spoke, her thin, reedy voice so different from Eleanor's rich contralto. "Nay. We saw no reason to impose on the McShannons while Greer was an infant, but she's gettin' older now. If you'll let them know at the forge that we'll be calling, we can begin gettin' to know the child."

Keeping a tight rein on his temper, Martin stood. Thinking past his shock, he guessed that the Paxtons had gotten a whiff of gossip. Someone had criticized them for allowing their granddaughter to go to strangers, and they wouldn't stand for it. It would be a cold day in hell before he'd send Greer to them to be raised in the same rigid, cheerless way they'd raised Eleanor, but they could make trouble for him if they chose. He'd be wise to mollify them.

"I'll tell Caroline the next time I see her that we've spoken. You can visit Greer, and we'll see how you get on before I make a decision."

Apparently satisfied, Hugh and Margaret rose together. Hugh cleared his throat one more time. "Aye. We'll see how it goes. We'd best be on our way if we're to get home before dark. We'll call at the forge the next time we're in Mallonby."

After watching them drive away, Martin lit the lamp. He burnt his finger with the match and clouded the chimney with smoke before he got the wick properly set. He muttered a few choice words, dumped the chimney in the wash basin and scrubbed it clean.

*You might be a poor excuse for a father, but no child of yours will grow up in their house while you're still drawing breath.* But time was passing. He wouldn't be able to put off making a decision about Greer's future much longer.

\* \* \* \*

Chelle stood in the shade of one of the churchyard oaks, wishing herself back in her room at Uncle Jack's or better yet, down by the creek at home. When you took the 'social' out of them, church socials really were depressing affairs. Almost everyone in Mallonby was there, on the lawn or on the church steps, dressed in their well-starched Sunday best, but the chatting groups seemed closed to her.

Jean's mother was watching the babies. Chelle's father had found some old cronies, and of course, Uncle Jack's family knew everyone. She was the only outsider.

Brian and Jean had introduced her to some of their friends, other young married couples, but Chelle still felt out of place. Eventually she'd retreated to the refreshment table to nurse her loneliness.

Nearby, another young woman stood alone, wearing a rosebud-embroidered muslin gown, the perfect shade of pale green to set off her creamy skin and auburn hair. She certainly wasn't dressed like anyone else there. Chelle mustered her nerve and said hello. Jade-green eyes coolly looked her up and down. Clara Hughes at home couldn't have done it better.

"Have we met?"

"No. I've only been in Mallonby a few weeks. My name is Rochelle McShannon."

The other girl smiled; a smile as cool as her eyes. "Yes. I'd have known you by your accent. You're the blacksmith's niece, aren't you? My maid has mentioned you."

In contrast to the broad Yorkshire Chelle heard everywhere in Mallonby, this girl spoke like the product of a good finishing school. Chelle doubted there were more than two or three families in the district who could afford that kind of education for a daughter.

"Yes, I'm Jack McShannon's niece, and from *your* accent, I'll hazard a guess you're Miss Westlake."

A graceful nod. "I am. Actually, since Susan mentioned you I've been curious to meet you. I'm going to have my tea under that tree over there. Will you join me?"

Seated on the grass under another spreading oak, Chelle balanced a plate of food on her lap, sipped her punch and waited, wondering why Miss Westlake would be curious about her. Then it occurred to her how lonely the mill owner's daughter likely was. She couldn't put herself on a level with her father's employees or the local farmers, but the two or three landed families in the area were old gentry and probably wouldn't accept her, either.

Miss Westlake nibbled on a cucumber sandwich as she took in the details of Chelle's dress. It was one Jean had commented on, made of navy blue challie in a small flowered print, its plainness relieved by hand-tatted lace and an embroidered leaf pattern on the collar and cuffs.

"Did you make your dress yourself? It's very well done. I must get you to do some sewing for me. I've no vocation for it at all."

Chelle's hackles rose a bit at Miss Westlake's patronizing tone. "Thank you. My mother taught me to tat and embroider as well as sew, and I've always enjoyed it, but the only handwork I've ever done has been for myself, and with two babies at the forge, Aunt Caroline and Jean really need my help at home."

"Of course." Miss Westlake dropped her gaze for just a moment, long enough to tell Chelle she'd made her point. "I've been curious to meet you because I've been following the war overseas in the London papers. I do hope the Confederacy wins. I'm sure our government would prefer to deal with a nation of gentlemen. Do you think it will be over quickly?"

Chelle looked Miss Westlake over in turn. They were about the same age. Miss Westlake had polish, but not quite enough to avoid seeming like she was putting on airs. She could have learned a thing or two from Cathy Sinclair. Chelle couldn't help feeling a bit sorry for her in spite of her patronage.

"I'm afraid not. I know the boys I grew up with. They're proud and determined, but they're badly outnumbered and there are far too few factories and foundries in the South to supply them. The Confederacy could do with fewer gentlemen and more manufacturers right now. They won't give up until they have no choice, but I think that time will come."

Chelle's mind conjured an image of her and Trey's eighteenth birthday party last September. She saw her brother and Justin sitting on the porch steps, feeling the whiskey Justin had pilfered from his father's stock, shaking with laughter while Charlie Bascomb did a killing imitation of Mrs. Hetty Palmer. Meanwhile, Tony Ferrar stood under the big pine in the yard, looking daggers at Everett Marshall for flirting with Cathy Sinclair. And Rory leaned against the porch railing, smiling, a drink in his hand, his smoky eyes fixed on Chelle…Rory and Justin and Tony and Ev and the others were all in the troop. How many would come back?

Miss Westlake broke into Chelle's thoughts. "Miss McShannon, I have to say that you don't carry yourself like a blacksmith's niece. My Susan told me that your father has a plantation at home. You must find life very difficult here."

Chelle covered her surprise with a smile. She should have expected to be a subject of exaggerated gossip, or was it downright fabrication? "I'm afraid Susan was misinformed. We had a mid-sized farm, that's all."

"I see. How many slaves did it require?"

Chelle fought off a blush. Slavery might be a fact of life at home, but she'd never been comfortable with it. Her family had always walked a fine line around the issue, but if she had married Rory she would have become a slave owner. She'd thought about it, pictured herself learning from Mrs. McAfee how to manage the plantation, and it had always made her very nervous.

"None. My father and brother worked our place themselves, and many of our neighbors did the same."

"I see." Miss Westlake's tone became a touch more patronizing, as did her smile. "I daresay Susan *was* misinformed. So you are a farmer's daughter. You'll probably find life all the easier in Mallonby, then. The villagers don't have much use for slavery."

Chelle had her own share of Surette temper. It flared, prompting her to speak before she thought.

"I shouldn't wonder. They don't appear to live as well as many slaves I've known. I don't see much difference between slavery in name and slavery in fact."

It was satisfying to see Miss Westlake's flawless cheeks color. "You've been here a very short time to be making that kind of judgment, don't you think?"

Chelle couldn't disagree, but she wouldn't back down. "Perhaps, but I read the papers too, Miss Westlake. The war has drawn attention to the textile industry and its working conditions, and when I look at the people here, I tend to believe what the papers are saying. Of course, I've never been inside a mill myself. Have you?"

"No. Father would never allow it." Miss Westlake rose, clearly annoyed. "It's been interesting chatting with you, Miss McShannon. Good afternoon."

Chelle felt a little ashamed of herself as she watched Miss Westlake walk away, but only a little. As her father said, Mallonby's mill was likely no worse than many others, but she wasn't going to let Miss Westlake walk over her. The shame came from the realization that the English girl had touched a nerve.

That evening, Chelle picked up the York paper Jack had brought home from the store on Saturday. When she came to a page of letters to the editor, she stopped reading. The mill children's plot in the cemetery, the things her father had told her, her conversation with Miss Westlake, all combined to prod her. Her father looked at her as she passed through the kitchen on her way upstairs.

"You've got a bee in your bonnet."

"Yes, I think I have." Up in her room, Chelle pulled out her pen, ink and paper.

*The Meaning of Slavery*

*Having arrived in England a month ago from a country currently embroiled in a civil war in which many, on both sides of the ocean, believe slavery is the divisive issue, I find myself considering the true meaning of the word in a way I never have before. At home, many of my neighbors were slave owners. Their slaves were paid no wages. In some instances, they worked under threat of punishment if they shirked their labor, and for all, the consequences of trying to escape were severe. They were born to their lot with no choice in the matter. To me, that has always been the essence of slavery.*

*In the Yorkshire village where I currently live, the large majority of the inhabitants from the age of twelve upwards work in the local woolen mill. They earn a wage, but it is too small to allow for anything but the barest necessities of life. They work longer hours under more onerous and dangerous physical conditions than any plantation slaves I have known.*

*Where a slave owner is obliged to provide at least rudimentary care to sick or injured slaves, mill owners have no such obligation to their 'free' employees when they suffer injury or ill health. These same 'free' employees sometimes work under threat of punishment, as do slaves, and though they are lawfully able to leave their jobs, most would face starvation if they did so. In reality, they have almost as little choice in their lot as those who are slaves in name.*

*In comparing the circumstances of these 'free' workers to those of the slaves of my former neighbors, I am forced to conclude that the differences are fewer than many who decry American slavery would like to believe. Does true freedom not require a real opportunity to earn a living wage, and more if one's ability allows it? I believe it does, and so I hesitate to call the mill hands in my new home free.*

Chelle read her finished letter through three times. She'd only wanted to write out her annoyance with Miss Westlake, but now that she'd done so, it didn't seem to be enough. Not one of the letters on slavery she'd seen in the English papers since coming to Mallonby had been written by a person who'd known a slave. Surely her opinion was just as valid. Why not send the letter to the York paper and see what happened?

*Chelle, you know what would happen. You'd have to use a man's name to get it published, but even so, people here would read it and assume you wrote it – or worse, that Dad did. You'd better think about it for a few days before you let yourself in for a lot of trouble.*

\* \* \* \*

"Oh, drat!" Chelle rolled her eyes at the wrapped pound of butter on the pantry shelf. Aunt Caroline had intended to take that out to Mr. Rainnie today, but she'd been called out to a birth and might not be home till tomorrow.

As part of their arrangement for keeping Greer, Mr. Rainnie supplied the McShannons with milk and cream. Caroline converted some of it to butter, most of which went to the Binghams' store, but she always kept some back for Mr.

Rainnie. He insisted on paying for it, which put Caroline's nose a little out of joint, but she forgave him because he said she made the best butter in the district.

The men were in the middle of a full day's work and Jean had gone to visit her mother for the afternoon, with little Peter. Greer had just woken from her nap. Chelle could deliver the butter, but she'd have to take the baby with her.

So, she would. It couldn't be a better day for a walk, and it was cool enough to keep the butter from melting on the way. Greer needed fresh air, and Chelle couldn't deny being a little curious to see Martin Rainnie's home as well. He wouldn't appreciate her appearing there with his daughter, but he'd likely be out haying anyway. Aunt Caroline had mentioned once that she just stepped in and left the butter on the table if he wasn't in.

Chelle tied a shawl into a sling for Greer, settled her in it and set off, carrying the butter by the string that bound the brown paper wrapping. The walk took longer than she'd expected, because she hadn't realized that the Rainnie lane wound a good half mile back from the road. When she came to the last bend, she stopped to adjust the sling and take the place in from a distance.

Its lines softened by the branches of an ash tree at either end, the house blended into the landscape from which its stone had come. The long, low byre, made of the same stone, stood across the cobbled yard. Rough grass grew up to the walls of the buildings, except for one spot by the house where the remains of a perennial bed showed a few splashes of color. As she got closer, Chelle made out one bright blue delphinium lifting its head above a riot of wild daisies and phlox. The garden clearly hadn't been given any attention this season.

Hens scratched busily in the dirt by the open byre door. Chelle stuck her head inside and saw only a ginger tabby cat skulking across the aisle. Through the open door at the other end, she saw Mr. Rainnie's Clydesdales, a shaggy black cob and a pair of Jersey cows grazing in a paddock. So he wasn't haying.

Chelle crossed to the house, knocked on the door and got no answer. She opened it a crack. "Mr. Rainnie?" She heard heavy steps on stairs and swung the door open.

He stood at the bottom of the staircase that led to the bedrooms, filling the opening with his broad shoulders. The surprise on his freckled face swiftly changed to annoyance, then pure anger when he saw that Chelle had brought his daughter with her. His sea-colored eyes fired sparks at her.

"I told your aunt and uncle –"

Chelle stood her ground, refusing to let him intimidate her. "Aunt Caroline got called away this morning and couldn't bring your butter. I decided I'd bring it, since it's a fine afternoon, but I couldn't leave Greer home with no one to mind her. Here it is."

She held out the package of butter. Just as Mr. Rainnie reached for it, the string broke. The wrapping fell away as the soft butter landed with a dull *splat* at Chelle's feet. Without thinking, she moved one foot forward, just enough for it to skid in the butter. Chelle felt herself falling and instinctively pushed Greer into Mr. Rainnie's arms.

By falling backwards, Chelle managed to stay out of the butter except for her shoe. She'd lifted her arms to let the shawl slip over her head. Mr. Rainnie stood as if he'd been turned to stone, holding the shawl and his daughter, while Chelle scrambled up from the floor.

"Is Greer all right?"

The baby gurgled when she heard her name, but Mr. Rainnie didn't answer. Her face burning, Chelle pulled her handkerchief from her pocket and wiped the butter from her shoe.

"I'm sorry. What a waste. Let me clean that up for you."

"No." He clipped off the word, his voice vibrating with anger. As soon as Chelle stood upright again, he thrust the baby back into her arms. "I don't know what you think you're

56

about, but I've no patience for meddlers. The butter could have waited till tomorrow. You'd best learn now rather than later that folk here mind their own business." He shouldered past her, strode across the yard and disappeared into the byre.

Her stomach knotted from the force of Mr. Rainnie's words, Chelle looked down at the wasted butter. She'd never felt like such a fool. Aunt Caroline wouldn't be pleased about this.

Greer gurgled again and held out her arms. Chelle slipped back into the sling, lifted the baby from it and cuddled her close.

"I should have known better. We'd best be getting home before we make things worse."

* * * *

Martin gave the girl a fifteen-minute head start, then stopped pushing straw about in Tessa's stall, left the byre and started down the lane. Perhaps a pint in the village would soothe his nerves. Nay, a shot or two of good Scotch was more like it.

The lass couldn't have known that he'd never held his daughter before. He was still reeling from it. So small and fragile and perfect. The sight of Eleanor's eyes in Greer's little face stabbed Martin to the heart, but that wasn't what terrified him.

Connection. He'd done his utmost to avoid feeling it, and now, the first time his child smiled at him, there it was, threatening to tear him open inside and leave him empty and exposed. His coloring, his chin, Eleanor's eyes and mouth…Greer was part of him, part of all that had been good in his life. He couldn't deny it. How was he going to live with it?

Martin settled himself at a back table in the Split Crow, grateful for the pub's cool dimness. He didn't relish the thought of anyone seeing him clearly right now. The familiar worn oak bar, the voices of two old men talking quietly over a pint across the room, felt more homelike than home did. He tossed back a shot of whiskey and called for another. Harry Tate, the owner, brought it. He glanced around the nearly empty pub and pulled up a chair.

"Have ye got your hay in then, Martin?"

"Aye, finished yesterday. Cheers." Martin took a swallow of strong amber nectar. Its mellow burn warmed away some of the tension in his gut.

"You'd best slow down, lad. It's early yet." Harry lifted a brow. "I don't think I've seen you drink aught but ale before."

Martin shrugged. "The sun's over the yardarm, and I'm not in the mood for ale today."

"Aye, I can see that." Harry held Martin's gaze for a moment, then pursed his lips and shook his head like a doctor assessing an unsatisfactory patient. "Martin, you finished shearing before anyone else in the district, and now haying. I've known you all your life, so I hope you'll forgive an old man for talkin' out of turn, but you can't keep this up. Sooner or later, you'll have to stop and face things."

The sympathy behind Harry's words roused Martin's temper. "I've faced them, Harry. The baby's taken care of. As for me, it's easier if I keep busy."

The edge to his voice didn't ruffle Harry. His lips quirked in a half-sad, half amused grin. "Aye, and safer too. You'll realize that in your own time."

The mill whistle blew for dinner break. Martin seized the chance to change the subject. "What are you hearing about the mill these days, Harry?"

Harry shook his head. "A lot of grumbling. You know Westlake's dropped his price for wool. There's some as says he wants to lower wages, but doesn't dare. If he isn't careful, he'll have a lot of angry workers to deal with. He ought to talk to some of the older folk who were here during the Luddite trouble and see what he's lettin' himself in for."

Martin hadn't been born when the Luddites had brewed up a storm in Yorkshire and Lancashire, destroying mill machinery and, in some instances, shedding blood as they protested the mechanization of the textile industry, but he'd heard the stories from his parents. His mother had been a mill hand in her youth, and she'd died before reaching forty, her life shortened by her years at the loom. A slow-burning anger pushed his daughter from his mind.

"What do you think he's about? I know the war in America has the cotton mills starved, but what's that to Westlake?"

Harry shrugged. "Just greed, I'd guess. If people can't get cottons they'll have to wear woolens, and he wants to take advantage of the market before things adjust themselves." He sighed, glanced down at the half-empty glass of Scotch on the table and put a hand on Martin's shoulder. "One more for the road, and that's all you'll be gettin' from me. On the house."

"Thanks, Harry." Martin finished his second drink, felt the sharp edge of his grief dull into merciful numbness. He nursed the third, images of his daughter's face blurring into the McShannon girl's, with her cheeks flushed due to his rudeness, her hair windblown from her walk, and those sapphire eyes…

*Lad, you're half drunk. Go home.*

## CHAPTER 7

Though she couldn't send letters to Trey until he settled, as time went on Chelle fell into the habit of writing to him. She'd mail the letters when she could, and some day they'd read them over together, when she went to visit him out West. Today she sat on her bed to write, taking advantage of the afternoon light that poured through her open window, breathing in the scent of the forge fire and the breeze off the fell.

*June 25, 1861*
*Dear Trey,*

*I hope and pray that you are safe and well. It's so difficult, not being able to get news of you. I miss you so much, and so does Dad.*

*It's finally summer here, and the countryside is in full bloom. I have to admit that Mallonby is a pretty place, and I wish you could see the fell. It's wild and lonesome and beautiful.*

Chelle stopped, imagining what Trey would think of it. Perhaps someday he'd come over and see the fell for himself, but she couldn't describe the witchery of it, or the way it made her feel as if some previously unknown part of her had found itself at home.

*I like Uncle Jack's family. He and Aunt Caroline have been good to me, and Brian has too, though he likes to tease almost as much as you do. His wife Jean is sweet, and so is their little boy. There's also another baby here, Greer Rainnie, a little girl Jean is nursing as she lost her mother.*

*Dad is working at the forge and it seems to be good for him, though there are times when he's very quiet and I know he's thinking of Maman and you. At least his work leaves him little time for brooding. I keep busy too, helping Jean with the children, especially Greer. She is a good little one for the most part, though I'm starting to suspect she has her father's temper. Mr. Rainnie is even more bitter than Luke Bascomb over losing his wife, and wants nothing to do with his daughter.*

*As for the village, people seem to make friends slowly here. I can't say I've really gotten to know anyone. At the church social last week, the only person I had a conversation with was the daughter of the man who owns the woolen mill. She was curious about slavery, though it had never occurred to her that her father's workers aren't much different from slaves themselves. I got so annoyed with her condescension that after I got home I wrote a letter comparing mill hands to slaves, and then a couple of days later I mailed it to a newspaper in York. Imagine me writing a letter to the editor. I wrote it in a bit of a temper, but I sent it because of the mill children I see here. They haven't had a childhood. I never really knew how lucky I was before.*

She shrugged off a whisper of doubt. Chelle wished now that she'd shown her letter to her father before deciding to mail it, but she hadn't told anyone about it. She'd signed it 'John Hughes' after Clara's brother at home. If by some unlikely chance it was published and people connected it to her, she'd just have to stand by her words and let the chips fall where they may.

*I wonder where all the boys from home are now. Are they fighting? Are they safe? I often think of the tricks you and Justin used to play, like the time the two of you hid in the ditch and frightened Mr. Bascomb's horses with your toy guns. Things like that pop into my mind at the oddest moments, when I'm reading or washing dishes or doing any other chore. It must mean you're thinking of me, too.*

A small sound came from the next room. Chelle pushed her fears away and added a last sentence.

*Greer just woke up, so I'm going to stop for now. Oh, I can see you reading this. If only you really could.*

She tucked the letter in her writing case and took Greer downstairs to Jean to be nursed. Afterwards Jean went out to sit in the sun with both babies, and let Kendra Fulton in at the same time.

Noticeably larger than she'd been the day Chelle returned her change, Kendra stepped into the kitchen. Chelle hadn't been able to think of a pretext to call on her, so she'd been waiting for Kendra to come to see Aunt Caroline.

"Come in and sit down, Miss Fulton."

"Nobody calls me that. Call me Kendra." She sounded a little grudging. Chelle gave her a welcoming smile. "All right, Kendra. And I'm Chelle. Aunt Caroline took some butter in to the store a while ago, but she should be home soon."

With a sigh of relief, Kendra settled in a chair at the table. Flushed and warm from her walk, with curly wisps of hair escaping from her bun to frame her face, she looked healthy and prettier than Chelle had ever seen her, but her blue eyes hadn't lost their wariness.

"I'll wait for her then, if I might. I don't fancy walking home and then back here again later."

She had to be close to her time. She did a good job of covering her fear, but Chelle felt it just the same. "Are you feeling well?"

"Aye, well enough. Just tired." Kendra ran a hand over her belly, then straightened up in her chair as if she were bracing herself for more questions. "Are you settling in, then?"

She looked as if she must be eight months along now. From what Jean had said, Kendra had good reason to be defensive. Earning her trust wouldn't be easy, but Chelle admired the girl's courage enough to try.

"Slowly. I don't think Mallonby is very used to newcomers."

"Nay, it isn't." Kendra's expression softened. "I've heard you lost your mother just before coming here. I'm sorry."

Chelle leaned forward, bridging a little of the distance between them. "Thank you. I miss her so much. And my brother. He went West instead of coming with us. I hope we hear from him soon. And my friends…almost all the boys are in the army."

"Aye. That can't be easy."

"It would be even harder if it weren't for little Greer. She keeps me occupied. Sometimes I almost feel like a mother myself." Chelle put on the coaxing smile that usually worked on her girlfriends at home. "Kendra, I've been wondering if maybe, after your baby comes, you'd bring it out here for walks. I've gotten to know the fell fairly well, but I'm sure you know it like the back of your hand, and we wouldn't have the village staring at us."

The sullen look Chelle had seen the day she arrived in Mallonby flashed in Kendra's eyes again. "If you want to make friends here, that wouldn't be the way to do it."

Chelle threw her a challenging glance and snorted. "I certainly don't care what the likes of Drew Markham think of me."

Kendra looked taken aback, then she smiled briefly. "Nor do I. No one in Mallonby cares a rap what Drew thinks, when it comes to that. The mill hands don't speak to him at work because he's in the office, and he's never gotten on well with his family. I'd feel sorry for him if he weren't so rude."

Chelle remembered the way Drew had run his eyes over Kendra at the store. "I think he could be worse than rude if given the chance."

Kendra shrugged. "Likely. Stay clear of him. There's your aunt now."

Caroline came in, dropped a few packages in the pantry and took Kendra upstairs for her examination. "Everything's fine," she said when they came back down. "I'd say you've got about three weeks left to go. Send your mother for me when you start having pains, and in the meantime, take care of yourself."

The relief on Kendra's face as Chelle walked her to the gate showed just how much fear she was hiding. "Do as Aunt says and take care of yourself, Kendra. And think about coming to visit. You'll be welcome."

Kendra started to walk away, then looked back over her shoulder with another brief smile. "Aye, I'll think about it."

\* \* \* \*

63

Kendra propped the door of the cottage open, did the same with the windows, then knelt clumsily and kindled a fire in the small stove. She'd have supper ready by the time Mam got home.

While she waited for the stove to heat, she settled into her mother's rocker under the front window and let the incoming breeze fan her. Three weeks. The thought brought an equal mixture of dread and impatience. How bad would the pain be? Would she survive?

*Don't be a coward. Babies are born healthy more often than not. And how good will it feel not to be fat and tired anymore?*

She should be used to fear by now. It had been her constant companion since she'd discovered she was pregnant, but she wouldn't give in to it. She couldn't afford to.

*Davy.* Whatever happened, Kendra wouldn't forget or regret those few weeks with him. She hadn't thought it possible to be that happy, to love anyone that fiercely. When she'd told him about the baby he'd offered to marry her, but she'd seen the trapped look on his face and known it was no good. Davy was nineteen, not ready to be a father, and with both of them dismissed from the mill, they'd nothing to raise a child on. He knew as well as she did that she would have been daft to say yes.

How did he spend his time now, when he wasn't at work? Visiting the pubs with the other lads from the warehouse? Chasing the local girls? He didn't owe her anything, she'd made that clear, but that didn't make the thought any easier to bear.

Kendra longed for someone her own age to talk to, and it seemed Rochelle McShannon did, too – enough to risk her good name. Kendra's friends from the mill, the girls she'd grown up with, had shunned her in fear for their own jobs. She'd have to go see Mrs. McShannon one last time after the birth anyway. She could hardly avoid seeing Chelle again.

Kendra sat up with a gasp as her baby kicked. The little one seemed strong enough, that was for sure and certain. They might both be outcasts, she and her child, but Chelle was an outcast, too.

\* \* \* \*

July came in with a heat wave, at least by Mallonby's standards. On sultry days, Jack, Brian and Colin made for the Split Crow after work to cool off with a pint or two. Aunt Caroline waited supper until they returned, and the family would eat in the late summer twilight.

One Friday night, Chelle and Jean were setting the table when the men came back from the village. Chelle's heart lurched when she saw the York paper in her father's hand and the odd look on his face.

"Lass, read this. We all read it at the pub." He handed the folded newspaper to Chelle. Her face burned as she took it.

She'd thought her letter must have died a painless death, but there it was, in irrevocable print. Even if she'd wanted to deny writing it, there was no point. How many newly-come Southerners could there be in Yorkshire? She blew out a breath and faced her father.

"I never thought they'd publish it."

"Publish what?" Caroline took the paper and scanned the letter. Her mouth opened in shock.

"Whatever possessed you to write this?"

"Miss Westlake, and the mill children buried in the churchyard, and the things Dad told me." Chelle forced herself to look her father in the eye. After all, he'd never hesitated to express his own opinions. "I had a little conversation with Miss Westlake at the church social, and she made me think—"

Her father quirked his brows. "You mean she made you angry."

"A little." Chelle lifted her chin. "I don't suppose she and her father will appreciate my opinion, but as far as I'm concerned, everything I said in that letter is true."

Jack and Brian joined them at the table, their faces mirroring her father's misgivings. Caroline finished reading the letter and laid the paper on the sofa, shaking her head.

"Aye, it's true, that's for sure, but the Westlakes likely aren't the only ones who won't appreciate it. The mill folk won't thank you either. It's their livelihood you're talking of, Chelle, and you've never set foot in the mill."

"I didn't pretend to know anything I don't. Everything I wrote was common knowledge or my own experience." Chelle got up, wearing the stubborn look her father knew well. "Anyhow, I can't take it back now. Dad, Uncle, you must be hungry."

She moved to the range and began serving up ham and scalloped potatoes. Why hadn't she left that wretched letter in her writing case?

*Don't be a coward, Chelle. You wrote it, you sent it to the paper, and now you'll have to face the music.*

\* \* \* \*

"There you are, lad. Stay." Martin lifted Gyp to the cart's seat and finished arranging the load of market day produce in the back. Being the last Saturday of the month the mill was closed today, and people were already coming out, lured by the fine morning. In another hour the street would be full, and by noon the pub would be as well.

Martin leaned against the cart and rolled his shoulders, trying to ease the stiffness in his neck. He'd fallen asleep in his chair by the fire last night and wakened at dawn, feeling like he'd been beaten enthusiastically with a stick. To improve matters he was starting a headache, too.

Other farm carts were assembling on both sides of the main street. Around the last bend, a plume of smoke rose from the forge fire. They were crowded enough there now, with Colin and his daughter as well as Brian and Jean and their little one, and Greer...

Greer. Was she awake yet? Crying? Nursing? An image of Eleanor with Greer at her breast flashed into his mind, making his breath catch with pain. Thanks to the McShannon girl Martin knew what holding Greer felt like, in spite of his best efforts never to know.

He welcomed the distraction when people began buying. A busy hour had passed when he noticed Colin McShannon coming out of Bingham's shop, just in time to collide with two men, who were busy discussing something in the newspaper one of them held.

Lester Connell and Charlie Walker were about Martin's age. He hadn't seen much of them since his school days, but he'd never liked either lad and didn't care who knew it. Lester picked up the newspaper he'd dropped and said something to Colin. Martin couldn't make out the words, but he picked up on the threatening tone and took a few steps closer. Charlie spoke next.

"You'd best stop meddling in things that don't concern you and pay heed to that daughter of yours. She wants watching, from what I hear."

Colin took a step toward him, fists clenched. "Don't say any more, Charlie, or I'll shut your ugly mouth for you."

Martin didn't wait to hear more. Both Charlie and Lester would have at least thirty pounds on wiry Colin, and it wouldn't occur to either to fight fair. He reached the group in three quick strides.

"Mornin', Colin. I couldn't help overhearin' you and Charlie exchanging greetings. What's the problem?"

Colin answered without taking his eyes off Charlie. "No problem at all, yet, but if either of these two says a word against my girl, there will be."

Martin looked from Charlie to Lester and back again, amazed at the aggression building inside him. He'd never done much fighting. All his life he'd been one of the biggest lads in the district, so few had challenged him, and he'd never felt the need to be a bully. But now, he was a hair's breadth from taking on two men in the middle of the street, in the middle of a crowd. And he was almost trembling with anticipation at the thought.

"You aren't goin' to do that, are you lads?" He spoke quietly, but Lester and Charlie sensed that he was on the edge. Lester glared at him briefly, then handed the paper to Martin.

"I never said a word." He turned and walked away. Charlie followed.

Martin looked down at the paper in his hand. He read a few lines, read the rest of the article.

*Bloody hell.*

"Colin, did you write this?"

Rochelle's father looked him in the eye. "Aye, I did."

"You're lying. Not that I blame you." Martin scanned the article again. "This isn't as short and to the point as you'd make it. It reads like it was written by a woman. Your daughter?"

Colin still held his gaze. "I'm not lying. I wrote it. Thank you for standing beside me, lad. You have customers waiting. I'd best be off."

He touched his cap and walked on toward the forge. Martin made his way back to his cart.

*I don't envy him keeping a rein on that one. Of course, she never gave a thought to how much trouble she'd cause. Preserve me from a flighty woman.*

He ruffled Gyp's fur and turned to the first housewife waiting. "Now then, Mrs. Tewkes, what'll you have?"

\* \* \* \*

Not long after her father left for the village, Chelle walked in with Jean and Caroline. The market day crowd had already gathered, and it didn't take long for Chelle to realize that Aunt Caroline had been right. She felt more than one hostile look as she navigated among the wagons and stalls to do her share of the family shopping.

She filled her basket with vegetables and was easing her way through the crowd on her way to the fishmonger's when she found her path blocked. Chelle looked up into Drew Markham's arrogant hazel eyes.

"Excuse me, Mr. Markham."

He didn't move. "Miss McShannon. The daughter of our village Luddite."

Chelle didn't know what a Luddite was, but Drew's tone made it an insult. She stepped aside, but he moved with her so she couldn't get around him. She let her eyes flash at him.

"Have you been reading the papers? I'm surprised. Actually, my father didn't write that letter. I did."

"I wondered about that. Your father was born here. I wouldn't expect him to bite the hand that fed him." Drew looked her up and down as suggestively as he had Kendra Fulton that day in the store. "You're a pretty lass, Miss, so I'll give you a word of warning. You'd be wise to keep your opinions to yourself." A smirk spread across his face. "You'd best think on the company you keep as well, if you care about your good name. Then again, it's likely you and Kendra Fulton are birds of a feather."

Beyond furious, Chelle glared at him. "I'll be speaking to my father about you."

Drew chuckled. "He's nobbut a small man, isn't he, lass?"

"Perhaps, but my uncle and cousin aren't." She threw all the contempt she could muster into her tone. "And anyhow, I'd have to say you're the smallest man I've ever met."

She started to turn away, but Drew reached out and caught her chin. "Saucy little baggage, aren't you? For tuppence I'd—"

"For tuppence I'd put your lights out here and now, Drew. Let her go."

Chelle knew that voice, though she'd never heard it laced with such cold rage. She jerked out of Drew's grasp and stepped aside, leaving him face to face with Martin Rainnie.

Chelle enjoyed watching Drew's aggression die as he measured himself against Mr. Rainnie's greater strength and heard the quiet venom in his voice. "Apologize to Miss McShannon. Now."

Drew turned to her, his swagger gone. "Sorry, Miss. I meant no harm."

Mr. Rainnie jerked his head toward the street. "All right then, bugger off."

Drew faded into the crowd. Mr. Rainnie turned to Chelle, his fists clenched, gray-green eyes snapping, his feet still slightly spread in a fighting stance. Chelle knew he wouldn't hurt her, but his anger hit her in waves, making her stomach flutter.

"Mr. Rainnie. How did you happen to be here?"

"My cart's just over there. I'm selling, though I have to say it's a job doing business today. Half an hour ago I had to talk your father out of a scrap over that fool letter of yours. He tried to pass it off as his work, but I knew better. He has more sense than that."

A cold chill settled in Chelle's stomach. Of course her father would try to shoulder the blame. Still in the grip of her outrage with Drew, she held Mr. Rainnie's gaze.

"Every word I wrote was true, wasn't it?"

He shrugged his heavy shoulders. "True or not, it's likely to make a fine lot of trouble for you and your family, but I don't suppose you considered that."

The biting words on the tip of Chelle's tongue died there. He was right. "I didn't write that letter to make trouble for anyone. I wrote it because it's what I believe."

He dismissed her beliefs with another shrug. "Have you ever been inside a mill, then?"

Chelle took a fresh grip on her temper. It really was galling to owe a debt of gratitude to such an abrasive man. "No, but I've read plenty about slavery in the papers here, written by people who've never seen a plantation. Is my opinion any less valid than theirs? Or is it simply because I'm a woman that I ought to keep my mouth shut?"

Mr. Rainnie's hard mouth curved in a humorless smile. "I've nothing against women speaking their minds, but they can expect to have the likes of Drew Markham to deal with if they do. Only chances are, they won't be the ones who have to do that. But that's your father's concern, not mine. As for your letter, it won't change anything. My mother was a mill hand before she married. She started when she was eight. The work ruined her health, and it isn't much different now. The so-called regulations are just words on paper and always have been."

"But conditions have changed, Dad says. The hours are a bit shorter now, and they don't take the children as young. Mr. Rainnie, what is a Luddite?"

"The Luddites were a group that formed to protest conditions when the mills were first mechanized. They didn't want their leaders known, so they conjured up a sham leader named Ludd and used his name. They went about Yorkshire and Lancashire destroying mill machinery, and there was some bloodshed. A lot of them were hanged or transported for their pains, and they accomplished naught, just as you will by writing to the papers. I'd best be getting back to my cart."

Mr. Rainnie turned abruptly and walked away. By the time Chelle realized she hadn't even thanked him, it was too late.

She watched him shoulder his way through the crowd, until she remembered that he might look back and see her. Why did every encounter with the man have to end in embarrassment? And his bitter cynicism was enough to curdle milk. Her stomach still knotted, Chelle hurried to finish her shopping before Aunt Caroline came looking for her.

# CHAPTER 8

"Mam, go to work. I'll be fine. Hurry on, or you'll be late and lose an hour's pay." Kendra closed the door gently in her mother's worried face and watched her out of sight from the window. She poured herself a glass of water and washed their few breakfast dishes, hoping that being up and moving would ease the pain in her back.

It didn't. When she'd finished the dishes, Kendra moved heavily to the rocker, reached into the mending basket and picked up the baby dress she'd made from an old childhood frock of her own, a soft yellow cotton that would do for a girl or a boy. The hem still needed to be finished.

*A girl or a boy? With blue eyes like mine, or hazel like Davy's?* Kendra had asked herself the same questions hundreds of times, and always came to the same answer—she didn't care, as long as her labor was safe and her baby healthy.

The one thing she'd never doubted was that she would love her child. She never thought of the baby without a wave of fierce possessiveness. *Her* child, hers to raise. To send to the mill at twelve? What other life could she give her baby, born on the wrong side of the blankets as it would be?

Perhaps she'd been rankly selfish, but she'd never forget the fear stamped on Davy's face, the way he'd backed away from her as he told her he wanted to do what was right. Kendra's answer was just as deeply etched on her mind.

"We've nothing to marry on, Davy. I've no work, and you won't be making enough in York to keep a family. A family! We're hardly more than children ourselves. We made a mistake, lad. Let's not make it worse."

"But it's my child, too!"

Yes, and Davy would never have considered proposing to her otherwise. Kendra wouldn't trap him, the child or herself in that kind of a marriage.

She'd just put the last stitch in the hem of the dress when pain knifed her in the back, making her gasp. It eased as suddenly as it hit, leaving her short of breath, eyes watering.

Perhaps sitting had been a bad idea. Kendra rose and circled the room, holding her back. As she reached the chair again, she felt warm liquid trickling down her thighs.

Her water. She found a towel, took off her dress, dried herself and settled in the rocker again, wearing only her shift. Should she send for Mam? Who would she send? The neighbors were all at work, and if they hadn't been, it wouldn't have surprised Kendra if they refused to help her.

She took a few deep, calming breaths and fought to still her racing heart. Any road, from what Mrs. McShannon had told her, chances were nothing much would happen until after Mam got home tonight. It would be time enough to send for Mrs. McShannon then.

\* \* \* \*

Not long after the mill whistle announced closing time, Chelle answered a knock on the kitchen door and found a flustered-looking woman who, from the resemblance, had to be Kendra's mother. She stepped inside, breathing hard as if she'd run all the way to the forge. "Is Caroline home, lass? Kendra's in labor. Has been all day and didn't send for me, the little fool. I hope she's no' done herself harm by it."

Chelle ran upstairs for her aunt, who'd been helping Jean settle the babies. Caroline found her shawl and washed her hands while Chelle and Mrs. Fulton chafed in the background.

"She should have sent for me at the mill. Her water broke this morning and she's having strong pains now."

"Then it's likely she's progressing well, Helen." Caroline laid a hand on Mrs. Fulton's shoulder, then picked up her birthing stool. "Let's be off, then."

Chelle rose from her chair. She didn't think she could sit here, powerless and wondering, until Aunt Caroline returned.

Not after what had happened to Ellen Bascomb and her little son.

"Aunt, I want to go with you. That is, if it's all right with you, Mrs. Fulton."

Caroline exchanged a look with Kendra's mother. "I'd say that's up to Kendra."

Chelle laced her fingers together, a small pleading gesture. "Please. If she doesn't want me there, I'll leave."

After a moments' tense silence, Mrs. Fulton nodded. "All right then, come along, and we'll see what Kendra says."

By the time they reached the Fultons' cottage, Chelle felt breathless from more than hurry. She'd seen animals born, but never a baby. Along with her fear for Kendra and the child, Chelle acknowledged a little selfish anxiety.

*Will she send me away?*

They found Kendra in the rocker, catching her breath after another contraction. She got to her feet, the relief in her eyes turning to doubt as she saw Chelle. She held Kendra's gaze, willing her to accept the friendship she was offering.

"Kendra, if you want me to leave I will, but I thought I'd rather be here with you than thinking about you at home."

Kendra sat again with her hands on her belly, weighing the sincerity of Chelle's words. Finally she nodded. "You can stay." Then her lips curved slightly in a reserved smile. "Thank you."

Chelle returned the smile without the reserve. "Thank *you.*"

Afternoon stretched into evening, and then night, while Kendra paced the floor between contractions and rested in the rocker when she got tired. Chelle and Mrs. Fulton took turns walking with her while Aunt Caroline checked her for progress every so often.

"You aren't dilated yet," Caroline told her at midnight, "but that's not unusual. The first one often takes its time."
By dawn, Kendra's pains had grown more severe, but the baby still wasn't moving. Mrs. Fulton took Chelle aside. "Will you go

to the mill for me and tell the floor supervisor that I won't be in today? I don't like this. She should be progressing by now."

"Of course I'll go, Mrs. Fulton." A short time later, when she looked from the window and saw the mill's employees starting up the hill, Chelle joined them. She did her best to ignore hostile glances and pretended not to hear the occasional murmured comment as she passed.

The mill yard was quiet, the din of the machinery not yet started for the day. Chelle didn't enjoy the thought of walking up to the man standing at the door, watching the workers as they came in. He'd probably read her letter in the paper—everyone in the village must know it was hers by now—and he didn't look as if he'd be very approachable at the best of times.

She glanced across the road at the Westlakes' house, wondering whether one of the windows she saw was Miss Westlake's—her name was Maria, Aunt Caroline had said—and whether she ever watched her father's employees arriving for work. Did Miss Westlake ever think about their conversation at the social? Could she be looking down at Chelle from the house right now?

*Nonsense. She wouldn't be out of bed at this hour.* By walking quickly, Chelle managed to reach the mill ahead of most of the hands. She chose a moment when there was a gap between groups of incoming workers, squared her shoulders and walked up to the man at the door.

"Mrs. Fulton sent me to tell you she won't be in today."

The supervisor eyed Chelle coldly. "Is she ill, then?"

"No, she's taking care of her daughter."

"Ah." His lips curled in a sneer, then he simply turned away. Looking past him through the open door, Chelle got a glimpse of the mill floor with its fulling tables, spinning machines and enormous power looms. The strong smell of lanolin pervaded the place. She couldn't imagine the noise of all that machinery working. She turned on her heel, as eager to get away from the mill as she was to get back to Kendra.

The day wore on with little progress in Kendra's labor. Her pains were intense now, but her womb still hadn't opened. She dozed in the rocker when she could, worn out after over twenty-four hours of pain and lack of sleep. Mrs. Fulton looked almost as tired, her face drawn with worry. "Something isn't right, Caroline. I know it's her first, and she's young for it, but…"

"This could all be perfectly natural, Helen. We don't want to frighten the girl." But Chelle saw concern in her aunt's eyes. She moved a chair to sit beside Kendra, wiped the sweat from her face with a cool cloth and gave her a reassuring smile.

"Have you chosen names yet?"

Barely awake, Kendra nodded. "Helen if it's a girl. And if it's a boy…"

Chelle squeezed her hand. "David?"

"Aye." A faint smile glimmered in Kendra's eyes. "Chelle, I've been thinkin' on what you said before about coming down to the forge, and there's a few places on the fell where I used to go when I was little…I haven't been to them for years, not since I started at the mill. Once the baby's strong enough, I could show them to you if you'd like."

"I'd like that very much." Chelle squeezed Kendra's hand again, just before another contraction hit her. Gripping Chelle's hand, she closed her eyes and tried to keep back a cry. When it was over, Kendra let her head fall back against the pillow behind her.

"That was the hardest one yet." Her voice became a whimper as tears sprang to her eyes. "I'm so tired. I can't do this much longer."

Her mother took her other hand. Caroline knelt, checked Kendra again and stood, smiling. "You won't have to do it much longer, lass. You're open now. Let's get you on the birthing stool."

After all the hours of waiting, the birth happened so quickly Chelle could hardly take it in. Kendra's mother kept her upright on the stool while Chelle held her hand. Kendra screamed with each pain as the final agonizing moments of birth came upon her, then she and her mother wept tears of relief as Caroline laid the baby in Kendra's arms.

"You have a son."

Chelle cried too as she looked down at the ridiculous, red-faced little mite squalling in Kendra's arms. "He's all yours, Kendra. You worked hard enough to bring him into the world."

She saw no fear in Kendra's eyes now, only wonder. "He's the spit of Davy's mother. Mam, I wish…"

Mrs. Fulton knelt by her. "What do you wish, love?"

Kendra shook her head and cuddled her son closer. "It doesn't matter. He's here and he's healthy, that's all that matters now."

Once Kendra and her son were in bed asleep, Caroline and Chelle walked home under a clear evening sky pricked with early stars. Now that all was safely over, Chelle felt let down and inexplicably homesick, acutely aware that her mother wouldn't be there to share the pain and wonder of it when— *if*—she ever had a child of her own. She recalled the talk they'd had not long before her mother's death, when Chelle had told her about Rory.

"It seems like only yesterday that you and Trey were babies." Her mother's tired dark eyes had taken on a wistful light. "Now, you're thinking of marriage, and your brother…it's selfish of me, I know, but I wish the two of you were five years younger." The wistfulness had turned to a smile. "Me, too, when it comes to that."

Sitting on the edge of her mother's bed, Chelle had forced a laugh. "Maman, haven't we caused enough trouble for you to be glad we're grown up?"

Her mother's answering laugh startled her with its strength. "Trouble? Ask your father what it was like when you were little." She'd reached up to cup Chelle's cheek. "Chelle, as a mother I should tell you to take your time, think everything through before you marry Rory or anyone else. But as a woman I can't, not honestly, because I didn't. I was so deep in your father's blue eyes that I couldn't think at all. And I've been happy."

At eighteen, Sidonie Surette had known her mind and heart without reservations. Would her daughter's feelings ever be as trustworthy? Chelle shook off the memory with a sigh.

"Aunt, I was so frightened for Kendra for a while."

Caroline put an arm around Chelle's shoulders. "So was I. First births are chancy, but it's safely over and she has a strong, healthy boy."

Chelle's mind turned to the little girl asleep at home. "I'm thinking of Greer. What happened to her mother?"

It was too dark to see Caroline's face clearly, but her regret came through in her voice. "She hemorrhaged. The doctor and I couldn't get it stopped. These things happen, but it never gets any easier to take."

Chelle had no idea how she'd react in a situation like that. She only knew how awed she'd been by Kendra's courage and the new life she'd brought into the world. "I don't suppose it does, but I'd like to go to other births with you and learn from you. Would you be willing to let me do that?"

Caroline stopped, her surprise obvious. "Aye, I'd be willing, if you're willing to be ready for anything. If you change your mind just let me know, and I won't think any less of you for it."

A warm glow built in Chelle's chest, an unexpected sense of purpose. This was something she could do to give her time here some meaning. "Thank you, Aunt."

Chelle and Caroline arrived home to Jean's welcoming hot supper of beef stew and dumplings. Ravenous, Chelle had half-cleared her plate before she noticed that the rest of the family seemed preoccupied, especially her father. She dropped her fork and looked around the table. Jean wouldn't meet Chelle's gaze. Something was clearly amiss.

"Dad, is something wrong?"

Her father cleared his throat. "We've had a letter from your brother, lass."

Fear ran through Chelle like ice water. "Is he all right? Where is he?"

"Yes, he's all right." Colin pulled the letter from his shirt pocket and handed it across the table. "Here, read it yourself."

*June 2, 1861*
*Camp Marcy, Maryland*

*Dear Dad,*

*By the time you get this, I will have been several weeks a member of the 60th Cavalry, 3rd Pennsylvania volunteers. A fine name for a bunch of raw recruits like us. Some of these boys had never even fired a rifle until they joined up. I only hope that our commanding officer, Colonel Averill, can turn us into soldiers before we're needed, which likely won't be until next spring. By the looks of it, he intends to do just that.*

*I've made some friends, but on the whole I can't think of anything more boring than camp life. It isn't particularly comfortable, but none of us would mind that much if there were anything to distract us from it. We drill constantly and no one can say we don't need it, but there isn't much else except picket duty, which can be dicey. We've already had a couple of recruits taken prisoner because they let themselves be caught unawares. I make sure I keep my eyes and ears wide open when I'm out there.*

*I don't suppose you'll be any more surprised at me than I am at myself. After you sailed, I took the next train back to Washington to pick up Cloud. I intended to buy my supplies and start West, but then the attack on Fort Sumter happened and I found myself surrounded by talk of the war. The recruiters were everywhere. I couldn't avoid it, couldn't turn my back on it.*

*I remembered our talks at home, and I remembered what we saw in New York. The more I thought about it, the more it seemed that if I walked away, I'd always wonder about myself. I don't want to spend the rest of my life with Nate Munroe's voice in my head, telling me I didn't*

79

*have the sand to stand up and fight for my home. And I thought, maybe we're right and the Confederacy is doomed, but home doesn't have to be. If the war ends quickly enough, it might never get that far South at all. So, I enlisted to do what I can to make that happen.*

*I know this means I won't be able to go back, but if the war ends soon, it will be worth it. I only hope you and Chelle can understand..."*

Chelle couldn't read any more through her tears. She dropped the letter and ran from the table, upstairs, to hurl herself on her bed. A few minutes later she heard footsteps and felt someone sit beside her.

"Come, lass, it's not as bad as all that."

Chelle sat up and laid her head on her father's sharp, bony shoulder. He folded his arms around her and rocked her as he used to when she was a little girl waking from a nightmare, but she didn't think she'd ever wake from this one.

"How could he do this? I understood that he couldn't go with Justin and the others, but to fight for the other side!"

Her father held her closer. "He told us his reasons, Chelle. To my mind, they're good ones."

"I could kill Nate Munroe," Chelle whispered fiercely against his shirt. "If it weren't for him, Trey would never have done this." Anger coursed through her, hot and satisfying, distracting her from her pain. Nate had goaded her brother all spring with slurs and insinuations. Trey had finally called him out and shut his mouth, but Chelle knew her twin well enough to be sure the slurs had still rankled deeply.

She felt her father shake his head. "I don't believe that, lass. Trey and I had some talks over the winter, and I know he talked to your mother, too. He thought it all over, thought about what the war would mean. It wasn't just Nate's slurs that drove him to do this."

"But he never talked to me. If he'd told me—"

"What would you have said to him, Chelle?"

That stopped her. She and Trey had always understood each other. They'd been playmates and close friends as well as brother and sister, but if he'd told her he was considering joining the Union army, it would have come between them. Perhaps permanently.

"You're right, Dad. He couldn't have told me." Chelle pulled away from him and wiped her face on her sleeve. "At least he's relatively safe until next spring."

Her father gave her another quick hug. "Aye, and it could all be over by then. Let's not worry until we have to."

## CHAPTER 9

"Then there's Mrs. Fred Connell, Mabel, her name is. Mam says there's lots of folk clever enough to mind everyone else's business if they neglect their own, but Mrs. Connell's capable enough to mind her own affairs and others' too."

Chelle giggled. "She sounds like Mrs. Hetty Palmer at home."

"Aye." Kendra leaned over her small son and adjusted the bonnet that protected him from the sun of the warm August afternoon. "There's plenty like that the world over, I'll warrant. And then there's Hiram Brantley. He goes by contraries. Whenever his wife wants him to do a thing, she nags him to do the opposite. They've been married twenty years and he still hasn't caught on."

Laughing, Chelle inched forward on her knees, holding Greer's chubby hands as she took a few steps over the rough grass. "Mother used to do that to Dad sometimes, but he knew it, and she knew he knew it. Greer, you'll be running me off my feet in no time."

They sat in a secluded spot on the fell, reached by a side path that wound off in the opposite direction from Mr. Rainnie's sheep pasture. In the two weeks she'd been bringing little Davy out for walks, Kendra had shown Chelle a few worthwhile new spots and told her the quirks of some of Mallonby's people in the process.

Kendra clapped her hands, cheering Greer on. "I think she's goin' to be a big girl, more like her father than her mother. She likely won't thank him for it when she's older."

With a little gurgle of triumph, her red curls running riot in the slight breeze, Greer plumped down on her bottom. Her brown smocked dress promptly blew up over her face, making her squeal. Chelle pulled it down, feeling a twinge of sadness for Mr. Rainnie, mixed with impatience. He shouldn't be missing his daughter's first steps.

"She seems to have her father's temper, too. I hope she's got enough of her mother in her to balance it out. What was she like?"

"Well, you know that Mrs. Rainnie was from Carston." Kendra laid Davy on the grass and clasped her arms around her knees. She'd recovered well from the birth, and she was slowly losing her defensiveness around Chelle. "I think Mr. Rainnie met her at one of the dances there. She had dark hair, and lovely gray eyes. She'd have been two or three years older than me. I never really knew her. She seemed a bit shy like, but I know she loved music. She had a fine singing voice, always sang solos in the church choir, and she and Mr. Rainnie went to all the dances. He played at most of them and they were the best dancers in the district. He's given up playing at dances though, now that she's gone."

Chelle picked Greer up with a sigh. Jean was weaning the babies now. It wouldn't be long until the little girl moved on.

"I can't imagine how anyone raised by the Paxtons could grow up to be a dancer. I wouldn't give them a dog I liked, but I'm afraid Mr. Rainnie is going to let them have Greer."

Kendra gathered up her son and held him close. "Are they so bad, then? I don't know them."

Chelle made a rueful face. "They aren't bad at all, just stiff and set in their ways, and judgmental. They disapproved of me on sight. I don't know if it's because of that letter I wrote, or just because I'm a newcomer." She wished she hadn't spoken when Kendra blushed.

"Or because they've heard you've been seen with me. They have, of course."

"Don't think that way, Kendra. I've done a good enough job ruffling feathers all on my own with that letter. Mrs. Bingham told Dad people were talking about it. Of course, no one's said anything to our faces. I wish they would, so I could fight back. You can't fight a whisper." Chelle wouldn't admit how much the whispers bothered her. They felt like the last straw, added to her fears for Rory and Trey.

She was almost certain that Drew Markham had spread the word about the letter. Chelle had told no one else except Kendra and Mr. Rainnie, and she knew they would both hold their tongues. Of course she would have been blamed regardless, but that didn't lessen her disgust with Drew.

"It's time I was getting home. I promised Aunt Caroline I'd start supper for her so she could run some errands. Oh, no, is that who I think it is?"

Chelle put her hand on Kendra's arm. The man coming toward them was too far away to see clearly, but there was no mistaking his arrogant walk or the auburn hair glinting in the sun. Kendra rolled her eyes.

"Aye, that's Drew sure enough. I don't like coming across him outside of the village like this, but there's nothing for it now."

"He can go to the devil," Chelle huffed. "Come on."

They reached the ford across the river at almost the same time as Drew. He crossed and waited for them, blocking the way to the stepping stones.

"Afternoon, Kendra." His voice was laced with insolence. Kendra replied in kind.

"Bugger off, Drew."

Drew grinned and glanced back at the stepping stones. "Looks like you *ladies* are in need of a little assistance." Before Kendra could react, he scooped her into his arms and carried her across the ford. With the baby in her arms she didn't dare struggle, and he knew it. When he reached the other side, Drew smiled down at her red, angry face and brushed his thumb over his mouth. "Should I or shouldn't I?"

Meanwhile, Chelle had stormed across the ford. Angry beyond thought, she shifted Greer to one arm, stooped and picked up a rock. As a little girl her aim had been as good as Trey's, and she doubted she'd forgotten how to throw.

"Put her down or I'll knock you out."

Drew gave Chelle an appraising look, then set Kendra on her feet. She promptly slapped him as hard as she could. His eyes blazed with anger, but Chelle stood poised with her rock still in hand. "You heard her. Get lost."

Drew's temper overcame his caution. He lifted a hand to the red welt on his cheek and took a quick step toward Chelle. Rather than throw her rock and leave herself unarmed, she elected to stick her foot out and trip him. With a satisfying splash, he toppled face down into the shallow river. Before he could get to his feet, the girls ran to the top of the hill, into sight from the village. Drew didn't follow.

Kendra looked shaken. The children were both crying. Chelle could hardly speak for anger.

"What I wouldn't give if any of the boys from home could have seen that! He'd be lucky if all he got was the thrashing of his life!"

Kendra cast a nervous glance back along the track as she hushed her son. "For your sake, perhaps, but not for the likes of me. Chelle, you'd be wise to say naught about this. That's what I'm going to do."

Chelle stopped and turned to face her. "I'll be…I'm not going to let him get away with this. I'd like to see Brian give him the beating he deserves."

Kendra's eyes turned pleading. "Aye, but it isn't you Drew would vent his spite on afterwards, Chelle. Please, just let it lie."

It went against the grain, but Kendra was right. Chelle would never forgive herself if Drew retaliated against her friend. At least they'd had the satisfaction of seeing him land in the river.

"All right, for your sake I'll be quiet, but I hope Drew goes home and catches pneumonia."

\* \* \* \*

Martin edged his way through the Saturday night crowd and nodded to Harry, who nodded back and pushed a full mug of bitter across the bar. Martin laid down his coins and tasted his drink as he took in the lively scene.

The rich smells of good food and beer permeated the air. Lamplight warmed the stone walls and glanced subtly off mugs and glasses, giving the room a welcoming glow. Mill hands and farm workers filled the tables and lined the bar. Later on Jason Tewkes would be in with his flute, and Henry Walker with his fiddle. Malcolm Blake was already here, over in the far corner, priming his rough but true tenor voice with a whiskey or two. Malcolm's memory was a storehouse of ballads to fill the gaps between tunes. And chances were, someone would bring a bodhran. Martin had always enjoyed playing along with the wild, pulsing rhythm of a bodhran. It seemed to unleash his imagination, lending its energy to his bow until he couldn't tell whether the drum followed him or he followed it. The music just flowed.

Eleanor would sing, too, *My Bonnie Light Horseman* or *Black is the Color* or some other favorite of hers. The Crow was the sort of pub where a woman could go with her husband and feel comfortable. Martin closed his eyes against the memories. He hadn't been to the pub on a Saturday night since losing Eleanor, but tonight he'd felt the walls of the farmhouse closing in on him and knew he needed to get out. A pint or two, and he'd be gone before the music started.

With no empty seats in the place, Martin put his back to a brick post and took his time over his ale. Perhaps this hadn't been a bad idea after all. The hum of voices and the cheerful atmosphere took some of the edge off his loneliness.

"Perhaps she just doesn't like your looks, Drew. Maybe I'll have a go and see if she likes mine better." The voice came from a table at the back of the room. Martin looked and saw Drew Markham sitting with three or four farm laborers about his age. Being in the mill office now, he wouldn't drink with the floor workers. These were lads Drew had known since he was still on his father's farm.

He laughed and clinked his glass against his mate's. "Luck to you, Tom. Only, if it works, you'll have to share. She looks to me like one who might enjoy spreading it around."

Tom looked a bit taken aback. "Keep your voice down, Drew. Her cousin's here somewhere."

"Nay, I saw him leave a few minutes ago, and what's the odds if he were here? I doubt if Brian McShannon's too interested in defending her, not if she chooses to cast in her lot with Kendra Fulton."

The same unfocused rage Martin had felt on market day came boiling up again. He scanned the room for Brian, but didn't see him. It was none of his affair, but tonight Martin didn't feel like containing himself. He'd been doing that for too long. He let the months of suppressed pain rise hot and strong in his chest as he made his way to the back of the pub. Tonight, just once, he'd give it free rein.

"Evenin', lads." Martin focused on Drew, throwing all the contempt he could muster into his tone and gaze. "Was Drew telling you how Jack's niece put him in his place last market day, then? I don't wonder you haven't forgotten, Drew. She called you the smallest man she'd ever met."

The way Martin spoke, Drew couldn't laugh it off. He leaned negligently back in his chair, a reckless gleam in his hazel eyes. He wouldn't be faced down a second time, and Martin knew it. Was counting on it.

"We're here minding our own business, Martin. Why don't you bugger off and do the same?"

"Fine, I will." As he spoke, Martin reached across the table, grabbed the front of Drew's shirt in one hand and backhanded him across the face with the other, sending him and his chair crashing to the floor. It felt good. In fact, it made Martin feel more alive than he had for months. He stood back and grinned at Drew's shocked companions. "Enjoy your evening."

He turned away, deliberately taking his time while Drew staggered up from the floor, his hand to his split lip. Martin had his back to him by the time he got to his feet, but he heard Drew coming around the table and spun at the right moment to bury his left fist in Drew's belly. He crashed to the floor again, gasping.

Oh, it felt good, more like joy than anger. Martin stood there smiling, savoring the energy pumping through him. Drew started to rise, then unexpectedly launched himself at Martin's legs, taking him down. His head snapped back as Drew's right fist connected with his jaw, followed by a left to his eye. Martin felt his own fists slam into Drew's body, then people were pulling them apart and Harry Tate stood over them.

"Martin, have you taken leave of your senses?"

Maybe a little, but he didn't care. Two of Drew's companions helped him up while Martin got to his feet under his own power. Still feeling the rush of the fight, he looked down at the wiry little pub owner and tried to grin, but his sore jaw rebelled.

"I'm sorry, Harry, but his filthy mouth needed shuttin'." He glanced at the toppled chair and the spilled beer on the floor. "Doesn't look like there's any damage to speak of."

"No damage? You should see your face, and Christ, look at Drew."

Martin didn't feel the blows yet, but no doubt he would soon. His left eye had already swollen shut, but through his right he saw Drew, blood from his split lip running down his chin and spattering his shirt. By the way he clutched his side, he might also have a damaged rib or two. Feeling no regret, Martin turned away.

"Perhaps he'll keep a civilized tongue in his head from now on. I'm goin' home. Sorry again, Harry."

A half-moon lit his way home, the cool night air helping to clear his head. By the time Martin reached the farm the rush of the fight had left him, making way for the old emptiness. He went inside, lit a lamp and tended to his battered face. The stillness began to weigh on him again, no matter how hard he tried to ignore it.

This had been a quiet house for as long as he'd known it. As an only child, Martin had spent more time with his fiddle than with any companions, but home had always been warm with love. When his parents' deaths had left him alone, he'd found Eleanor. Now, the silence was a fierce thing that gnawed at his heart.

Unbidden, the image of Chelle McShannon as he'd seen her last popped into Martin's mind. Cheeks blooming scarlet, eyes flashing scorn as she faced Drew, she'd been a sight to stay with a man. Truth was, she'd lurked in the background of Martin's thoughts since she'd dropped his butter on the floor and his daughter in his arms. She'd go through life upsetting apple carts, that one.

Martin put her firmly out of his mind. She'd caused him enough trouble already. He was starting to feel his hurts, and he didn't want to think about what he'd look like in the morning, but he wasn't sorry. Remembering the feel of his fist connecting with Drew's face did wonders to dull his pain.

As he expected, he woke in the morning aching fiercely all over, unable to open his left eye and with a good-sized lump on his jaw. Martin worked his way through the morning chores, then returned to the house, made coffee and sat at the table while it brewed, trying to decide how to spend the day. Not going to church, that was for sure and certain. He wouldn't have gone with a face like this even if he'd been in the habit.

If he wasn't going to keep the Sabbath, he might as well break it. With haying over and harvest not yet on, it was time some of the smaller jobs around the place got done. Perhaps he'd clean out the shed loft where he'd stored his fleeces. He'd ended up selling them to the mill after all, though it galled him.

Someone knocked at the door. Who the devil could that be at this hour on a Sunday? He toyed with the idea of simply shouting for whoever it was to bugger off, but that was bound to hurt his sore mouth. Less painful to tell them face to face.

The devil turned out to be Rochelle McShannon with another package of butter. "Good morning, Mr. Rainnie. May I come in?"

Her eyes widened at the sight of his face. She started to raise a hand to her mouth, then dropped it and blushed. In her yellow print, her face tanned by the summer sun, she lit up the whole yard. Martin took the butter and opened his mouth to tell her he was busy.

"Aye, lass, come in."

He didn't bother to ask himself why he'd changed his mind. Rochelle McShannon might be headstrong, rash and opinionated, but suddenly Martin just didn't feel like drinking his coffee alone. He set the butter on the kitchen dresser and pulled two mugs from a cupboard. "I'd have expected you to be in church this mornin'. I was just 'avin' coffee. Care for a cup?"

"We're going tonight, and yes, please."

He filled the mugs, brought them to the table and got cream from the icebox. Martin winced as the hot coffee hit the raw place on the inside of his cheek, where Drew had smashed it into his teeth. Color rose in Rochelle's face again as she took a sip.

"Gossip travels even faster in Mallonby than it does at home. Brian heard in the village last night that you were in a fight at the pub."

"Aye, I guess that's obvious enough."

"He also heard why. I offered to bring the butter today because I wanted to see if you were all right, and to thank you."

The half-grateful, half-ashamed look in her eyes left him feeling annoyed. Truth, Martin had started the fight because his anger goaded him into it. If Drew's remarks about Chelle hadn't given him an excuse he'd have found another, but here she was, looking at him as if he'd done it for her.

"You've naught to thank me for, lass. Drew has been asking for a beating for months now, and I happened to be there and in the mood to give it to him."

He watched irritation and a little hurt flicker in her eyes, but then her mouth quirked in a small smile. "You don't like being caught in a kindness, do you, Mr. Rainnie? Whatever your reasons, I do owe you thanks. Dad hasn't been too pleased with me over writing that letter, but now he's satisfied that it's been dealt with, which makes things a lot easier for me."

"I'll warrant he's had his times with you before now." Martin could well imagine that, with her obstinate will and flair for finding trouble. She'd be enough to give a father gray hair.

"My father admires people who say what they mean and stand by the consequences." Her smile blossomed into an impish grin. "Brian heard that Drew looks worse than you do."

Martin couldn't hold on to his annoyance. He shook his head, wishing he hadn't invited her in. Her humor touched places inside him that were still raw, places he forgot when he was alone. "I suppose he does."

He watched her look around his home, a feminine assessment that took in all the details, from the books on the mantle over the hearth and the green muslin curtains that framed the windows, to the well-worn oak floors and the fiddle hanging on its peg by the door. The place looked much as it had when Martin was growing up, though Eleanor's rag rugs had replaced the old ones and the sofa facing the hearth was new. The kitchen dresser bore the scars of time, as did the heavy ash farm table that had always been too large. The Rainnies ran to small families.

Rochelle spoke as if she'd been reading his thoughts. "This house is so much older than any at home. Has it been in your family a long time?"

"Aye, happen two hundred years."

"That's hard for me to imagine. Dad built our house twenty years ago." Then, as if it followed naturally, "I'm going to miss Greer when she leaves us. She's starting to walk now and—"

Her voice died away in embarrassment as she looked at him. Martin's anger welled up again. After her last visit here, she should know better.

"Aye, she'll be weaned soon. I'm obliged to you all for takin' such good care of her."

He deliberately let his annoyance show, but it seemed that Miss McShannon had an axe to grind. She lifted her gaze to his. "The Paxtons have called to see her once or twice. Will she be going to them?"

The concern on Chelle's face roused Martin's guilt. Would Greer be that much worse off with her grandparents than if he farmed her out elsewhere? He'd started making inquiries, and there weren't many families willing to take on a baby for what he could afford to pay. Greer couldn't stay with the McShannons. If Brian and Jean were to have another child, they'd have no room to spare.

"I haven't decided yet."

Elbows on the table, Chelle leaned forward, her blue eyes dark and troubled.

"Mr. Rainnie, how well do you know the Paxtons?"

The knife of guilt stabbed deeper. "I know them well enough. They made a decent job of raising Eleanor, and there's no reason to think they'll do worse with Greer if I send her to them."

The concern on Chelle's face deepened into something akin to anguish. "That was quite a few years ago. They're not exactly young now, and ..." With a visible effort, she stopped herself. "As you already know, I have a bad habit of meddling. I'm sorry. I should go. Thank you again for last night. Goodbye, and take care of that eye."

She got to her feet and hurried out. As he drank his lukewarm coffee, Martin felt the walls closing in on him again. Finally he grabbed his cap, whistled for Gyp and strode down the lane, away from Rochelle McShannon and her accusations...

*Hold on, lad. She never made any accusations.*

Perhaps not, but she might as well have. She'd certainly implied that she cared for his daughter more than he did.

Which was a good thing, Martin told himself as turned onto the track leading to the fell. He wanted Greer to be raised by people who cared for her, but where was he going to find them?

* * * *

*Dear Allan,*

*Can you possibly miss me as much as I do you? But I expect I will be returning to London by October at the latest, and it's less than a year now until we'll be together permanently. I've never looked forward to any spring as much as I do the coming one.*

*I hope the business troubles you mentioned in your last letter are resolving. Allan, I know you can't give me particulars without breaking your father's confidence, but I wish you would be more open with me about such things. After all, I will be sharing your future soon. I've given up asking Father about his business concerns, as he persists in treating me like a child...*

Maria Westlake put down her pen and glanced out the French doors of the breakfast room at the back garden. The perennials had finished blooming but colorful beds of dahlias filled the void, backed by tiger lilies. In the centre of it all stood the neat, whitewashed pigeon house, where her father kept his prized fantails. Since he'd given up shooting years ago, they were his only diversion.

A diversion he'd seemed to need lately. He'd been preoccupied for weeks now. Susan had told Maria there'd been grumbling in the village about the mill dropping its price for wool and lengthening hours, but her father always brushed aside her questions.

Now Allan was doing the same thing, and it was becoming more than tiresome. Maria put her letter in the drawer of the desk, opened the doors and stepped out into the sunshine. When she crossed the lawn to the pigeon house, her father came to the door with a white fantail in his hands.

"Maria, were you looking for me?"

"Yes, I was. I want to talk to you."

"Of course, dear." He ducked inside, returned the fantail to its nest box and came out to sit on the bench in front of the pigeon house. "Sit down."

She sat beside him, searching for words. Her father's salt-and-pepper hair was still impeccably clipped, his features as sharp, his face no more wrinkled than it had been for years now, but somehow he seemed older. There'd been a time when Maria found it easy to talk to him, but somehow, over the last couple of years they'd grown apart.

*When did we lose each other?*

"Father, I'm worried about you."

He smiled and patted her knee. "Really? Why?"

She held his gaze, determined to get him to take her seriously. "Because I can tell you're uneasy about something. I always have been able to, you know. Are there problems at the mill?"

Her father smiled again. Perhaps he did have a few more fine lines around his mouth and eyes. He was fifty now, after all.

"Nothing you need to concern yourself over, my dear. Market conditions change. It's a fact of life. Things will right themselves in their own good time."

Maria held on to her patience. He'd spent so much of himself over the years, climbing the business ladder, managing the mill to prosperity, but he'd never learned to manage his family, never knew when an easy answer wasn't enough.

"Perhaps, but I'd still like to know. Allan's letters are full of enough evasions and half-truths as it is. I know his father's cotton business must be suffering, but he won't talk about it, and you're no different."

He took her hand, squeezed it. "Maria, you're young and getting ready to be married. Enjoy this time, and don't worry yourself over my dull business concerns."

Maria let her exasperation show. "But Father, I don't find them dull. Your business concerns affect me as well, and I'm curious. There's so much in the papers these days about the mills, and I've never been through the door of ours."

She watched her father's face turn stern. "There's nothing much to be curious about. The mill is unpleasant, loud and dangerous, no place for a lady."

"But women work there." Maria didn't like to admit it, but her conversation with the McShannon girl had started her thinking. And then that letter in the paper had disturbed her even more. She *was* curious.

Clearly vexed, her father stood. "Yes, but they're brought up to it. Bred for it, you might say. You aren't. Now stop worrying over nothing. If you nag Allan like this once you're married, you'll make him old before his time."

She heard the dismissal in his tone. Of course he was right in a way; the mill hands started young and grew used to the work as time went on, and most of their families had been mill hands for generations. Maria gave up and went back to the house, weighed down by a sense of foreboding she couldn't shake.

* * * *

"Calm down, child. Your mam's had three babies. She knows what she's about. Chelle, are you ready?"

"Yes, Aunt, I'm right behind you." Chelle followed Caroline and the agitated seven-year-old messenger, Annie Wilson, out into the fine summer night. It only took fifteen minutes to reach the Wilsons' home near the other end of the village. Annie's mother, Sarah, met them at the door. Square-built but comely, she stepped aside to let them in.

"Now then, Caroline. I didn't want to send for you so soon, but John insisted. I've barely started painin' yet. Annie, be a good girl and take your brother and sister down to your Gran's now, will you?"

"But Mam—"

"Go on, Annie, and do as you're told. I'll be all right." Sarah looked at Chelle with some doubt, but the Wilsons weren't mill people and Chelle guessed they knew Caroline well enough to weigh against any gossip they might have heard. "Come in, lass. I'll do my best not to keep the two of you here all night."

Mr. Wilson stood in the background, a tall, lean fellow who owned the harness shop next to the Bingham's store. He seemed to be the nervous type of father. Once Annie had reluctantly left the house with her younger siblings in tow, Caroline took him in hand.

"John, why don't you go down to the Crow for a pint? You'll only be five minutes away, and I'll send Chelle for you if you're needed."

"Aye, John, go," his wife urged. "Caroline doesn't need you underfoot."

"All right, then, run me out of my own home." He took his cap and made for the door, but out of his wife's sight he beckoned to Caroline. She followed him out to the step for a moment. A few minutes later, under pretence of checking the water heating on the stove, she whispered to Chelle in the kitchen.

"John told me he thinks Sarah's heart has been acting strangely. She's been putting her hand to her chest now and then, and her hands and feet have been swelling, though she denies anything's wrong. Let's hope it's just him being jittery."

The next few hours gave Mr. Wilson's fears the lie. Sarah's labor progressed like clockwork. By midnight she was in the final stages, ready to push her child into the world.

And then the unthinkable happened.

In the middle of a strong contraction, Sarah relaxed and stopped breathing. Caroline turned to Chelle, her face stark white.

Run for Dr. Halstead, then go fetch Mr. Wilson. Hurry, lass."

Chelle ran. She found the doctor home; he left for the Wilsons' before she'd even finished explaining. Then she had to face Mr. Wilson.

As soon as he saw her outside the pub window, he ran to the door. Seeing the fear on his face nearly dried up her voice.

"You're needed at home. The doctor should be there by now. I called for him first. Hurry."

She stood, trying to catch her breath, while Mr. Wilson disappeared down the street. All Chelle wanted was to go home, crawl into bed, pull the covers over her head and hide. She'd helped Aunt Caroline with first births, long, painful births, dicey births, but the outcome had always been a healthy baby and a happy, if exhausted, mother.

*Chelle, you promised Aunt Caroline you'd be ready for anything.*

Moving as stiffly as an old woman, she returned to the Wilsons'. Mr. Wilson sat on the sofa, his shocked face pale in the dim light of the lamp on the mantel. He didn't seem to see Chelle as she passed into the kitchen. Aunt Caroline was there, sitting at the table with the doctor. She looked ten years older.

"There you are, lass. The baby survived. A healthy little lad."

Dr. Halstead laid a hand on her shoulder. "Will you call for Sarah's mother on your way home, Caroline? I'll stay here until she arrives."

"Aye." She picked up her bag and handed her birthing stool to Chelle. In the sitting room, Caroline knelt beside Mr. Wilson and put a hand on his knee. "I'm so sorry, John. You have a fine new son."

He didn't acknowledge that she'd spoken. Caroline rose and left him there, staring stonily into space.

At home, Chelle hurried upstairs to her room. She went in to light the lamp, but instead of undressing she crept across the hall into the children's room and lifted Greer from her crib.

*The baby lived. Remember that. The baby lived, and he has a father.*

Just as Greer did. Chelle thought she understood Mr. Rainnie a little better now. She almost wished she hadn't taken Greer to the farm that day.

Almost.

She sat in the rocker and held the sleeping little girl close for a few minutes. In spite of what had happened tonight, Chelle didn't want to stop helping Caroline. And she didn't want to stop hoping that someday, Greer really would have a father.

# *CHAPTER 10*

Jean looked over her shoulder as she finished pinning Peter's diaper. "What's wrong wi' that one this mornin'?"

Chelle struggled to get Greer's arms through the sleeves of her dress as she kicked and whimpered. "I don't know. She's normally so happy in the morning."

By the time she was dressed, the little girl's whimpers had turned to peevish sobs. She settled briefly after breakfast, but started fussing again later in the morning and refused to eat at dinnertime. Jean and Caroline were puzzled. Weaning had gone well for both babies, with no upsets, and Greer had never been whiny. She screamed when she was angry and usually smiled otherwise.

"There's summat not right," Caroline said. "She's always eaten well."

By late afternoon, Greer was running a low fever. Chelle put her to bed and managed to get her to sleep. When she checked on the baby half an hour later, she ran down to Caroline as fast as her legs would take her.

"Aunt, that child is burning up."

Caroline followed her back to the children's room. Greer's face was flushed, her eyes glazed with fever. Caroline's lips set in a worried line as she changed the baby's diaper.

"I'm at a loss. She and Peter have been eating the same things and he's fine, but summat's certainly upset this one. Run and get some cold water, Chelle."

Greer screamed when Caroline started bathing her with icy well water. Chelle's heart started to race. She'd helped Aunt Caroline with one or two ailing babies, but she'd never seen a child this ill.

"Aunt, do you think someone should go for her father?"

Caroline laid the baby in her crib, naked except for her diaper, still shrieking. She hesitated for a moment. "I don't like

99

to alarm him, but aye, lass, perhaps so. I don't like the look of this. Go get one of the men to saddle Lady, and tell Jean to make some agrimony tea. And send someone for the doctor."

Brian, who'd been in the kitchen when Chelle first came downstairs for his mother, anticipated her and had the mare saddled by the time Chelle got out to the yard. When he made to mount, she stopped him.

"I used the saddle last. The stirrups are still set for me. I'll go for Mr. Rainnie, and you can go for the doctor."

"All right, go on, then." Brian stepped back and gave her a leg up. "And try not to frighten Martin too much. These things happen wi' young ones."

It would be difficult not to scare Mr. Rainnie when Chelle was thoroughly frightened herself. She'd known she'd grown attached to Greer, but now she knew just how deep that bond ran. She'd watched Greer learn to walk, spent hours with her daily, put her to sleep at night. Chelle wished with all her heart that Uncle Jack's elderly Lady were her father's fleet Jezebel as she galloped along the road to the Rainnie farm.

After an afternoon spent digging potatoes, Martin had come in for an early supper, intending to go out to the sheep afterwards. Only he'd had a poor night's sleep, and after eating he'd dozed off on the sofa. He woke with a start at the sound of a knock at the door.

He got up, rubbing the sleep from his eyes. He'd half a mind not to answer it, to let them think he was still out in the fields. He must look like the old Nick, with two days' growth of beard, his hair standing on end and the remains of bruises still discoloring his face. But whoever it was might have seen him through the window, so he really shouldn't.

He came fully awake when he opened the door and saw Rochelle McShannon standing there, breathless with worry. She struggled to find her voice.

"Mr. Rainnie, Greer's ill. She's running a dangerous fever. Aunt thinks you should come in."

He must be still asleep and dreaming. Martin stood there gaping at her like a half-wit until she spoke again. "Mr. Rainnie, please."

The fear in her voice snapped him out of his trance. Instinct took over. He pushed past Rochelle, ran to the byre, bridled the black cob and swung up bareback. The girl followed him down the lane at a gallop.

The horses' hooves pounded out a beat that became words in Martin's mind, a frantic, repeated prayer. *Please, God. Not her too. Please.*

Was this punishment? The price for turning away from all that was left of Eleanor? From a part of himself? He knew nothing of his daughter, had cared nothing for her except to keep her housed, fed and out of his sight. He'd given her nothing of himself, and now he was going to lose her.

Brian came out of the house to take the horses as they clattered into the forge yard. Martin slid to the ground, his legs threatening to buckle as he followed Rochelle inside.

Caroline hurried down the stairs. "You're here then. She's about the same. Jean's with her right now."

Martin's heart hammered in his ears at her obvious concern. Caroline had been bringing Mallonby's babies into the world for the last twenty years, and she wasn't easily shaken.

"I want to see her."

"Aye, come with me."

When Caroline didn't protest, Martin's fear rose a notch. He followed her and Chelle up to the children's room. Greer lay in her crib, crying fitfully, her fine red curls plastered to her head with sweat. When Martin reached out to touch her hand, she opened her gray eyes wide and screamed.

Eleanor's eyes, looking at him with terror. Martin thought his heart would tear loose in chest. Why wouldn't he frighten his daughter, showing up like this when she was ill? He was a complete stranger to her.

Chelle picked the baby up, wet a cloth in the basin on the nightstand and laid it on the back of her neck. In familiar arms,

Greer stopped screaming. Martin laid his hand on her back, his palm covering her from shoulder to shoulder, feeling the heat radiating from her. She looked to be a sturdy little thing, but she was too young and small to fight for long against a fever like this.

"Haven't you sent for the doctor, Caroline?"

Jean answered, indignation in her tone. "Aye, of course we did, but he's out on a call. His wife said she'd give him the message as soon as he returned."

Martin wanted a target for his fear and anger, but he knew the McShannons had cared for Greer as if she were their own. The only person he could blame was himself. He tried to speak around the lump in his throat and couldn't. Caroline took him firmly by the arm.

"Come downstairs and wait for Doctor Halstead, Martin."

With a last look at Rochelle cradling his daughter, he let Caroline lead him from the room. Colin and Jack had arrived home from a job on one of the farms. They came in laughing and bantering, but the laughter died when they saw Martin there and Caroline's grave face. Jack crossed the room and put his hands on his wife's shoulders. "Is summat the matter with Greer, then?"

"Aye, she's running a high fever. Jack, will you run round to the surgery and find out what's keeping Dr. Halstead?"

"Aye, I won't be long." Jack hurried out again. Martin slumped on the sofa, rested his elbows on his knees and hid his face in his hands. By the stove, Colin and Caroline spoke quietly, their voices too low for him to follow. Then Martin heard the clink of glass, the sound of pouring liquid, followed by Colin's voice.

"Here, Martin, I think you could use this."

The fragrance of good whiskey made him look up. He took the drink, welcoming its bracing burn. Colin sat beside him, his thin hand surprisingly strong as it gripped Martin's shoulder. "Dr. Halstead will be here soon. Don't think the worst, lad, it won't help."

Martin turned away from the sympathy on the older man's face. He didn't deserve it.

"I can't lose Greer, Colin. I haven't had time to get to know her. I haven't *taken* the time to get to know her."

Colin swirled the whiskey in his own glass, then gave his head a rueful shake. "We don't always make the most selfless decisions when we're hurting. I've got a son caught up in the war at home who might have been safely out of it if I'd said or done some things differently when Sidonie was ill, and Chelle had expectations. I don't think she realized I knew, but she might have married if she hadn't felt obliged to come here with me. She's never told me what happened. Perhaps her young man didn't want to wait. Maybe I did the right thing for my children by leaving and maybe I didn't, but what's done is done."

So Chelle had been disappointed? *Fool, it's no concern of yours. A glowing young lass like her, with that figure and those eyes—she likely had her pick of the men.* Any road, he had no right to be thinking of Chelle that way, least of all now. Martin fisted his hands in an instinctive response, as if he could use them to battle the illness menacing his little daughter.

"Aye, but you were a father to your children when they were small. What if I don't get a chance to be a father to Greer? I've turned my back on her—on Eleanor's daughter."

Colin downed his drink and gave Martin's shoulder a bracing squeeze. "Yes, but you're here now, when she needs you. You're being a father to her right now. Don't think on it, Martin. Just hope."

\* \* \* \*

Jack returned with the news that Dr. Halstead couldn't leave his current patient and didn't expect to be home until morning. "Not that he could do much more than we're doing," Caroline said. She filled the kettle and set it back on the stove with a clatter. "We'll just have to wait."

103

Her eyes met Martin's. She started to speak, but changed her mind. Feeling her eyes on his back, he got up and climbed the stairs.

His shaky hand fumbled with the knob as he opened the bedroom door. Chelle sat in the rocker with Greer, humming quietly as she rocked the baby. Afraid he'd upset his daughter again, Martin stayed in the shadows as he crossed the room. Chelle looked up at him as he stopped behind her.

"There isn't any change. Is the doctor coming?"

"Not before morning." Martin laid a tentative hand on Greer's hot little back. He didn't want to frighten her again, but he had to touch her. When she whimpered and pulled away, he retreated to the bed against the wall. From there, all he could see of Chelle and the baby was a gently rocking silhouette in the dim lamplight.

"I want to stay here with her."

He braced himself for an argument. He got simple acceptance. "Of course you do."

She humbled him. Whatever she might have thought of him before tonight, she was willing to give him a chance. Chelle had reason to be bitter, too, but she had strength, a kind of strength Martin hadn't been able to find through his own grief.

"You're one as looks for the best in people, aren't you, lass?"

"Yes, I am." The silhouette shifted as Chelle ran her hand over Greer's back. "You might like me to think otherwise, but you aren't the sort of man who has no feelings for his children."

"Nay, I suppose not." In the concealing shadows, the words seemed to say themselves. "When Eleanor found out she was going to be a mother she was beyond pleased, and I wasn't far behind her. She was an only child, as I am. We wanted a big family." Martin never allowed himself to think of those months, the happiest he expected ever to know. It hurt to think of them now, but somehow the pain opened him. He felt alive, and that life found its focus in the baby dozing fitfully in Chelle's arms.

She stopped rocking and turned toward him. "Mr. Rainnie, I think you need Greer as much—maybe more—than she needs you."

"It isn't that simple, lass. I've got a farm to run, and good housekeepers aren't easy to find."

Martin knew how hollow the excuse sounded as soon as he spoke. Chelle must know it too, but she stayed silent, waiting while he found his way to the most frightening decision of his life.

"Any road, I'll find someone, and as soon as I do, Greer's comin' home where she belongs."

Holding Greer close, Chelle rose. She took a step toward him, then another, until she could see his face clearly. A soft smile tugged at her lips.

"Get some sleep, Mr. Rainnie. I'll wake you if there's any change in her. You'll need your strength to deal with Aunt Caroline tomorrow."

* * * *

Caroline, Jean and Chelle took shifts tending Greer through the night, bathing her, giving her sips of agrimony tea and juice to settle her digestive tract and replace the fluids she'd lost. By dawn, Chelle could hardly keep her eyes open. Her anxiety hadn't allowed her to sleep when she wasn't with the baby. Rocking slowly, she started to drift off, but the harsh cawing of a crow jerked her back to wakefulness.

She blinked and looked around the room, clearly visible now in the growing light. She must have slept in spite of herself. And Greer…

Greer slept deeply, her little face pale, her bare skin damp with cooling sweat. Her fever had broken.

"Oh, thank God." All night Chelle had tried to face the possibility of losing the little girl, and failed. As for Mr.

Rainnie, she'd never forget his stricken eyes when she'd gone to fetch him. He really did need Greer as much as she needed him.

The baby didn't wake while Chelle changed her, laid her in her crib and tucked a blanket around her. Mr. Rainnie lay on the bed, his hair rumpled, a shadow of a beard on his jaw. He hadn't moved since he'd stretched out there last night, but she had no idea if he'd slept. Chelle crept over to him and laid her hand on his shoulder.

"Mr. Rainnie, Greer's fever has broken."

His eyes snapped open. Relief seemed to strike him like a blow. The color drained from his face as he sat up.

"I—it has?"

His whole face lit up as the news sank in. Chelle wouldn't have dreamed he could look like that. Dizzy with relief herself, she nodded toward the crib.

"Yes. Look for yourself."

Just as Mr. Rainnie carefully lifted his daughter from the crib, Caroline entered the room. Her hands clamped on her hips as her brows lifted. Chelle shot her a pleading glance and held a finger to her lips.

"She's better, Aunt. I was just going to come down to tell you."

Holding his daughter close against his chest, Mr. Rainnie stood his ground. As formidable as Chelle had ever seen him, he looked defiance at Caroline.

"As soon as I can find a housekeeper, Greer's comin' home with me."

Chelle's stomach knotted when her aunt's mouth drew into a thin line. Caroline could be as stubborn as Mr. Rainnie when she chose.

"Martin, you can't think we've neglected her."

Mr. Rainnie spoke in an urgent whisper. "Of course I don't think that, Caroline. I'm the one who's neglected her, can't you see that? I'll always be grateful for all you've done for her, but she belongs at home."

There wasn't much Caroline could say. After all, he was Greer's father, but she wouldn't yield immediately.

"We'll discuss it over breakfast. Now put the child back in her bed and come downstairs. She needs to rest."

While Caroline and Jean made porridge and toast, Mr. Rainnie sat quietly at the table. Absorbed in his own thoughts, he watched Chelle set out plates and cutlery. Colin and Jack came in from the yard and broke into relieved grins when Caroline told them that Greer was better.

"Good news." Colin scraped a chair back and sat next to Mr. Rainnie. "She'll pick up as quick as she took ill. She's got your constitution as well as your temper. Caroline, what's the matter?"

Caroline had been bustling around the kitchen in silence. Her wooden spoon rattled against the porridge pot as she stirred it with unnecessary vigor.

"Nothing's the matter, except that Martin needs to find a housekeeper as soon as possible. He's decided to take Greer home."

Jack crossed the room and laid his hands on Caroline's shoulders. Chelle knew her aunt would miss Greer every bit as much as she. Mr. Rainnie turned to her, looking just as determined as he had upstairs.

"Not long after Greer was born, Jessie Mason told me she'd be willin' to keep house for me. I said no at the time, and I'd all but forgotten the offer. She's still living with her sister's family, isn't she? I haven't heard otherwise."

Jean set a plate of toast on the table. She looked tired and relieved. Chelle felt a pang of guilt at her own selfish regrets. Jean would miss Greer the most of anyone at the forge, having nursed her along with her own child.

"Aye, she is. Jessie likes children, but I think she'd be pleased to have just one to look after instead of her sister's six, and to be paid in the bargain. Her husband didn't leave her much, and you know her brother-in-law doesn't exactly have his name up for generosity."

Caroline stepped away from Jack and started dishing up porridge. She threw Martin a challenging glance over her shoulder. "What about Eleanor's parents?"

He shrugged. "I'll pay a call and tell them what I've decided. I doubt they'll be pleased, but I'm not sure how much they really want her, when it comes to that. More than anything, I think they don't want their neighbors talkin', sayin' they let their granddaughter be raised by strangers. Any road, it isn't up to them. I'm Greer's father."

Watching him, it came home to Chelle that this was no overnight change. Mr. Rainnie had always loved Greer, but it had taken almost losing her to make him face the fact. Knowing how much he cared made it a lot easier to see Greer go.

* * * *

Out in the yard with the children in the sweet-smelling August dusk, Chelle glanced up at the sound of the gate clicking shut behind Mr. Rainnie. In the two weeks since Greer had been taken ill, he'd stopped by every day, until even Caroline began to believe he deserved to take his daughter home.

Greer ran to meet him. She'd recovered as quickly as she'd gotten sick, and she'd already gotten over her shyness with her father, helped by the treats he usually brought for her. As always, his face lit up with a smile as he squatted down in front of her and touched the tip of her nose.

"How's my lass today?"

Chelle never saw him smile like that for anyone but Greer. To everyone else he remained as distant as before, but perhaps this one chink in his armor would widen with time to include others. If it did, no doubt that smile would melt the heart of some local girl and Greer would have a mother again. Chelle felt a pang of loneliness at the thought.

Bending down, Greer's tiny hand engulfed in his, Mr. Rainnie crossed the yard and sat beside Chelle on the doorstep.

"Evenin', Miss Rochelle. This one seems right as rain again, doesn't she?"

Greer and Peter both climbed into Chelle's lap, but Greer reached out to grasp her father's sleeve. Chelle couldn't help grinning at the gratified look on his face.

"Yes, she does. She likes you, Mr. Rainnie."

Suddenly ill at ease, he turned towards her. "She seems to be getting used to me, any road. Lass, there's summat I want to ask you."

"What's that?"

He took a deep breath as if he needed to gather his courage, keeping his eyes on his daughter. "Well, Jessie Mason has agreed to come and keep house for me, startin' on Monday. So I'll be takin' Greer home, and I was thinkin' it would be easier for her if you could come out, too, for two or three days to help her get settled."

Clearly uncomfortable with the request, Mr. Rainnie raised his eyes to Chelle's for a brief moment. "If you're willin', I'll step in and see if it's all right with your father and Caroline."

Chelle's heart lifted at the thought of being able to help Greer adjust to her new home, but she couldn't imagine her father or her aunt agreeing. She'd created enough talk already, and staying at Mr. Rainnie's with only a housekeeper there would surely cause more. With a baby in each arm, she stood.

"I'd be willing, but I can't speak for Dad and Aunt Caroline. Come in."

Caroline hesitated when Mr. Rainnie broached the idea. "It wouldn't be proper, Chelle, a young girl like you, with only Mrs. Mason there. No offense meant, Martin, but people would likely talk."

Chelle's father surprised her. "It's only for two or three days, hardly something for the old hens to cluck about," he said with a shrug. "You've known Martin and Jessie all their lives, and so has everyone else in Mallonby. I'd say go, lass, if you want to, and let the hens cluck if they choose."

Before Chelle could respond, Mr. Rainnie held out his hand. "All right, then. I'll come in for you and Greer after chores on Monday morning."

His warm, hard fingers closed around hers. Something in her thrilled to the emotion she sensed in him. Any doubt that he'd be good to Greer melted away. As for the hens, Chelle agreed with her father. Let them cluck if they chose.

* * * *

"You'll like Jessie. That's what she prefers to be called, by the by. And when it comes to that, it's time you started calling me Martin, if you're going to be staying under my roof."

Chelle shifted the baby on her lap and let her shawl slip from her shoulders. The day promised to be a warm one, with the sun burning away the delicate mist that hung over the fell. It still blanketed the river, adding allure to the fine morning as they rolled along in Mr. Rainnie's pony trap behind the black cob, Major.

"And most people call me Chelle. My brother started it when we were little, and it caught on. Martin, how long have your parents been gone?"

"Mam's been gone for happen ten years now, and Dad for six."

Ten years. He'd been younger than Chelle when he lost his mother. "I miss my mother so much," she said softly. "When I was seven or eight, a girlfriend of mine said that Mother had 'charmth.' Warmth and charm, that describes her pretty well."

Martin glanced sideways at her, a brief, summing look. "I'll warrant you're more your father's daughter."

Chelle lifted a brow at him. "Meaning?"

He shook the reins, a hint of a grin on his face. "You look like him, and I'll warrant that you can be just as hard-headed as Colin when you choose."

Chelle had been told all her life how much she resembled her father, but it surprised her coming from Martin. After all, he hardly knew her. "I suppose so. Trey—my brother—was always more like Mother. He has her coloring and her temper."

Getting too warm in her coat, Greer started to squirm. Her fussing progressed to annoyed shrieks by the time Chelle got the garment unbuttoned. "Speaking of temper, Greer certainly has one, but it never seems to last for long. A bit of a storm, and then the sun comes out. And she's determined. When she wants something she doesn't give up easily." She flashed Martin a smile. "It goes with the hair, I suspect."

His eyes settled on Greer, full of possessive pride. "No doubt."

When they reached the farm, a stout, fiftyish woman came out of the house to greet them. With her salt and pepper hair pulled back in a tight bun that accentuated her narrow face, Jessie Mason would have looked rather grim if not for the twinkle in her round hazel eyes.

"So this is Greer." She smiled when the baby hid her face against Chelle's shoulder. "She'll come around soon enough." Jessie's gaze followed Martin as he took the horse to the barn. Her voice dropped to a conspirator's whisper. "I'm glad to see her father startin' to come around, too. Come in, lass. I expect you're ready to put that one down. She looks heavy enough."

Martin brought Chelle's bag and the baby's things in, then took the sandwich Jessie made for him and headed out to the fields to make up for lost time. "I'm cuttin' the oats today, so don't expect me before dark." After he left, Jessie led Chelle upstairs to the room she and Greer would share. A crib stood ready in the corner, obviously old and well-used. Jessie ran a hand along one dark-stained side rail.

"It's the one Martin slept in himself. He told me so."

Chelle struggled to imagine Martin's long legs and broad shoulders ever having been small enough to fit in the crib. The room was larger than her room at Uncle Jack's, with a crab-apple tree outside the window that would be lovely in its spring bloom. Now, the leaves and branches filtered the incoming light, making shadow patterns on the floor.

Together, taking turns holding Greer, Jessie and Chelle made up the crib with the linens Jessie had bought in the village. Chelle opened the window to let in the breeze before they returned downstairs. The house didn't have the airy feel of her old home, but it had the same warmth. Right now, it smelled of the soup Jessie was simmering for lunch. When she set about making scones Chelle offered to help, but Jessie waved her away.

"You just keep an eye on the little one, lass, and leave the cookin' and the house to me. That's what Martin's payin' me for."

After her busy morning, Greer was ready for a nap. Chelle settled her on the sofa, then scanned the books on the long mantel. She found an old copy of *Ivanhoe*, curled up beside Greer and started leafing through it.

The story took her back to her eighth winter, when her mother had read it to her and Trey in the front room while the fire snapped and the wind rattled around the house. Chelle turned to Jessie and held up the book.

"Have you ever read this?"

Jessie looked up from her dough with a shrug. "No. I've never had much time or inclination for novels."

"My mother read it to me when I was small. She had a gift for telling stories. She made you feel like you were right there."

Jessie shrugged again as she kneaded. "You've got an imagination, lass. I was born without one."

"No one's born without an imagination, Jessie." Chelle smiled at her memories. "There was one story Mother used to tell, about a phantom wolf—*loup-garou*, she called it—it scared Trey and me half-silly, but we asked her to tell it over and over again. She could use her voice to make you feel a dozen different things at once."

Jessie wiped her hands on her apron and began cutting her dough into neat triangles. "These will be a treat with the strawberry jam I brought. I suppose you'd say Martin has a gift. When he plays his fiddle he can make you feel a dozen things at once, like you say."

"See, Jessie, you do have an imagination. I'm going to take Greer upstairs, and then I want to know what you put in that soup. I'm getting hungry just smelling it."

\* \* \* \*

Martin stopped on the track in the late twilight, scythe in hand, watching the lamplight glowing from the windows of his house. It hurt him and drew him both. It wasn't the same, never would be the same as coming home to Eleanor.

But now Greer was there. He started off again, quickening his stride at the thought of seeing her. He still didn't understand what had happened to him or why, but he knew something inside him had shifted permanently the night Greer was ill. He had no choice but to accept it, even while he acknowledged that it scared the hell out of him.

He came in to the aroma of Jessie's ham and leek pie and the sight of Rochelle—Chelle, he reminded himself—on the sofa, cradling his sleepy daughter on her lap. When he crossed the room and crouched beside her, Greer turned away with a whimper. Chelle rocked her slowly back and forth, stroking her back.

"She doesn't want me to put her to bed. I tried, but she started screaming. This is the first time she's been away from Uncle Jack's overnight."

Feeling foolishly inadequate, Martin just stood there. His daughter hadn't been home a full day, and already he was at a loss. Jessie took the pie from the oven and set it on the table.

"Why don't you try playing for her, Martin?"

His chest tightened at the thought. He hadn't picked up his fiddle since the day he'd met Chelle up on the fell. It had torn something open in him then. Would it hurt as much now, or had that changed too? He couldn't make sense of his feelings anymore.

But Jessie was watching him with an encouraging smile, and Chelle's deep blue eyes were on him, too. How could he refuse without looking like a fool? He took down the fiddle, tuned it, keeping his eyes on Greer.

"Does she recognize any songs?"

"Jean used to sing the Skye Boat Song to her and Peter," Chelle told him.

Eyes closed, Martin began the familiar melody. In his mind he heard Eleanor's voice blended with the singing of the fiddle, as he'd heard it on so many evenings.

*Tho' the waves leap, soft be your sleep*
*Ocean's a royal bed*
*Rocked on the deep, Flora will keep*
*Watch by your weary head...*

He looked and saw Greer staring at him, eyes wide. Forgetting his own feelings, he slid into a slow air and watched her as he played. Her fascinated gaze never left him. Then, her lids drifted down and she laid her head on Chelle's shoulder. She stood slowly and carried the baby upstairs.

Martin watched her out of sight before he hung the fiddle back on its peg. He looked down at the bow in his hands. Instead of the crushing grief that had overwhelmed him the last time he'd played, he felt only simple contentment. What kind of alchemy was Greer working on him, then?

He hung the bow with the fiddle and turned away. Since Eleanor's death, there'd been no solid ground under his feet. Now, he felt more at sea than ever, all because of a child still too young to speak.

He sure as hell didn't want this ache in his heart, this raw, stinging vulnerability, but it seemed he had no choice.

# CHAPTER 11

Martin woke to the sound of women's voices drifting up the stairs. It took him a moment to remember who they were and why they were there. He'd brought his daughter home yesterday.

She must have had a relatively peaceful first night, since he'd slept through. He knew already that if Greer had decided to cry, he would have heard her. She wasn't one to hold back.

Martin rose, opened his door a crack and found a pitcher of warm water waiting for him in the hall. Of course, with women in the house he couldn't go down undressed to get water himself. Another small thing to get used to.

*Better shave, too.*

The savory aroma of browned sausages and potatoes floated up to him with the voices. Stomach rumbling, Martin hurried to wash and dress. Downstairs, he found Jessie ready to serve breakfast and Chelle leaning over Greer as she scuttled across the floor on all fours, laughing, her bottom in the air, her green calico dress all askew. Chelle hadn't put her hair up yet; it swept past the curve of her cheek like a sunny curtain to mingle with the baby's bright curls.

She wore a plain cotton dress in a quiet rosy shade that would have made most blondes look washed-out, but not her. The gown's simplicity emphasized the grace of Chelle's slender young figure, and the subtle color brought out the bloom of her skin. Watching her, Martin felt his blood warm, a straightforward male response.

He averted his eyes. It brought up too many confusing feelings—resentment, sadness, appreciation—to watch someone else take Eleanor's place with Greer. As for his body's response, that was natural enough, but it only added to the confusion.

Greer saw him, stopped her game and scampered to him with Chelle behind her, flushed and smiling.

"Good morning."

Something of his uneasiness must have showed. Her smile fading, she stepped back as Martin picked up his daughter.

"Mornin', young lassie. Have you had your breakfast yet?"

"Yes, she has." Chelle retreated to the table, pulled her hair over her shoulder and began braiding it, her movements quick and, Martin thought, a little nervous. She pulled a ribbon from her pocket, tied her braid and began setting the table. He still hadn't spoken to her.

Jessie set a pan of sizzling sausages and potatoes in the middle of the table. Martin hugged Greer, put her down and included both women in a nod of thanks.

"This looks a treat. How'd the little one fare overnight?"

Her face flushed from her game with Greer, Chelle handed him the plate Jessie had just filled. "Fine. She only woke once, and she went right back to sleep when she realized I was there."

"Good. Jessie, I'll be goin' in to the store for the mail this afternoon. Let me know if you need anything."

He hadn't realized he was so rusty at ordinary conversation. Or perhaps it was his new awareness of Chelle that kept him silent. Declining to analyze his reasons, Martin applied himself to his breakfast and watched Greer while she played around the table. Altogether, it was a relief to get out of the house when the meal was over.

\* \* \* \*

After settling Greer for her afternoon nap, Chelle found herself at loose ends. Jessie had already taken care of the housework and started a pot of corned beef and cabbage for supper. Now she was concocting a milk pudding. She hadn't allowed Chelle to do anything useful other than look after the baby. She wondered if Jessie was afraid Martin would decide he didn't need her if she slowed down.

The only chore waiting now was milking. Greer would sleep for at least an hour, so Chelle slipped out without saying anything to Jessie, found the milk pails in the cellar and brought the two cows in from the paddock behind the byre. She breathed a sigh of relief when she got them safely inside without Jessie appearing to see what she was about.

Chelle approached the first Jersey cautiously, but the cow gave her no trouble. She seemed to be used to a woman's hand. Likely Martin's wife had done the milking. Chelle shook off a vague feeling of guilt as her hands worked the cow's teats. It was cruel that Eleanor Rainnie hadn't been given the chance to enjoy her baby and her marriage.

Chelle had hoped to see a picture of Greer's mother when she came to the farm, but hadn't come across one yet. From Kendra's description, Eleanor had been close to Chelle's physical opposite. Her cheeks warmed, remembering the way Martin had looked at her this morning when he came downstairs. Was it her imagination, or had she seen a glimmer of attraction there?

He was almost as different from Rory as she was from Eleanor, but something in Chelle had responded to that look. She shrugged off the thought. She'd had enough attention from men at home to know that these stray attractions came and went. Martin was no carefree boy looking to flirt, and she had no intention of getting involved with a man who needed a mother for his child. When she left the farm, this pull between her and Martin—if she hadn't imagined it—would die as quickly as it had formed.

The same ginger tabby Chelle had seen before came skulking into the byre, looking expectant. At home, they'd always given the cats a treat at milking time. It seemed Mr. Rainnie did the same. Sure enough, the tabby came closer and opened his mouth for a squirt of milk. Chelle obliged him with a grin, just before she heard the clatter of heavy hooves and the creak of a wagon coming to a halt.

A few minutes later, Martin led his team past the stall where Chelle sat. Walking between the two massive mares, he didn't see her. Gyp followed.

"Now then, Tessa, get over, there's a lass." Martin's voice was low and easy, followed by the sounds of him removing the mare's harness. Gyp barked, earning a quiet chuckle. "Daft old lad, are you ever going to act your age? Go on now."

Chelle discovered that she'd stopped milking to listen to him. Irritated with herself, she turned back to the cow and sent milk hissing into the pail. When Martin stilled, she knew he'd heard her. He appeared at the entrance to the stall, blocking her light.

"Go on inside. I'll finish out here."

Chelle looked up. She wasn't sure why—perhaps just because it reminded her of home—but she felt childishly determined to finish the chore.

"Mr. Rainnie...Martin, I grew up on a farm. I'm used to milking, and Greer's asleep. I have time. Why don't you start with the other cow?"

His eyes flashed irritation as he took a step closer. "You're here to look after Greer, not the stock. If she wakes early, Jessie will have to tend to her in the middle of getting supper. Go on inside."

His voice held no warmth now. Clearly, she'd overstepped a boundary. Without replying, Chelle stood and edged past him.

In the cramped space, he seemed larger than ever. His legs would make two of hers in thickness, as would his forearms, revealed by the rolled-up sleeves of his cotton shirt. He exuded power along with the scents of clean sweat and fresh air. Chelle knew he'd intended to intimidate her, and he'd succeeded. The thought irked her, so she stopped and rested a hand on the cow's side.

"If I've done something to annoy you, tell me and I'll try not to do it again."

Martin took Chelle's place on the stool and looked up with an exasperated scowl. "Can't take no for an answer, can you? I'm used to doing my own chores, is all, and I'd prefer that you leave me to it."

"Of course." Chelle flashed him an irritating grin and took her time leaving the byre. *If you and I were to spend a week together, Mr. Rainnie, we'd be at each other's throats by the end of it.*

She fed Greer when she woke, then convinced Jessie to let her make buttermilk biscuits to go with the corned beef and cabbage for supper. Poignant memories of her mother crowded in as she mixed and cut the dough. Chelle wasn't used to a coal range, but the biscuits came out better than she'd feared, if not quite as well as she'd hoped.

Martin came in as she was taking them from the oven. Greer ran to him, clutching the rag doll he'd bought her last week. Chelle's annoyance dissipated as he scooped the little girl up. He might feel the need to be prickly with her, but Greer already had him wrapped around her little finger, and she knew it. The man was infatuated. It didn't seem possible that less than two weeks ago, he'd wanted his daughter out of his sight.

*Maybe that's why he resents me. I was close to his daughter while he was keeping her at arm's length, and he's jealous of that.*

Chelle chatted with Jessie over supper while Martin ate in silence. Then, with the meal over, the dishes done and the baby settled for the night, she slipped out and sat on the doorstep to enjoy the cool breeze sweeping down from the fell. The Rainnie house didn't boast a summer kitchen and perhaps in this climate didn't really need one, but today it would have been a blessing.

Minutes later, a few stray notes from Martin's fiddle drifted from the open window. He began a tune, stopped awkwardly and began again, feeling his way through the waltz as if he hadn't played it in a long time. Then he played it again with more assurance. The lilting melody rang out, warm and full of expression, until Chelle felt like getting up and dancing. Jessie was right. Martin had a gift.

He slid from the waltz into an arrogant march that he played with a hint of a bounce, as if he were making sly fun of the tune's seriousness. Chelle closed her eyes and smiled. Martin followed the march with a haunting air that sent her soaring over the fell in her imagination, looking down at its windswept emptiness.

One tune blended into the next until twilight faded and the stars came out. When Martin stopped playing, Chelle came back to earth with a jolt. How long had she been sitting there?

The house behind her was dark. Jessie must have gone to bed. Through the open door, she heard Martin hang up the fiddle and come to stand in the doorway. Then she felt his presence behind her. His voice touched her ear as he sat next to her.

"You'd best come in, lass. It's gettin' late."

Chelle pulled up her knees and clasped her arms around them, instinctively sheltering herself. From what? She wasn't sure. She should do as he suggested and go in, but somehow she couldn't.

"Martin, I wonder if you realize what a gift you have. You could be playing in concert halls, I'm sure of it."

Chelle felt as much as heard his slight chuckle. She could barely pick his form out of the surrounding darkness, but that seemed only to heighten her awareness of him. She felt his warmth, heard the scrape of fabric on stone as he settled beside her.

"Nay. I haven't the background for it, or the inclination. If I put on a suit and collar once a week, that's enough for me. I haven't even done that for months."

"Have you never wanted to make a living playing?"

She caught the fragrance of tobacco as he pulled a pipe from his shirt pocket and filled it. A match flared, illuminating his face for a moment.

"Nay. I spent a few months in London one autumn, playing in pubs, but by Christmas I was ready to come home. I'd tired of the food and the company, and I'd realized that most of the people I played for weren't listening to me anyway. Then Dad took ill and I had no choice but to stay home, unless I wanted to give up the farm."

"And you've never had any regrets?"

"Nay. I belong here."

The glow from the pipe's bowl faded, leaving him in darkness again, making the hint of wistfulness in his voice more compelling. Chelle remembered what Kendra had told her, how Martin used to play at the local dances and how he and Eleanor had liked to dance. What a hole she must have left in his life.

"What's the furthest you've been from Mallonby, Martin?"

"London. I'd like to travel a bit someday, though."

"So would I, but I always thought I'd settle close to home. I've never wanted to live anywhere else." Chelle understood Martin's sense of being rooted here. She'd felt the same way about her home, more deeply than she'd known before she'd had to leave it.

He blew out a breath of fruity smoke. She felt him turn toward her.

"What was it like, your home?"

Chelle wondered if Martin knew his voice had lost the edge it always took on when he spoke to her. It must be the dark. It made even strangers less reserved, and she and Martin weren't exactly strangers anymore. She'd seen this side of him with his daughter, and now he was showing it to her for the first time. At that moment, it would have felt very natural to move closer to him, share his warmth, perhaps feel Martin's hand over hers…Chelle forced her mind back to his question.

"It was peaceful. There never seemed to be any need to hurry. When Trey and I were growing up we had the run of the woods and fields. We rode, swam, and climbed trees. It was a wonderful place to be a child."

She *had* moved closer to him, without realizing it. Chelle edged away and shivered as cool air filled the space between them, replacing his warmth. They really should go in, but at the moment, Martin didn't seem inclined to move. He drew on his pipe again.

"Your father told me your brother ended up enlisting."

Chelle winced in spite of his gentle tone. Her father and Uncle Jack had told a few people about Trey's change of plans, and she wished they hadn't. Not that she was ashamed—not any longer—but it still hurt to think of it.

"Yes, he did. He'd planned to go West and stay out of the war, but he changed his mind and joined the Union army."

"Being your brother and Colin's son, I'm sure he had good reasons." The simple statement brought unexpected comfort. "Is it true, what we read in the papers over here about the West—all that land, free for the taking?"

"The land is there, but it isn't exactly free for the taking. The Indians consider it theirs, and they're fighting for it. Trey wouldn't have been a whole lot safer if he had gone West instead of enlisting."

"Perhaps not, but it's one place I'd like to see."

"So would I. I likely will someday, if Trey survives. He won't be going home. He'll be selling our place when he can."

He turned to her again, his voice like a sympathetic touch. "You'll see it then, for sure. Don't let yourself think otherwise."

Silence settled between them. Martin finished his pipe and then, just as Chelle decided she'd really have to go in, he rose. "Now come inside, lass. We'll have Jessie wondering, sitting out here like this."

She got stiffly to her feet and followed him in. Jessie might well wonder, if she was still awake. They'd sat outside much longer than was proper, but neither of them seemed to care.

With the ease of long familiarity, Martin made his way through the dark room to the mantle and lit two candles.

"Good night, Chelle."

"Good night."

Chelle watched him climb the stairs, heard his door close. She'd never imagined they could talk like they just had. She'd never imagined that sitting out in the dark with him would feel so comfortable. She set her candle on the nightstand and faced herself in the mirror before undressing.

"Rochelle, it would not be wise for you to spend much time around Martin Rainnie."

* * * *

After chores and breakfast, at which Martin was silent as before, he told Jessie he was going out to the sheep. Chelle gave him a half-hours' start, then bundled Greer up against the brisk wind and set off for a walk. If Jessie didn't want her help in the house and Martin wouldn't have her work outside, she'd rather occupy herself out on the fell.

Without any conscious intent, she turned into the track that led to Martin's pasture. At a distance, Chelle paused, set the baby down and rested her tired arms while she watched Martin and Gyp cut a ewe and her twin lambs from the flock. Absorbed in their work, neither man nor dog noticed her when she took Greer's hand and walked closer.

Together, Martin and Gyp maneuvered the sheep close enough for Martin to get a good look at them. Apparently satisfied, he called to Gyp and let the mother and offspring run back to the flock. Chelle waited with Greer near the bramble bush that had precipitated their first meeting, now showing a crop of ripening berries. When she called and waved, Martin closed the distance between them in a few long strides.

"What brings you here?"

His gruff self again. Perhaps he felt a bit awkward about sitting out together so long last night, too. Chelle held his gaze with a hint of a challenge.

"It isn't too soon for Greer to get to know where you work and what you do, is it?"

"Nay, it's not." Seeing Greer's eyes widen with fear as Gyp sniffed at her feet, Martin knelt beside her. "He won't hurt you, lass. See?" He ran his hand over the dog's back. "He's soft."

Greer reached out, touched the Collie's head and squealed. Martin swung her up to his shoulder and turned to Chelle, his face unreadable. A chill seemed to have fallen between them.

"You likely want a rest after carrying her out here. I'm glad to see her, but you could have kept her closer to home."

"Yes, I could have, but I didn't want to. Martin, how old is Gyp?"

"He's nearly ten now."

Chelle bent to ruffle the Collie's fur. "We didn't have a dog for the last few months at home. Our old Molly died, and we didn't have the heart to replace her. I enjoyed watching the two of you work. Was there something wrong with those lambs?"

"Nay. They were born small, so I've been keepin' my eye on them. They've picked up well over the summer. As for Gyp, he's the best dog I've ever had. It's time I got him some help, but I can't bring myself to do it."

"It would break his heart if you replaced him." Chelle fell into step with Martin as he started back toward the farm. Greer giggled, fisted her hand in his hair and pulled.

"Ouch! You little monkey, that hurts." Martin shifted her to sit astride his neck. "There now, hold on. Aye, Gyp wouldn't like giving way to a pup, that's certain."

Chelle smiled over a pang of jealousy. After all the time they'd spent together, it hurt a little to see Greer warming up to her father so quickly. She seemed to sense his affection for her and respond to it instinctively.

"She's taking to you so quickly. It's as if she wants to make up for lost time."

"So do I." Martin slipped back to last night's reflective tone. "The night she was ill, your father and I had a talk. I was beside myself, thinking how I'd turned my back on my daughter—on Eleanor's daughter. He said he wondered if he'd done the right thing himself, coming here, leaving your brother behind and taking you away from…" Martin stopped, looking embarrassed. "He told me you'd been considering marriage before you left."

Chelle felt herself blushing. "I wasn't sure he knew."

"I'll warrant there isn't much that gets past Colin, though likely keeping track of your young men was a chore. I admire you for sticking by him, Chelle. A lot of girls would have put themselves first with a war coming."

*If you only knew.* "Thank you, but I don't want Dad blaming himself. I made my own choice. Martin, I hope you'll let me visit Greer every so often. I really will miss her."

"Aye, and she'll miss you, too. I'm not fooling myself about that. Of course you can visit her." Their eyes met for a moment, long enough to bring back all of Chelle's doubts from last night. Surely she hadn't imagined the flare of warmth in Martin's gaze before that unreadable mask dropped again.

## *CHAPTER 12*

Martin stopped by the open door of his daughter's room, heard nothing but her soft breathing and stepped in. They'd had a time getting her to sleep for a few nights after Chelle went home, but tonight he'd put Greer down without a fuss and she hadn't wakened.

After two weeks, he couldn't fathom his house or his life without her. She'd soothed the ache of grief deep inside him, and she'd given him back his music. Martin had no desire to play in public again, but it no longer pained him to play for himself. He came home every night to Greer's smiles, Jessie's good food and his fiddle, and he counted himself content. Once the memories of Chelle faded from his mind, he'd ask for nothing more.

Images of her kept invading his thoughts at random, when he was working, shaving, eating, playing with Greer. They would fade. He understood what had happened to him the night they'd sat outside together. After eleven months, was it surprising that his body was waking up again? He'd rediscovered his music and, full of all the feelings that released, he'd stepped out to tell Chelle to come inside and....he hadn't.

He'd gotten caught up in her voice with its soft drawl, her scent, her nearness. He'd seen it happen at dances time and time again, couples under the spell of a summer night. Chelle, with those sapphire eyes and those slender curves, would tempt any man. And she'd felt the pull between them, too. He'd sensed it.

She had substance as well as looks. Not every girl would have put her own wishes aside to stand by her father. She'd already lost her mother, and now her brother was at war. Martin prayed she wouldn't lose him as well. As for her lover, that young man must have been a double-dyed fool not to appreciate Chelle as she deserved.

He heard the front door open, heard Jessie asking someone to come in. Martin closed Greer's door behind him and went down to find Eleanor's parents standing there with Jessie.

Tension knotted in his chest. He'd intended to call on the Paxtons to tell them he'd decided to bring Greer home, but he'd put it off, wanting to get her settled first. Now they'd heard the news elsewhere, and it was plain as plain that they weren't pleased. Jessie's face as she retreated to the kitchen spoke volumes.

*Damn and damn again.* "Hugh, Margaret, I'm glad you're here. I was going to call on you this week. You know Jessie Mason."

"We've met." Hugh sent a less than friendly glance in Jessie's direction. She held his gaze, undaunted, until he turned back to Martin.

"So it's true then, what we heard at church on Sunday? You've brought the baby here?"

"Aye, I've brought Greer home." Martin deliberately stressed the word 'home' as he gestured toward the sofa. "Sit down. I'm sorry you heard the news elsewhere, but I wanted to see her settled before comin' to tell you."

"Aye, well, that's as may be, but we also heard you had that brazen niece of Jack McShannon's staying here." Stiff with disapproval, Margaret perched on the edge of the sofa beside her husband. Dressed in black merino, she reminded Martin of a grackle with her grating voice and jerky movements. "I'd have thought you'd have better sense."

Martin opened his mouth to give her a sharp dressing down, but remembering sitting outside with Chelle in the dark, he couldn't. Embarrassment gave his voice an edge.

"Aye, she was here for three days to help Greer get settled. Miss McShannon knows the child as well as anyone. Her father and her aunt were willing for her to come, so I saw nothing improper in it."

Hugh pinched the bridge of his nose and sighed as if gathering his patience. "Martin, you're nobbut twenty-six. Any time now you'll be castin' your eye about for another wife, and that's as it should be, but we don't want our granddaughter taking second place behind your new family. And from what we've heard and seen of Miss McShannon, she's not fit to raise Greer. She has no regard for her reputation, and her family lets her do as she pleases, keeping company with folk she ought not to speak to and writing nonsense for the York paper —"

So this was about Rochelle. Martin fought back the same anger that had made him sail into Drew at the pub.

"I'm not looking for a wife, but Miss McShannon is a lass any man would be lucky to win. Caroline told me that you'd been to see Greer. If you have eyes, you'd have seen that Miss McShannon has been as good to the child as most mothers. Have you troubled yourselves to get to know her at all, or have you just listened to a lot of idle tongues wagging?"

Margaret's sallow face colored. "There's no need to get your back up. We have a right to be concerned about our granddaughter."

Martin took a step toward the door. If he didn't end this now, he knew he'd say something he'd regret.

"Aye, you do, so I'll tell you. I'll be raising Greer. I want her to know her grandparents, but if that's to be, you're going to have to trust me to do what's best for her. Now, I'll say goodnight."

Jessie was beside the Paxtons with their coats as soon as they rose from the sofa. Visibly keeping his temper in check, Hugh held Margaret's coat for her. "Very well. She's your child, of course, but we'll be keeping an eye on her, Martin. Remember that. Goodnight."

\* \* \* \*

128

*Sept. 3, 1861*

*Dear Trey,*

*Our birthday today. Happy nineteenth. I wish we could throw a party like we did last year, but I'm sure you'll find a way to celebrate, if only you're well and safe.*

*I know Dad's written to you since we got your letter telling us you'd enlisted, but I haven't. I couldn't. At first I was too angry, and then too frightened for you and ashamed of myself.*

*I didn't want to believe you'd chosen sides against Justin and your other friends. That you'd cut yourself off from home completely. I wondered if you'd done it because of Nate Munroe, but I know you better than that. Your reasons were every bit as good as Justin's and Rory's, and I'm proud of you. But oh, next spring will be hard. Do you suppose there's any hope it will end before then?*

*We got news of the battle of Bull Run back in July. The papers here reported it as a rather bungled affair on both sides, but it seems that this is going to be a much longer and crueler war than anyone at first anticipated. It's not likely to end before you see action. Trey, I'm glad you still have Cloud. I know you'll do your best to keep him safe, and that will mean keeping yourself safe, too.*

Chelle looked up at the sound of little Peter laughing downstairs. It was good to hear. He'd been out of sorts since Greer left, sensing how much his mother and Chelle missed her.

*Things are much the same here, except that little Greer Rainnie is no longer staying with us. She was sick a few weeks ago and frightened us all badly, but the old bromide about an ill wind proved its truth. The scare brought her father to his senses and he decided to take Greer home. I spent a few days at his farm helping her settle in, and he's asked me to visit. I have to say he isn't the unfeeling man I took him to be. You'd like him.*

*Trey, we've both had difficult choices to make. Do you still feel that you made the right one? I do, though I can't help wondering if Rory is safe and if he thinks* he *made the right choice. I wonder if I'll ever hear from him again, and what I'll say if I do.*

*I'm looking forward to the day when I can visit you out West and we can celebrate our birthday together again. Until then, I'm sending you a glimmer of moonlight on the creek at home. Can't you just see it? We'll always be able to, whether we're ever there again or not.*

*As ever,*
*Chelle*

Chelle folded her letter, thinking of all the things she wanted to know, but couldn't ask Trey without annoying him. Was there any sickness in his camp? Was the food decent? How were his fellow recruits treating him as a Southerner in their midst? Did he lie awake at night, thinking of what lay before him?

She looked out at the gray, wet September afternoon. Autumn came much earlier here than it did at home. The nights were already growing cool, the leaves showing a hint of color here and there. If her father hadn't exaggerated, the winter would be something to reckon with. For the first time in her life, Chelle dreaded the spring that would follow.

Peter laughed again, giving her a pang of loneliness for Greer. Chelle had been to the farm three times since she'd come home, and found the little girl happy. "As she should be," Jessie said. "Martin is setting about spoiling her till salt won't save her. I've never seen a father dote more on a child."

When Chelle had repeated that to Caroline, she'd responded with an indulgent smile. "He can't see anything but Greer right now, but that'll change ere long. He's healin' in spite of himself. Give him another year and he'll be looking for a new wife, just wait and see."

Chelle hadn't seen Martin since her stay at the farm. He was always working when she visited, but her heart still beat a little faster when she remembered sitting with him in the dark, the scent of his pipe wafting around them, his nearness so palpable they could have been touching. As little time as they'd spent together, Chelle knew she wouldn't forget him. She wasn't as sure as Caroline that Martin would marry again soon, but whenever he did, Chelle hoped he'd choose someone who'd love Greer as she deserved.

The rain continued all afternoon and into the evening. When Chelle went to bed she lay listening to the soft hiss of water against her window, until it became the sound of the ivy rattling against the front window at home. Then the sound faded and the familiar room became a farm field, green and peaceful under a bright blue sky.

Only the field's peace was an illusion, its silence the ghastly aftermath of battle. Bodies lay piled like cordwood along a pole fence, scattered over the land as if dropped there by some obscenely cruel hand.

*Rory. You have to find him.* Chelle focused all her will on putting one foot in front of the other until she came to the first gray-clad form in her path. A blond boy younger than Trey, he stared sightlessly up at the sun, part of his throat shot away. Chelle turned away, fought to quell her churning stomach, and moved on. The next man, bearded and forty-odd, clutched a tintype in his hand. She didn't stop to see the faces of his loved ones. Somewhere in this carnage, she had to find Rory.

The third man in her path wore blue. Dark-haired, he lay on his stomach, his arms flung out to his sides. Just as she passed him, Chelle saw his back lift slightly. He was breathing.

She stopped, turned him over, sank to her knees with a cry. Trey's eyes, barely conscious, looked up at her. Blood soaked the front of his uniform jacket. Choking panic rose in Chelle's throat. Then she was sitting up in bed in a sheen of cold moonlight, shaking, gasping for breath.

Her father's words came back to her. *Mam was one of those people who seemed to know things before she was told.* Fingers trembling, Chelle lit her lamp. Could she have inherited a touch of foresight from her father's Irish ancestors?

She refused to think so. Ever since leaving home, she'd worried constantly about Trey and Rory. This dream had to be the result of that worry and her overactive imagination, nothing more. Her father would say the same thing if she told him.

She lay awake until the sky began to lighten, then blew out the lamp and fell into an uneasy sleep. She woke to find the sun up and voices rising from the kitchen where Caroline and Jean were getting breakfast. Feeling tired and muzzy-headed, Chelle washed and dressed. By the time she took her place at the table, everyone else was already eating.

"I'm sorry I'm late, Aunt. I didn't sleep well. I had a nightmare."

Her father looked up from his ham and eggs. "What was it, lass?"

Chelle hesitated. She didn't want to worry him. "I was on a battlefield. I don't really remember much, but I couldn't get back to sleep afterward." She helped herself to toast and a slice of ham. "I think I'll go for a walk after breakfast to clear my head."

Caroline nodded. "Aye. There's the butter to go to Martin, if you like."

Since Greer had gone home, Chelle had taken over the task of delivering Martin's butter every week. Those were her times to visit the baby. After breakfast she started out, with a brisk wind almost blowing her along, driving last night's rain clouds before it.

About a quarter of a mile from the Rainnie lane, the track branched, one fork leading on to the fell and the other winding down around its base to the village of Carston. When she reached the branch, Chelle met the Paxtons' buggy coming from Carston toward Mallonby. Mr. Paxton pulled the horse to a stop.

"Mornin', Miss McShannon."

"Good morning." Chelle's stomach clenched, as it always did in their presence. She knew they didn't like her, but today their disapproval was more marked than ever. Mr. Paxton's voice was laced with it.

"Now that Martin has Greer at home, I want to thank you and your family for your care of her."

His tone conveyed a lot of things, but thanks wasn't one of them. Chelle ventured a quiet "You're welcome."

Mrs. Paxton chimed in. "We were planning on stopping at the forge before going home. We know you stayed at the farm for a few days when Martin took Greer home, and, to be honest, we were surprised. We spoke with him yesterday, and he agreed it would be best for Greer if your visits stopped. It will only confuse the child to have you coming and going. He would have told you himself, but now he won't have to."

Chelle's face flushed with temper. Who did these people think they were? "He certainly will have to tell me himself if he wants me to stop visiting Greer. He's had plenty of chances to tell me if he wanted me to stay away. Why don't you tell me honestly why you don't want me visiting your granddaughter?"

The woman looked down at her with gray eyes that resembled Greer's except for their coldness. "That should be obvious enough. It's not right, a young girl like you calling on an unmarried man like Martin. But then, judging by the company you keep, and the way you embarrass yourself in the papers, you aren't too concerned about what's right. Martin doesn't want to get mixed up with the likes of you."

Chelle infused her voice with ice. "Martin is a grown man, Mrs. Paxton. He's quite capable of making his own decisions, but if it will ease your mind, he's never in the house when I visit Greer." Chelle felt a surge of satisfaction at the surprised looks on their faces. She knew she was damning herself further in their eyes by speaking out like this, but she was too furious to care. "I'm not going to stand here explaining myself to you. Good day."

She started to walk on, but Mr. Paxton's words stopped her. "Keep this in mind, Miss. We'll go to court to get custody of Greer if Martin proves himself unfit to raise her. I'd advise you to think about that before you go there again."

Shock hit her like icy water, but Chelle refused to show it. She faced Greer's grandfather and kept her voice calm.

"That would be a good way to alienate Martin and Greer for life. I doubt if you'd accomplish anything else, if all you can complain of is my visits. I'll stay away when Martin asks me to, and not before. Good day."

She turned and walked on without looking back, struggling with anger and doubt. Surely Greer's grandparents would have no chance of taking her from Martin when they had nothing substantial to complain of, but they could certainly make things unpleasant for him. She wondered if the Paxtons had realized she was on her way to the farm when they crossed her path.

When Chelle walked into the farmyard, Martin came out of the byre. She saw warmth flare briefly in his gaze. Something in him responded to her, just as she responded to him. It was pointless to deny it.

He'd changed. She felt it as much as saw it. He carried himself differently, his shoulders less tight, his movements more relaxed. Having Greer home was good for him.

What was it about him that drew her? The things that would draw many women, Chelle supposed. His solid strength, though men with his build had never appealed to her before. The intensity of his blue-green eyes. His voice. But more than that, the side of him that came out in his music, the depth of feeling that showed when he was with his daughter. No, she wouldn't forget him.

"Mornin', lass. Jessie and Greer are inside. Go on in." He turned to go back into the byre, but Chelle called to him.

"Martin, I need to talk to you. It's about Greer's grandparents."

He stopped, displeasure on his face. "Oh? Well, go in and I'll be there in a minute."

She found Jessie washing the breakfast dishes while Greer played nearby. Chelle scooped her up, held her close and ran a hand through her hair. She didn't want to think about losing contact with Greer.

"You're bigger every time I see you. Good morning, Jessie. Here's your butter."

Jessie looked over her shoulder, smiling. "Just put it on the table, lass. Aye, she is, and she's tryin' to say a few words now, too. Sometimes we can even understand them."

Martin came in, hung up his jacket and washed his hands. "So you've seen the Paxtons, then. Did they come to the forge?"

"No. I met them on the road on my way here." Chelle sat at the table with Greer on her lap. "They told me you'd decided it would be too 'confusing' for Greer if I kept visiting her, and that I wasn't a fit person to be around their granddaughter."

Martin's thick brows lowered and his fists clenched on the table. "I said no such thing! They were here the other night, talkin' about Greer. They're worried that I'm goin' to start looking for a second wife soon, and that Greer will lose out to my new family, or so they say. They've never shown much concern for her before now. I don't know what's driving them, unless it's just that they don't like the idea of anyone taking Eleanor's place."

Chelle glanced down at her hands. She hated to think that she was even partly responsible for this. "They mentioned me too, didn't they?"

Martin avoided her gaze. "Aye, they did. They'd heard that you'd stayed here."

"And they've heard about my friendship with Kendra. I know that from what they said today."

"Aye. Gossip travels between Mallonby and Carston as fast as the swallow flies."

Chelle felt a blush rising. "I don't care what they think of me, but they also threatened to try to take Greer from you. Do you think they'd actually try it?"

135

Martin's eyes turned stormy. "They made threats? They didn't dare when they were here. I'm sorry, lass, but don't let it bother you. The next time I see them, I'll tell them that if they make any more trouble, they won't see Greer until her wedding day. I won't have them interfering in my life like this."

Since she'd met them, Chelle had tried to fathom how the Paxtons could have raised a daughter like the young woman Kendra had described. Now it seemed even more improbable.

"Were they very close to your wife?"

"Not especially. As far as I could tell, her father thought her too fond of music and dancing, and not fond enough of his brand of religion." A hint of a grin showed through Martin's anger. "Eleanor had a mind of her own, something like you."

Chelle smiled. "I'll take that as a compliment."

"Naturally. Eleanor's parents were willing enough for us to marry, but I never thought they cared over much for me. I was the respectable husband they wanted her to have, that was all. After the wedding we rarely saw them, and I think Eleanor liked it that way. She never talked of them much, before or after we were married."

Still busy with the dishes, Jessie spoke up. "They took me by surprise when they showed up here the other night, that's for sure and certain. Just jealousy, plain and simple, if you ask me."

Greer started to squirm on Chelle's lap. Chelle put the little girl down and rested her elbows on the table.

"Martin, if it would be easier, Jessie could bring Greer to the village when she comes in, leave her at the forge to visit and pick her up on the way back."

"Nay, lass. I won't let the Paxtons think they can bully me like that. We'll carry on as we have been."

Their eyes met, and Chelle looked away. She read Martin's tone to mean that he wanted her to keep coming to the farm for his sake as well as for Greer's, even though she rarely saw him when she visited. She wasn't sure what to think of that.

# CHAPTER 13

Kendra lit the lamp, laid the baby in his cradle and set about getting supper. Her hands worked automatically, peeling carrots and paring potatoes, but her eyes kept straying to the unopened letter lying on the table. David's letter. His first, and since it arrived with the morning post she hadn't been able to summon the nerve to open it.

Though she hadn't asked him to write, she couldn't deny that she'd been disappointed when he didn't, especially after she'd written to tell him he had a son. She knew she'd forfeited her right to his help by refusing to marry him, but deep down she'd thought he'd at least acknowledge the baby's birth.

The paring knife slipped, nicking her finger. Muttering under her breath, Kendra rinsed the small cut, put a bit of sticking plaster on it, then took the offending knife to the table and slit the seal on the letter.

*Dear Kendra,*

*I'm sorry it's taken me so long to write to you. I wanted to wait until I had something to send you, and to be honest, I didn't know what to say. It still knocks me flat to realize I'm a father. I imagine you feel the same way about being a mother.*

Kendra peered into the envelope and found a one-pound note. Tears sprang to her eyes. It must have taken Davy the whole time he'd been away to save that much out of his wages. She gathered her apron in her hand, wiped her eyes and read on.

*I'm puffed that you named him after me, Kendra. I'll send you more money when I can. Uncle says that if I keep on the way I am, I can rise in the company with time. I'll do my best to see that I do.*

*I'll be coming home for a visit at Christmas, and I'll come by to see you then. Take care of yourself and the little one.*

*As ever*
*David*

Kendra's stomach clenched. She didn't want to see David. Not because she was too proud to accept help from her baby's father, or because she didn't want him to see his son, but because she was afraid to see him. David had been able to charm her from the beginning, and no doubt he still could. She didn't want to rake up all those feelings again. She put the letter back in the envelope with the money, put it on the shelf by the stove and went to tend little Davy, who'd started to fuss.

"Are you hungry? Come here then." Kendra unbuttoned her dress and put the baby to her breast. "Your father will be proud of you. He'll have to be. You're a charmer, just like him. I'll be easier in my mind when he's been and gone, that's for sure and certain."

\* \* \* \*

Chelle set the can of sand back in its place behind the range and glanced over the kitchen floor. Scrubbing and sanding had never been her favorite chore, but she didn't think she'd missed any spots. The raised knots in the floorboards showed how they'd been worn by years of scouring.

She swept the last remnants of sand out the door just as her father came through the gate. There wasn't a lot of work waiting this morning, so he'd gone to the store for a newspaper and a chat with Mr. Bingham.

He shrugged out of his wool jacket as he came in. There had been frost overnight and the air was still crisp with it, but the house was warm with the smell of Jean's apple tart baking in the oven.

"What did you hear at the store, Dad?"

Her father pecked Chelle on the cheek and handed her a small bag of Mrs. Bingham's toffee. "I brought you a treat, lass."

Chelle rolled her eyes, but she couldn't help grinning. He'd always brought her candy when he went to the store at home.

"You must be plotting with Aunt Caroline to fatten me up. You know I can't resist toffee."

"You never could." Her father's smile faded. "As for news, there was an accident at the mill yesterday. One of the workers got her arm badly mangled in one of the spinning mules."

Chelle's heart plummeted with sudden fear. "It wasn't Kendra's mother, was it?"

"Nay, it was a lass about your age, maybe a bit younger. Mary Tate is her name. I went to school with her father."

"What's being done for her?"

Her father stepped past her and stood by the stove to get warm. "Well, the doctor's done what he can and told her family not to worry about the bill. They'd heard that much at the store, but there was no mention of anything else."

So Mary's employer wasn't even going to acknowledge her accident. Chelle slammed the kitchen door to vent her temper.

"The mill isn't going to do anything?"

Sympathy showed in her father's eyes. Though he hated to show it, Chelle knew it hurt him to see anything living suffer, animal or human.

"I expect they'll give her something. They usually do. Don't jump to conclusions, Chelle."

"Aye, they'll give her something," Kendra affirmed when she arrived with little Davy for a walk later that afternoon. "Two or three weeks' wages, likely. Mary's the same age as me. Mam says she might lose her arm."

Chelle's stomach clenched as she recalled her glimpse of the spinning mules with their long, heavy rollers. "I saw those machines the day you had Davy. I can't imagine getting caught in one. A few weeks' wages? That's an insult."

Kendra gave a bitter little shrug. "Perhaps, but they aren't required to give her anything."

Chelle shut the forge gate behind them. "Do you know how it happened?"

"Aye. The threads on the spinners have a habit of breaking, and when they do, you've got to retie them. I was a spinner, and it's easy enough to get caught in the works of the machine if you aren't careful. That's what happened to Mary." Kendra's voice dropped. "We used to be good friends."

Chelle put a hand on Kendra's shoulder. "Let's hope she'll be all right."

Over the next few days, reports on the injured girl circulated around the village. Her condition wasn't improving. A week after the accident, the doctor amputated Mary's arm in an attempt to halt the infection she'd developed. Two days later she died, killed by the poisons in her blood.

Chelle stood beside Kendra and her mother under a leaden autumn sky while Reverend Nelson laid the seventeen-year-old girl to rest. Maria Westlake was there, standing a little apart from the other mourners. She looked pale and troubled. When Chelle tried to meet her gaze, she averted her eyes. Chelle's opinion of Maria softened a bit. Mary's death obviously bothered her.

Chelle caught a few contemptuous glances from the villagers gathered in the churchyard, but since Martin's fight with Drew back in the summer, no one had shown her any actual hostility. It seemed that his word, or at least his fists, carried some weight in Mallonby. As for Drew, Chelle hadn't seen him since their encounter on the fell—until today.

He stood on the other side of the grave, beside two thickset men, obviously farmers in their best suits. Resemblance marked them as Drew's father and brother, though their faces were dour and hard where Drew's was careless and arrogant. Chelle didn't find it hard to believe that there'd been no love lost between Drew and his family. The rift must have been deep to drive him off a comfortable farm, even if he was the younger son.

After the funeral Chelle walked home with the Fultons, Kendra carrying little Davy in her arms. When they reached the cottage, Mrs. Fulton went on to visit a friend. Kendra added coal to the stove, then sat in the rocker and cuddled her son. Chelle pulled up a chair beside her and shared her silence, knowing Mary's death had hit Kendra all the harder because of their fractured friendship.

After a few minutes passed, Chelle reached out and took one of Davy's small hands in hers. "Kendra, I'm sorry."

"I know." Kendra shifted the baby and lifted his other hand to her lips. "He looks more like his father every day." Color crept into her cheeks. "I had a letter from Davy a fortnight ago."

*She still cares for him.* With an effort, Chelle held her tongue and waited for Kendra to go on. "He sent me some money. He said he wants to help us. I wrote him when the baby was born, but I didn't expect to hear from him. I have no claim on him, after all."

Chelle spoke on a spurt of frustration. "Kendra, you and Martin Rainnie are just the same. Is stubbornness an epidemic in Mallonby? Of course you have a claim on him. You're the mother of his son. He cares, just like Mr. Rainnie cared for Greer all along, though he wouldn't acknowledge it."

Chelle stopped, inwardly cursing her impulsiveness, but Kendra looked thoughtful instead of angry. "You and Mr. Rainnie have become good friends, haven't you?"

"I don't know if I'd go that far. He's hardly ever home when I visit Greer. We just see each other in passing, but yes, I like him. And you're changing the subject."

Kendra gave her a long look that raised a blush, then turned her attention back to her son. "Davy said he wants to visit when he comes home at Christmas. I can hardly say no, but I don't like it."

Chelle forgot her discomfort in another rush of frustration. Martin certainly didn't have a corner on obstinacy in Mallonby. It couldn't have been clearer that Kendra still cared for David.

141

"Why not?"

Kendra's chin lifted. "He's moved on. He doesn't live in Mallonby any more. There are plenty of girls in York to catch his eye. I appreciate his help, but if I wanted him in my life I would have married him when he asked me."

"I'm still not sure why you didn't."

"I had my reasons. Now let's talk of something else."

"All right. I'd like to know more about Mary. What did she look like?"

Kendra's eyes clouded with grief. "She was a bit taller than me, but not as tall as you. Her hair was black, and she had blue eyes—her father's people were Highland Scots, and she took after them." She held the baby a little closer. "At the mill, Mary and I used to sit together on breaks and at lunch, until I started keeping company with Davy. Things got cool between Mary and me then. I thought she was jealous, but now I think she was just a little hurt because I hadn't told her about him. And then, after I found out I was expecting...I never saw any of the girls from work after that. They didn't want to be tarred with the same brush. I can't blame them."

In fairness, Chelle couldn't blame them either, as much as she would have liked to. Not with their livelihoods at stake. "What was she like as a person? Was she shy? Outgoing?"

Kendra's mouth curved in a sad smile. "Mary didn't have a shy bone in her body. She loved to laugh and tease. The boys noticed her, but she was a canny one around them. No one pulled the wool over her eyes. Not everyone liked her; a few thought her proud for a mill hand, but they were the sour sort that disliked most of us younger girls." She glanced at Chelle over the baby's head. "It's a world of its own, the mill, with its own set of rules. You keep to your station and don't speak to those above you, and you mind your tongue with the rest. The jobs are handed down through families as often as not. Mam is a spinner, and so was her mother, and so was I."

Chelle thought of the one person she knew who'd stepped into that world of his own accord, and found a way to bend the rules. "How did Drew Markham manage to get into the office, I wonder?"

Kendra shrugged. "Oh, a man can get promoted off the floor if he's sharp and competitive, and if he's had some schooling, but there's not much chance for a woman. If there's a place for one in the office, it goes to a girl with more background. Most of us on the floor hadn't more than three or four years of schooling before we started, though some kept reading and learning. Mary did. Otherwise you become as much of a machine as the spinners and looms."

That evening at twilight Chelle sat at her window, looking out through a driving rain at the cheerless, sodden gray landscape. Restlessness goaded her. She heard the homelike clatter of dinner preparations downstairs, but something in her rebelled at the thought of joining the family in the warm kitchen.

Unbidden, the image of Martin's big, open main room popped into her mind. Was he sitting by the fire tonight, playing his fiddle while Jessie got supper and the wind hurled rain against the old stone house? Something akin to homesickness came over her at the thought.

*Chelle, this won't do.* She gave herself a stern mental shake and turned her thoughts back to Mary Tate.

A machine. As far as Mr. Westlake was concerned, Mary had been nothing more. Not a person, not the daughter of people who had worked for him for years, not the lively young girl Kendra remembered. Mr. Westlake hadn't even paid Mary the respect of coming to her funeral.

But Maria had. Why? Because her father sent her to represent the family, or because she cared? Chelle recalled the troubled look she'd seen on Maria's face. Whether her father had sent her to the funeral or not, she cared.

Tomorrow was Sunday. Maria would likely be at the morning service. If Chelle could manage a moment alone with her, perhaps she could convince Miss Westlake to do something for Mary's family. Determined to try, Chelle hurried down to set the table for Aunt Caroline.

In the morning, Maria Westlake appeared at church alone. Chelle watched her out of the corner of her eye and soon decided she'd been right. Miss Westlake looked decidedly uneasy.

When the service ended, Chelle told the family to go on without her and waited in the yard. Nearly everyone else had gone by the time Maria came out. She gave Chelle a glance, then started for home at a quick pace. Chelle ran a few steps to catch up with her.

"Miss Westlake, do you have a moment?"

Maria stopped. Close up, the strain on her face showed all the more plainly. "What is it, Miss McShannon?"

Chelle took a deep breath and plunged in. She'd wondered if Miss Westlake would even speak to her after their last encounter. Maria looked wary, but not hostile.

"I saw you at Mary Tate's funeral yesterday. Did you know her?"

"No."

Maria started toward home again, slowly this time. Chelle walked beside her.

"A friend of mine did, quite well. She told me Mary was a hard worker and well liked at the mill. She kept learning and trying to improve herself, and she stayed out of trouble. My father also told me she was an only child. He grew up with her parents."

Maria threw her a glance from skeptical green eyes. "I'm sure you're telling me this for a reason."

Chelle nodded. "Yes, I am. Miss Westlake, I know I offended you the last time we spoke, and you may not believe this, but I don't hold you responsible for the workings of the mill. I also know accidents happen. I'd like to try to raise some money for Mary's family, and after seeing you yesterday, I hoped you might be willing to let bygones be bygones and help me."

"Father prefers that I don't get involved with mill business."

"But it isn't mill business. If Mary had been struck by a runaway cart or had some other kind of accident, he wouldn't object to you trying to help her family, would he?"

"That would be a completely different situation, Miss McShannon, as I'm sure you're aware." Maria squared her shoulders and met Chelle's gaze. "But I do feel badly for this girl's family. I can't promise anything, but I'll speak to my father about it and see if he'll agree."

Chelle hadn't hoped for anything more. "Thank you, Miss Westlake. That's all I can ask."

# CHAPTER 14

*The water is wide, I cannot cross o'er*
*And neither have I wings to fly*
*Build me a boat that can carry two*
*And both shall row, my love and I...*

"Martin, here's Jason Tewkes to see you."

Jessie's call brought Martin back to earth with a start. He stopped singing and looked down at Greer. The song, one of Eleanor's favorites, had done its work. The little one was sound asleep.

His mind filled with the memory of Eleanor's strong, sweet voice shaping the melody, Martin tucked the quilt around his daughter and went down. Jason sat at the table, his spare frame as awkward and angular as ever. Martin hadn't seen him more than twice since Eleanor's funeral.

"Now then, Jason, aren't you off to Carston tonight?" The annual harvest dance was happening in the Carston hall, and Martin knew Jason hadn't missed it for years. They'd played at the dance together for the last six.

Jason didn't look like a man on his way to a good time. Sober-faced, he shifted in his chair.

"Aye, but Charles Brantley isn't. His wife's ill and he can't leave her. Henry Clark and Pierce Jacobs will be there, I'm sure, but they won't bring their fiddles and they live too far away to go home for them. I don't fancy playing the dance alone with just my flute, but there it is, unless you'll do it with me."

Martin felt a chill in the pit of his stomach at the thought. Playing at home was one thing, but facing a crowd of merrymakers at a dance...No. "Borrow my fiddle, Jason. You'll do well enough."

"I don't know a whole night's worth of fiddle tunes, Martin, you know that."

"Then get Henry or Pierce to play it. I'm out of practice."

Martin knew Jason wouldn't believe that for a minute, but he had too much tact to argue the point. He got up with a sigh.

"Well, I'll be off then. I'll take your fiddle if you don't mind. One of the other lads can play it."

Martin rose to walk him to the door. Then....

"Go." Eleanor's voice, as soft and clear as if she'd spoken in his ear. His vision blurred for a moment with the shock of it. He blinked and brought the room back into focus. Jason was staring at him.

"Lad, what's the matter?"

Martin blinked again. Jessie's sharp eyes were on him too, questioning.

Nothing like this had happened to him before. He must have imagined it, but then why did he still feel Eleanor's presence in the room? It didn't matter why. Sitting home now would be more difficult than going to the dance.

"Nothing's the matter. Hold on a minute, Jason, I'm going with you."

\* \* \* \*

"You've got a button undone. Hold still. There." Jean looked over Chelle's shoulder and grinned at her in the mirror. "I'll have to tell Brian to keep an eye on you tonight. You're likely to cause a stir."

Chelle looked down at her royal blue challie with its off-the-shoulder ruffled neckline, no lower than Jean's. "Why do you say that? I'm sure there'll be dresses less modest than ours there tonight."

"Aye, there will, but there won't be figures like yours inside them." Jean's brow puckered as she fastened a gold chain around her neck. "I've gotten thin since Peter came, but what's the odds? Brian doesn't seem to mind."

Jean wore a sunny yellow gown that set off the sparkle of her amber eyes and the sheen of her golden-brown hair to perfection. The princess-seamed bodice accented her slender waist and breasts enhanced by motherhood. Chelle didn't wonder that Brian had no complaints.

"He'd better keep his eye on you, I think. Are you ready? I hear him outside."

Out in the twilit yard, Brian helped them both onto the cart seat and wrapped his arm around his wife. "I don't know as I want to take you out tonight, Jeannie. I think I'd just as soon keep you home."

Jean smiled flirtatiously and rolled her eyes at him. Brian shook the reins and started old Lady at a sedate pace towards Carston.

Chelle wrapped her mother's embroidered shawl more tightly around her to ward off the chill of the fine evening. A plump crescent of a moon hung in the crystal sky ahead of them, surrounded by early stars. She couldn't help a little twinge of shame at the glow of anticipation building inside her. They were going to the harvest dance at the Carston hall, the first dance Chelle had attended in over a year. For the first time since her mother's death, she remembered that she was nineteen years old and attractive, without the responsibility of a household on her shoulders.

As they passed the Rainnie lane, Chelle got a glimpse of lamplight from the farmhouse windows. She looked back as they drove past, picturing Greer asleep in the little room upstairs. Smoke curled from both chimneys. Jessie usually baked on Saturday evenings, and Martin was likely settling down to spend the evening by the hearth.

She ignored the tug at her heart and turned back to the road, now bathed in moonlight. The night seemed made to be enjoyed, and Chelle intended to do just that. For a few hours, she wouldn't let anything else matter.

They reached the hall to find the yard full of farm carts, wagons and buggies. Inside, the benches lining the stone walls were already filling up. Lanterns hung from the rafters, adding to the heat already building in the room.

The platform at the opposite end of the hall was still empty. The McShannons found space on a bench. Leaning back against the wall, Chelle scanned the room. She didn't know any of the Carston people.

Three older couples stood chatting near the platform. When they separated, laughing, to return to their seats, Chelle's heart did a queer little flutter. His broad back turned to her, fiddle in his hand, Martin stood there, deep in conversation with a man about the age of her father. He nodded to his companion, then the two of them stepped onto the platform.

The first sharp, clear notes of the flute caught the crowd's attention. They fell silent, then burst into cheers when Martin joined Jason in a fast, driving rant. Someone shouted out "Welcome back, lad!" They settled into a reel and in a blink, two sets of dancers formed. Chelle didn't know the steps to this particular figure, but they looked simple enough to learn. When a third set formed, Brian led Jean out onto the floor.

As she had at the farm, Chelle lost herself in Martin's music. Tapping her foot in time, she forgot the dancers until the reel ended. As the sets re-formed, someone tapped her shoulder.

"May I have the pleasure?"

Chelle started and looked up at a stocky young man with a shock of blond hair and a pleasant smile.

"Yes, I'd be glad to."

The music began again. Her partner was a good dancer, and Chelle soon caught on to the steps. The music carried her along until she felt lighter than she had in many months.

She wondered if Martin would dance tonight. If he did, would he ask her? Her pulse quickened at the thought. This must be the first time he'd played in public since losing his wife. How was he feeling? A little ashamed of the glow of warmth that came over her, Chelle turned her thoughts back to her partner and the music.

* * * *

Martin played the first reel through a storm of conflicting emotions. The welcoming cheers from the crowd touched him. Memories overwhelmed him. It wasn't until the beginning of the third tune that he dared to look out over the dance floor.

His gaze settled on Chelle as she moved neatly through the figures, flushed and smiling, her bright hair gathered in a soft knot on top of her head, exposing the slim line of her neck. He hadn't thought about her being here. It would surely make tongues wag, this soon after losing her mother, just as people would talk about him playing. He didn't give a damn what the village biddies said about him, but Chelle's reputation was another matter.

Martin had a speaking acquaintance with her partner, who came from one of the farms on the other side of Carston. Lester Barrow was a decent lad, and Chelle seemed to be enjoying herself with him. When the tune ended, another Carston man took Lester's place. By intermission time, Chelle had danced with eight or nine different partners and Martin's nerves were as taut as the strings on his fiddle.

*You're daft, Martin. What's the odds who she dances with? You're not in the market.* But his jealousy wouldn't die down. It tangled with all the other feelings raised by being here, and it wouldn't be rooted out.

He stepped off the platform and joined the line at the refreshment table. He'd just gotten his punch when he caught sight of Drew Markham lounging against the wall across the room, watching someone intently, a predatory light in his eyes. Martin followed Drew's gaze to where Chelle stood with her cousin and his wife. His fists clenched, eager to make the man's teeth rattle.

Jealousy. Protectiveness. Martin had no call to be feeling either, but they overwhelmed him. He returned to the platform, picked up his fiddle and held it out to Jason.

"Break time's over. Play a couple of tunes to start off, will you?"

Jason quirked an eyebrow as he took the fiddle. "Fancy joining a set? Go on, then."

Martin didn't answer. He eased his way through the crowd, his pulse drumming in his ears like it had at eighteen when he asked a girl to dance. The color on Chelle's face deepened and spread to her throat when she saw him. Standing beside her, her cousin held out his hand.

"Good to see you here, Martin. You haven't lost your touch."

"I'm not so sure of that, but thanks." He shook Brian's hand, then turned to Chelle. "Miss Rochelle, Jason's going to start off the next set. Might I have the pleasure?"

Chelle smiled and mimicked his broad Yorkshire. "Aye, sir, I'd be flattered."

Jason began a jig. Martin took Chelle's hand. The warmth of it spread through him instantly, and stayed with him as he guided her through the steps. She had on some kind of citrusy perfume that made him think of warm, exotic places. Some of her hair had worked loose to float in soft wisps around her face, delicate and alluring.

She could dance. She had rhythm, and she knew how to relax into the music. Caught up in her nearness, Martin felt like only seconds had passed when the tune ended.

Their eyes met. Chelle averted her gaze right away, but not before he saw her pupils dilate. Jason began a waltz. A squeeze of her hand brought her back into Martin's arms.

Holding her, even lightly like this, was heaven and hell combined. No normal man could be impervious to the warm flush on Chelle's skin, the creamy shoulders and distracting hint of cleavage revealed by her dress. Martin hadn't bargained on the strength of the pull between them. It threw him. It had been a long time.

"I'd say you've done a lot of this."

She looked up, her gaze casual and friendly again. She might be young, but she knew how to play the game.

"Yes. I'd say you have, too."

"Aye, Eleanor and I used to go to most of the dances hereabouts." How many evenings had they spent in this hall? So many that Eleanor's presence lingered here, pulling at his heart while his senses focused on the girl in his arms.

"So I've heard. I was a little surprised to see you here tonight."

Somehow, Chelle's voice helped to calm the turmoil inside him. "I'm surprised to be here. I wouldn't be if the fellow who was supposed to play had been able to make it."

Her hand shifted on his shoulder, a slight, unconscious comforting movement. "How does it feel?"

"It's difficult." Martin guided Chelle around a younger couple who were too wrapped up in each other to have any notion of where they were on the floor. He caught a look at the boy's face and hoped to God he didn't look just as thunderstruck. "But I'm glad I'm here."

Chelle looked up at him. "I think Eleanor would be, too."

Martin recalled that strange moment at the house. Could that have been Eleanor telling him it was time to move on? If so, why did he feel this wrenching sense of disloyalty at the way Chelle affected him?

"Perhaps."

She averted her eyes again. As the waltz went on, Martin got more and more caught up in the feel of Chelle under his hands. The way she followed him, unconsciously moving closer than was strictly proper, told him she felt the same. Martin knew people were watching them, but they'd watch him no matter who he danced with. He should care for Chelle's sake, but he couldn't. Too many contradictory feelings swamped him, drowning out the voice of common sense.

Those feelings culminated in physical need, followed closely by shame. She couldn't help but sense it. What must she think of him? He had to talk to her, try to explain himself before he lost her friendship for himself and Greer.

When the waltz ended, Martin took Chelle's hand and led her to the door. She went with him willingly, as if she knew something had to be said. They stepped out into the chilly, starlit dark of the yard and walked down the lane, away from the lights and from any couples who might have sought privacy around the back of the hall. Hadn't he and Eleanor done that more than once?

Chelle hadn't said a word. Martin felt the frantic rhythm of her pulse through the satiny skin of her wrist, racing like his own as they stopped in the shadow of an oak.

"Chelle, I'm sorry. I…"

His voice failed him. If he could have seen her face clearly he might have been able to stop, but he could only feel her warmth, hear her breathing. His hands dropped to her waist, trembled at her swift intake of breath. Then his mouth found hers and they melted together like spring snow on sun-warmed earth.

Chelle's body tightened, then relaxed on a soft sigh. Her hands came up to grip Martin's shoulders, as if to keep from falling. She'd been kissed before, by someone who knew how, that was for sure and certain. She explored his mouth with a sweet fervor that made his blood pound in his ears.

Martin didn't know how much time passed before the power of thought returned. This was wrong and, moreover, foolish beyond excuse. He broke the kiss and stepped back, his breathing ragged.

"Chelle, on my word, I never meant—"

"I know." The catch in her voice betrayed her own passion. "Don't apologize, Martin. I didn't stop you."

Martin gathered his scattered wits and struggled for words. "I haven't touched a woman since Eleanor, and I guess I'm not ready to. I shouldn't have asked you to dance, but I'm not sorry I did."

She was getting her feet under her now. Her voice steadied.

"There's something between us, Martin. We can't pretend there isn't."

"No, but I was a cad to act on it. Lass, don't let this stop you from comin' to see Greer. I'll stay out of your way." He glanced back toward the hall. Every minute they lingered here was putting another nail in the coffin of Chelle's good name. "I'd best get back inside. People will be wondering as it is. Goodnight, Chelle."

He left her standing there. How long had they been gone? Too bloody long. Curious eyes turned his way as he strode into the hall. Jason gave Martin a sharp look as he took back his fiddle.

"You know how to pick 'em, lad. Watch yourself. She could be trouble."

Martin snorted as he rosined his bow. "Don't be daft. She's danced with half the lads here, why shouldn't I take a turn?" Angry with himself for snapping, he drew his bow across the strings. "Come on, let's keep the party goin'."

\* \* \* \*

A few minutes later, Chelle strolled up to the hall, sat on the steps and took a few slow, calming breaths. She had no intention of getting involved with Martin, but she still wanted to melt at the thought of his kiss. What kind of a woman did that make her?

Before she could gather her thoughts the door opened behind her, releasing a gust of warm air. Chelle turned around as two young women stepped out, drawing their shawls around their shoulders and fanning glowing faces. One, a buxom, hazel-eyed brunette, flashed a bright smile.

"It's hot in there, that's for sure and certain. Mind if we join you?"

With her feelings in chaos Chelle certainly did mind, but she could hardly say so. She gestured to the step beside her.

The dark girl and her blond companion sat down and settled their skirts around them.

"Thank you. We haven't met, so I'll warrant you're the American girl who's come to Mallonby. Welcome."

The brunette's voice matched her smile, Chelle thought—bright and insincere. "Thank you. I'm Rochelle McShannon. Are you from Carston?"

"Aye. I'm Delia Putnam." The brunette jerked her thumb at her companion. "This is Win Fuller. I've heard your name—you wrote that letter in the York paper, didn't you?"

"Yes."

Delia and Win exchanged a look before Win spoke. "Are you enjoying the dance, Miss McShannon? You certainly don't seem to be in any danger of being a wallflower."

So these girls had been watching her. They'd probably seen her and Martin disappear. Chelle put on a smile and wished them both to the devil.

"Yes, I'm enjoying it very much."

"The music's certainly good tonight. It's a treat to have Mr. Rainnie playing, though I'm surprised to see him here so soon after losing his wife. And you…I understand your mother passed on a few weeks before you arrived here. I'm sorry."

The false sympathy in Win's tone grated on Chelle more than the veiled insinuation that she should be home in mourning. She instilled some sweet venom into her voice.

"Thank you. Mr. Rainnie and I got acquainted when his daughter lived with my family. She's really an adorable child. As you say, it is a treat to have Mr. Rainnie playing tonight. He's a good dancer, too, but then I'm sure you've danced with him before." *If you had, I'll wager you wouldn't be sitting here right now.* "I understand his wife was from Carston, so you and she would have grown up together, or perhaps she was a year or so behind you."

If that were true, it would make Win several years older than she looked. Her smile turned icy.

155

"Mrs. Rainnie was several years older than me, actually. I'll warrant it's not really so surprising to see Mr. Rainnie here, when it comes to that. He always did have a roving eye."

"And he's a good catch, too, with a fine farm. I don't doubt that a good many Carston and Mallonby girls set their caps for him before he married, and will again now that he's widowed." Chelle stood and threw a grin Delia's way. "I must go in. It's chilly out here."

Back inside, Chelle found a seat and caught her breath. It wouldn't do for her to look flustered. When new sets formed for the next dance, her first partner, Lester Barrow, reappeared. She danced the rest of the evening away with a succession of partners, but she didn't dare look toward the platform.

What had happened outside was as wrong as the war that had brought her here, for Martin as well as for herself. Her old world was irrevocably changed. She no longer fit in there, and she certainly didn't fit in here.

But she fit in Martin's arms. Oh, she fit there, far too well for the good of either of them.

# CHAPTER 15

Martin knew sleep wouldn't come easily that night, if it came at all. He stepped into the dark house, pulled a chair close to the stove and sat there in the warm glow, waiting for the storm of feelings inside him to settle, but they kept swirling. The memories that had come rushing back at the dance, the feel of Chelle in his arms, it was all too much for one night.

Finally he gave up, stoked the stove for the night and tiptoed upstairs to Greer's room. She slept soundly, bathed in the moonlight filtering through the muslin curtains.

As much as the child resembled him, Martin saw Eleanor's looks in Greer more and more each day. The shape of her mouth was his, but her full lips were her mother's. She had his square jaw, but the makings of Eleanor's gently rounded chin. More than that, Greer had her mother's vivacious spirit along with Martin's dogged stubbornness. Her smiles and laughter were so like Eleanor's they stabbed him to the heart sometimes, reminding him why he'd almost let her go to others.

Could he ever feel about another woman the way he'd felt about Eleanor?

No. The pull between him and Chelle was physical, nothing more. Martin only hoped she could forgive him for playing the cad.

*She's not for you.* He left Greer's room and crossed the hall to his own. About to draw the curtains and undress, Martin glanced out the window toward the village and froze in place.

An orange glow lit the sky beyond Mallonby. The ominous brightness grew and spread as he watched. It had to be a fire, and there was only one building within miles large enough to burn like that. Martin hurried downstairs and out to the byre, bridled Major and started down the lane at a gallop.

Lamplight shone from every window in the village by the time he got there, but the streets were empty. He tethered his horse in front of the store and jogged up the long slope toward the mill. Most of the village men stood waiting and watching in the yard.

Flames shot from the windows of the back end of the brick building, where the raw wool was stored. Some of the onlookers had formed a human chain down to the river, buckets at the ready, but the heat near the building was too intense for them to get close. Martin spotted John Watson, Westlake's agent, nearby and shouldered his way through the crowd to reach him.

"Is there anyone inside?"

"Nay. Smoke's pourin' into the production room from under the warehouse doors. It's too dangerous."

"Has anyone seen the watchman?"

John frowned. "I haven't, but he must be here somewhere."

Martin scanned the crowd in the torch-lit yard and saw no sign of Ethan Bowes, the mill's elderly night watchman. Surely Ethan would have been the one who'd spread the alarm, but where was he now?

If he'd gone back into the warehouse to try to fight the fire, he was already lost, unless he'd found some kind of refuge. Martin had never been on the production floor of the mill, but he'd been inside the warehouse many times when he brought in his fleeces. There was a small office on one side where delivery records were kept. A brick-walled corridor separated it from the storage area, a corridor with no exit. If Ethan had gotten trapped by the fire, he might have shut himself in the office. Martin put a hand on John's arm.

"I'm going round to have a look in the delivery office window, just to be sure."

John nodded. "I'll come along."

They walked around the front of the building. The moon shone fully into the yard on the other side. The heat wasn't as intense there, with the corridor separating the outer wall from the fire. Martin and John made their way along the wall until they came to the office window. Smoke obscured their view of the small room, but Martin caught a glimpse of white near the floor. It looked like a shirt cuff.

"He's in there!" Martin picked up a nearby brick and smashed the window. It wasn't big enough to crawl through, but they'd passed a larger one on their way. He knew it opened on the corridor. "Come on."

With John following, he ran down to the river. They stripped off their shirts, wet them and tied them over their mouths and noses. When they returned Martin broke the larger window, cleared away the glass with the brick, laid his folded coat on the sill and crawled through, with John right behind him.

Thick smoke and stifling heat filled the corridor. Eyes stinging, Martin shook shards of glass from his coat and pulled it on. He crouched low and felt his way along the wall until he came to the office door.

"Still with me, are you, John?"

"Aye."

He opened the door. Ethan lay huddled on the office floor. Much of the smoke in the room had escaped though the broken window. Enough moonlight came in to show burns on the older man's face and arms. He must have tried to fight the fire. Martin crawled to him and laid a hand over Ethan's heart.

"He's still alive."

John crawled up beside Martin. "He must have passed out before he could break the window." He wiped his sweaty face and glanced upward. "Let's get out of—"

A thunderous crash drowned him out. Martin's throat constricted with shock.

"Bloody hell! The ceiling's giving way." He shrugged out of his coat, draped it over Ethan's head, then slung the older man over his shoulder. Thankfully, Ethan was lightly built, not much of a burden.

159

Martin paused in the office doorway. Bloody hell said it all. A smoking rubble of brick and wood lay in the corridor where part of the ceiling had fallen. A thick wooden crossbeam on top of the heap burst into flames as he watched, blocking their only path of escape.

The acrid air burned Martin's lungs in spite of breathing through his wet shirt. He coughed and wiped sweat from his eyes. Heat poured into the corridor through the hole in the ceiling, already almost unbearable. If he didn't move that beam now, they weren't going to get out. He coughed again and fought to speak.

"Here John, you take Ethan." Martin got the watchman settled over John's shoulder, covered them both as well as he could with John's jacket, then took his own coat off to protect his hands and arms. The protection only lasted a moment. He closed his nose to the stench of his own scorching hair and skin, shut his mind to the blinding pain as he shoved the burning beam aside with his forearms, then he and John were stumbling over the smoldering mess toward safety.

If the fire hadn't already flashed by, they wouldn't have made it. When they reached the blessedly clear air by the broken corridor window, Martin took Ethan again while John crawled out. Between them they got the unconscious man through, then Martin followed.

He stumbled to the river and plunged in to cool his hands and arms, then collapsed on the bank, coughing and gasping for air. His head swam with the effort of trying to draw air into his protesting lungs, but the chill of the autumn night and the shock of the icy water kept him conscious, along with the searing pain of his burns.

After Greer, his next thought was of Chelle.

* * * *

Driving home from the dance, Chelle listened to Brian and Jean's banter and forced herself to join in now and then. She couldn't wait to close the door of her room behind her and stop pretending nothing was wrong.

Martin had made a quick escape when the dance ended, as Jason had to drive him home before heading back to his own farm. The McShannons lingered to chat with some of Brian and Jean's friends. Luckily for Chelle, Brian and Jean had been too wrapped up in each other to notice the byplay between her and Martin. They didn't get out alone together very often.

Halfway to the village, they caught the tang of smoke on the air. It smelled heavy and greasy, not like coal or peat. The fire's glow blossomed in the sky as they drove.

"That's got to be the mill." Brian sent the horses along at a canter. Jack and Colin met them in the yard. They jumped into the cart and headed for the fire, leaving the women to sit up through what was left of the night.

The men didn't return until dawn. At the sound of wheels, Chelle, Jean and Caroline hurried out to meet them. Chelle's father held her off when she ran to hug him.

"There now, lass, I'm black as a chimney sweep."

"I don't care. Was anyone inside?"

He rubbed at a sooty streak on his face, making it worse. "Aye. The watchman had gotten himself trapped inside, and the smoke got to him. Nobody thought to look for him—he'd raised the alarm and then gone back in, and everyone assumed he was somewhere in the crowd. Lucky for him, Martin and John Watson thought of him and got him out."

"Martin—"

"The watchman had some trifling burns and breathed in some smoke. Martin got some nasty burns on his arms. I don't know how bad."

Stomach churning, Chelle forced herself to speak calmly. Her father was watching her, and he'd always read her too well.

"What started the fire?"

Holding Jean and little Peter close against his chest, Brian answered. "I doubt we'll ever know. There's not much left inside the warehouse for evidence, but a few oily rags in the wrong place would have been enough. There's a few grumbling that the watchman was likely smoking on the job, but there's more that think it was set."

Set? Chelle's mind reeled. Martin hurt, perhaps seriously, after what had happened between them—she couldn't take it in.

"But who would gain by that? Not the mill hands, certainly. And the mill was making a profit, so the Westlakes wouldn't want it shut down."

Tight-lipped, Caroline slipped her arm around Jack's waist. "I'll warrant the mill was insured, but that won't help the folk who are out of work. Well, we'll likely never know, as you say. Brian, Jack, Colin, come in and get out of those clothes. It's a mercy no one was killed."

It took all of Chelle's self-control to wait until the next day to go to the farm. Martin might not want visitors, especially her, but she had to see him. As soon as breakfast was cleared away and the dishes done, she announced that she was going for a walk and braved her father's keen glance on the way out.

She walked fast until she reached the Rainnie lane, then stopped to catch her breath and calm herself. She didn't want to appear on Martin's doorstep looking like she'd run to see him.

Jessie came to the door, a worried crease in her brow. "Now then, Chelle, come in." At Jessie's heels, Greer held out her arms and said something very loosely translatable as "Up, Chelle."

"Clever girl, you're talking!" Her pulse racing again, Chelle lifted Greer and hugged her. "Jessie, how badly is Martin hurt?"

The crease in Jessie's forehead deepened. She nodded toward the sofa. "He's asleep. Doctor Halstead has me giving him laudanum for pain. The burns on his hands aren't much, but the ones on his arms are bad enough. They'll scar, and he's running a bit of a fever."

Chelle swallowed a lump in her throat, handed Greer to Jessie and stepped into the sitting area. Martin lay on the old horsehair sofa, a blue-and-white patchwork quilt thrown over him, both forearms swathed in bandages down to his palms. His brows had been singed and a few raw places showed on his hot, flushed face.

Jessie came to stand beside her. "They nearly didn't get out. He's lucky." She studied Chelle for a moment, a thoughtful look that made her face heat. "Will you sit with him for a while? I have work to do upstairs. I'll take Greer with me."

When the sound of Jessie's feet on the stairs died away, Chelle knelt on the floor next to Martin. She didn't intend to wake him, but he shifted and opened his eyes. They were glassy from the laudanum and dark with pain.

"Just like a bad penny. You keep turning up."

His voice was raspy from the smoke he'd inhaled. Chelle manufactured a smile and restrained an urge to lay her hand over his on the quilt. She couldn't let him see how shaken she was.

"I guess so."

Martin's mouth quirked in a slight smile. His eyelids drooped as the drug worked to pull him back under. "I've never thanked you... for giving Greer back to me."

Chelle looked down at his strong-featured face, a face accustomed to hiding his feelings. She remembered how he'd looked at her the day they'd met, the bitterness in his eyes. He hadn't looked at her like that since the day she'd pushed his daughter into his arms.

"You would have come to it yourself eventually, Martin."

He blinked, fighting to stay awake. "I'd like to think so— but I'm not sure."

Chelle shook her head. Anyone who heard Martin's music, anyone who knew him at all would know better.

"I am. You just needed some time."

"Perhaps, but thank you... just the same, lass."

163

His gaze locked on hers. Perhaps it was the drug talking, but Chelle couldn't look away. Not when he touched her cheek. Not when his fingers slid into her hair.

Jessie might come downstairs at any moment, but Chelle couldn't pull back. She leaned down and brushed her lips over his, once, twice, just a whisper of contact. Martin sighed, fisted his hand in her hair and held her still while he captured her lower lip between his. His tongue touched the corners of her mouth, coaxing her to open for him. It was slow and gentle, not like the passionate kiss they'd shared at the dance, but it made Chelle's blood run thick and hot. When it ended, she saw a glow in Martin's eyes that burned through the drug.

"I'll never look at Greer... without thinking of you. Chelle, you didn't just give her back to me. You've... given me more than that. I can't explain, but—"

"You don't have to, and you don't owe me anything. That's what friends are for. Now close your eyes."

He did. She waited until he drifted back to sleep, then gently pulled her hand from his.

What had she done? She should have been the one to stop this. Martin wasn't himself. She'd already proven that she wasn't ready to be a wife, let alone a mother, so she had no right to accept—no, *encourage* his kisses.

She got to her feet and slipped out. Perhaps the Paxtons were right after all, and it would be best for all concerned if she simply stayed away. She'd be setting herself, Martin and Greer up for heartbreak if she didn't.

# CHAPTER 16

"Louden, I said I didn't wish to be disturbed. What is it?"

"I'm sorry, Mr. Westlake, but there's a young man here asking to see you, one of the mill office clerks. I told him you were occupied but he said you wouldn't thank me for turning him away, and I thought it might be something about the fire. Shall I send him on his way?"

"Who is he?"

"Drew Markham, sir."

Phillip took a moment to get a grip on his temper. He really didn't have time for this right now. The week since the fire had been packed with extra paperwork. He knew Drew Markham as an efficient clerk, though he'd been told the lad had a bit of an unsavory reputation in the village. Louden's face certainly showed no liking for Drew, and Phillip had learned long ago to trust his valet/butler's instincts about people.

"No, I may as well see him. Send him in here."

Phillip cleared the papers from his desk and spun in his chair to look out the office window. Driving rain obscured his view of the mill with its smoke-blackened warehouse. Perhaps this whole episode was a message, telling him the time had come to bow out.

Truth be told, he was tired. The climb from a junior office clerk in Lancashire to wealth had taken his illusions as well as his youth, and all but the shell of his marriage. He'd been born a shopkeeper's son and always would be, at least in the eyes of the people whose society his wife courted in London. What more did he have to prove to the world?

A discreet cough made him turn around. Louden came into the office, followed by Drew.

"Mr. Markham, sir."

Phillip nodded toward the chair on the other side of the desk. "Well, sit down, Markham, and tell me what's so very urgent."

Louden retreated and closed the door behind him. Markham sat and crossed his legs in front of him, a smile on his face. "Aye, I have summat to tell you right enough, Mr. Westlake. It's about the night the mill burned."

Bile rose in Phillip's throat. He'd gone to the mill himself that night, not wanting to trust the job to anyone else. He'd put on an outfit of old shooting clothes he hadn't worn in years, waited till the watchman was at the other end of the property, touched a match to some oily rags in the warehouse and hurried home, certain he hadn't been noticed. It had never occurred to him that the watchman would be fool enough to try to fight the fire himself.

"I see."

Markham's smile widened as he leaned forward. "Do you? Aye, well, let's be sure. It was a fine moonlit evenin'—remember?—and it so happens I'd walked over to Carston to the harvest dance. On my way home, I passed the mill just as the fire was takin' hold. I looked over here and saw the light go out in the window of this room—but not before I saw you standin' there, watchin'."

Phillip relaxed in his chair and fit his fingertips together, willing himself not to react. It was possible...just possible. He *had* watched from the window for a moment to see the fire take hold, but only for a moment. If by some fiendish chance Markham had been on the road, he could have seen Phillip in the window without being seen himself.

"And now you want me to buy your silence, am I correct?"

"You're a quick one, Mr. Westlake."

"I'm flattered. I wonder if you thought of this little scheme yourself. I suppose you did—I doubt you'd have the cleverness to think of anything better. What reason could I possibly have to try to destroy a business that was turning a healthy profit?" Thankfully, Phillip had always made sure to keep his speculation in cotton separate from mill business. Everything was in his partner's name. Stuart McBeath, his oldest friend and the father of Maria's fiancé, could be trusted absolutely. The insurance investigators had already examined the fire scene, looked at the mill's books and seen no need to look further. They had no idea that the dearth of cotton caused by the Union blockade of Confederate ports had left him in a dicey position. As for Drew, he wouldn't even have the name of the insurance company.

Phillip rose from his chair. Even if Markham had seen him that night, the man couldn't prove anything. No one who mattered would believe him.

"You're wasting your time and mine, Markham. I have business to attend to. You may see yourself out."

Still smiling, Drew got to his feet and doffed his cap. "Have it your way, sir. I'll give my regards to Miss Westlake the next time I see her, then. She'll likely listen to me. If not, she'll get that high nose of hers taken down a notch or two."

Phillip fought down an urge to strike the man and smiled back. He considered firing Markham on the spot, but then he'd have nothing to lose by spreading his story. It would be wiser to keep that card in reserve. Markham had to know he'd rot in prison or hang if he tried to harm Maria. As for anything he might say, Maria would no more believe him than the magistrate would.

"Oh, I don't think you're quite that stupid, Markham. Now are you leaving, or shall I have you removed from the house and arrested for uttering threats against my daughter? And be assured, if I hear any more about this you will lose your situation. Good day."

\* \* \* \*

Maria reached the top of the hill outside Mallonby and stopped for breath. The early November twilight had faded to a chill dusk, with a half moon rising pale and clear over the fell.

She should be getting home, but her walk to Carston and back seemed to have increased her restlessness instead of easing it as she'd hoped. She hated the thought of going in. She might as well run an errand to Bingham's first.

She started down the hill, watching the light in her father's study window. She hadn't bothered to tell him she was going out. He'd been short-tempered and preoccupied for months, since long before the fire. Maria knew all wasn't well with his financial affairs.

Allan had written that his father's business was shaky, and she knew her father had invested heavily in Stuart McBeath's ventures, but Maria had given up asking questions. She couldn't ask Allan to betray his father's confidence, and her father continued to brush her off, leaving her feeling frustrated and helpless.

She walked faster, wishing she could outpace her worries. Lamplight glowing from windows brightened the dark, empty street. Most Mallonby people were at their evening meal at this hour, such as it was in this bleak autumn. The mill would be closed for the rest of the winter while the warehouse was rebuilt and the roof on the whole building replaced. She'd convinced her father to let her set up a relief fund for the unemployed mill hands, and at church the same week, Maria had asked Rochelle McShannon to help her. She'd accepted with a warm smile.

"I'd be glad to, Miss Westlake. I'm sure we can get the local farmers to donate some food, and we'll purchase more with whatever funds you can provide." Rochelle had enlisted her cousin's help, and between them they'd organized food distribution meetings at the church to take place every Saturday. They'd also arranged a settlement for the family of Mary Tate. Maria's mother had sent some money as well, though she hadn't seen any need to leave London to be with her husband during this crisis. Maria gave a resigned little shrug at the thought. She'd known for years that her parents' marriage was only a hollow show. They led completely separate lives.

In the village, Maria purchased the hair combs she intended to give her maid, Susan, as a birthday gift. She left the store just as a group of young men spilled from the Split Crow. For a moment they stood in the circle of light at the open door, laughing and talking, their dialect almost unintelligible to Maria. She'd never troubled herself to learn broad Yorkshire.

The smell of food that issued from the pub made her stomach rumble. She turned toward home, thinking of the chicken pot pie cook had planned for dinner. She heard one of the men from the pub coming along behind her, but paid him no mind. Then, just outside of the village he caught up and stepped in front of her, blocking Maria's path.

He was an arrogant-looking, auburn-haired creature, wearing a mocking smile. She looked him coolly in the eye.

"Will you get out of my way, please?"

"In a moment, Your Highness. I've summat to say to you first. Your sod of a father belongs in gaol for arson."

Scorching heat rushed to Maria's face. How could he dare? Too outraged to remember how far beneath her he was, she drew back her hand and slapped the man across the face as hard as she could.

"You're a disgusting liar!"

He just grinned at her. "Ask him yourself, Miss. I'd like to be there to see him try and deny it."

Too shocked to move, Maria watched the man head back toward the village and turn onto the side path leading to Carston. Could he possibly believe he could get away with treating her like that? He'd be in gaol by tomorrow morning.

*Unless it's true.*

When her legs would carry her, Maria hurried home. After dinner, when she would normally have left her father alone in the dining room, she stayed in her seat while he tasted his port.

"Did you wish to speak to me about something, Maria? You looked as if you had something on your mind all through dinner."

"Yes. Father, on my way home tonight a young man stopped me on the road and was...really odious to me. He said that you should be in gaol for arson." The man's words came back to Maria as she watched her father's face pale. *I'd like to be there to see him deny it.* "He said he'd been to see you, but you wouldn't listen to him." A suffocating lump rose in her throat when she saw that he couldn't meet her gaze. "He was telling the truth, wasn't he?" She rose and moved to kneel beside him.

"Father, why?"

He rubbed a hand over his eyes, still unable to look at her. "It's complicated, Maria. I needed money, and the insurance settlement was the only way to get it quickly enough. I never meant for anyone to get hurt."

Her heart cracking, Maria stood. "That just isn't good enough. Three people almost died. Does this have something to do with your dealings with Allan's father?"

Her father spoke in an odd, detached voice she'd never heard him use before. "Allan's father and I made some investments in cotton. When the war overseas started, those investments lost their value. I needed money to cover the interest on the short-term loans I'd taken out to finance my share of the venture. I approached one or two lenders, but Allan's father's firm is in a very uncertain position right now. Cotton made up a large portion of his business. The lenders I spoke to considered it a poor risk. I wasn't able to get the funds I needed. I was desperate."

"Desperate? Father, you know my trust fund matured last year. You could have come to me."

"I would have needed all of your money, Maria. I couldn't do that to you, with you and Allan planning to be married next summer. I put that money away over the years to give you a future."

Maria wanted to shake him, to jolt him out of his self-absorbed stupor and make him see what he'd done. "A future? If Allan finds out about this, if his father's company becomes insolvent because of it, I wouldn't blame him if he broke our engagement. Does Mr. McBeath know?"

"No. He believes the fire was an accident. He trusts me." Her father rose and moved to the window, looking out into the darkness. His reflection in the glass looked old and defeated. "That man's name is Drew Markham. He works in the mill office. He did come to see me, but I never imagined he'd speak to you. I thought he was only bluffing. I'll send for him tomorrow and offer him something. I've borrowed against the insurance settlement, so my cash flow problem is taken care of for the time being. Once the mill reopens, if he asks for anything more I'll tell him I'll let him go. By then it will be too late for him to try to have me charged. His job will be worth more to him."

Maria stood and returned to her chair. She supposed that would be the best way to handle the situation. "Likely it will. Susan told me there were rumors flying about the village that the fire was deliberately set, but with no evidence, rumors will do no harm. There's no trust between you and the mill hands to be lost."

She couldn't keep the bitterness out of her voice. A spark of temper lit her father's tired eyes.

"Maria, you have no idea how these people have to be handled."

"No, I don't, but they are people, not machines. You weren't very far above them starting out. Have you forgotten that?"

"No, I haven't. That's exactly why I have to be hard, Maria. I couldn't keep any authority if I wasn't. You've led a very comfortable life because I've succeeded."

She joined him at the window, her reflection next to his in the glass. Things would never be the same between them. She'd lost both parents in every way that mattered.

"I would have been content with much less, Father. So would Mother, I think. I wonder if that isn't where things went wrong between you."

* * * *

The spoon Chelle held slipped unheeded into the soup pot at the sight of Jessie hurrying into the forge yard. Two weeks had passed since the fire—weeks in which Chelle had kept her promise to herself and stayed away from the farm, knowing that she'd surely hear if Martin's condition worsened. Her breath caught with dread. Jessie certainly didn't look like a bearer of good news.

"Nay, lass, he's healin'. He ran a low fever for three or four days, but that was all." Jessie came in, stepped past Chelle to the stove and chafed her hands to warm them, looking over her shoulder. "I'm in a bit of a pickle, though. I got word this morning that my sister Charlotte tripped over one of the children's toys and broke her ankle. She's sent for her oldest daughter to come and help her look after the little ones, but she can't get here until tomorrow at the earliest, so I'll have to go in the meantime. Is Caroline home? Martin is going to need someone until I get back, and none of Charlotte's brood is old enough."

"Aunt was called out to Mrs. Dawes early this morning. I went with her, but it looked like being an easy birth, so she sent me home." In the grip of her relief, Chelle didn't stop to think. She'd been desperate to reassure herself about Martin. "I'll go out to the farm. I haven't much to do today anyway. I'll just tell Jean and be on my way."

"Thank you, Chelle." Jessie blew out a breath and gathered her shawl around her again. "I won't dawdle. Charlotte's youngest is probably in a fair way to burn the house down by now."

She bustled away, leaving Chelle prey to sudden doubt. She ran upstairs, where Jean was putting Peter down for his nap.

"If Aunt isn't back by suppertime—"

"Maybe I should go. I could take Peter with me. You've had enough grief from gossip as it is." Jean turned from Peter's crib and gave Chelle a sharp look that softened to understanding. "You really want to go, don't you?"

Chelle couldn't hold Jean's gaze. "Peter's just settled. It doesn't make sense to move him, and it'll upset him if you're not here when he wakes. If Aunt Caroline doesn't get home this afternoon, send Dad along. If that doesn't satisfy appearances, I don't care. I'd better be going."

When she reached the farm, Gyp rose from the sun-warmed doorstep and barked a greeting. Martin came to the door to meet her, frowning, the sleeves of his dark green linen shirt rolled up above his bandaged forearms.

"Now then. I was expectin' Caroline."

He looked tired, and pain lines showed around his mouth and eyes. Chelle couldn't read him, couldn't tell if he was angry, disappointed or just disconcerted to see her. He might not even remember her last visit, but he certainly couldn't have forgotten what happened at the dance.

"She's out at a birth, so I came out in the meantime."

"Aye. Come in. Greer's asleep. Jessie put her down just before she left."

Chelle followed him into the sitting room. As the silence wore on, Chelle decided he didn't know what to say to her. Perhaps he remembered everything.

"Jessie said your bandages need changing this afternoon. Whenever you'd like me to do it, let me know."

He nodded. "We may as well do it now, while Greer's sleeping. Jessie left everything ready."

Martin went upstairs and brought down two bowls, one holding a roll of gauze soaked in an oily mixture and the other

173

a roll of heavier linen. "The linseed oil helps keep the gauze from sticking to the burns. The dry bandage goes over it all."

Chelle got the scissors and sat next to him on the sofa. She cut and unwound the outer bandage on Martin's right arm, then started peeling away the oiled gauze underneath. Her hand went to her mouth as his raw, angry burns began to show through the fabric.

"Get on wi' it, lass." The irritation in his tone made her set her lips. She wouldn't show squeamishness in front of him. She continued removing layers until she started to meet resistance. In spite of the oil, the gauze had stuck to his skin in places. His arm tensed and Chelle heard his breath catch, but the bandage had to come off.

"This is going to have to be soaked." She couldn't imagine how much that would hurt. On unsteady legs, Chelle rose and fetched a basin of warm water. Not only did Martin have to bear his pain, she had to bear it, too.

Not daring to look at his face, she wet the gauze in the worst places. She didn't want to pull quickly and tear the healing flesh on his arm, but doing it slowly had to be agonizing for him.

Working as gently as she could, she managed to free the bandage, revealing the full extent of his injuries. Chelle's stomach turned over. She'd never seen a bad burn before. Martin held himself rigid, his fist clenched, until she'd finished applying the new oiled strip. Chelle had to stop and take a few deep breaths before her hands would obey her well enough to add the outer bandage. She tied it off and looked up, her voice almost failing her.

"I didn't know…"

Ashen beneath his freckles, Martin shrugged. Pain and annoyance mingled in his stormy-sea eyes.

"It's nothing that won't heal."

Yes, he'd heal—if he avoided blood poisoning—but he would be badly scarred. He likely wouldn't care, but Chelle hated to think of him marred. At least his hands weren't badly damaged.

Martin had become his old self again, edgy and remote. He wasn't comfortable being alone with her, and she didn't blame him. She could only blame herself. She moved to his other side and went through the whole wrenching process again. His left arm was worse than the right. By the time she finished bandaging it, his face was beaded with sweat and Chelle thought she might faint for the first time in her life.

She closed her eyes and sat still until the dizziness passed. She felt Martin get up, heard him climb the stairs. Chelle moved to the hearth, dumped the soiled gauze in the grate, set a match to it and watched it burn. How many times would Martin have to go through that?

She put the used linen bandages in the laundry and returned just as Martin came down again with his face washed. He looked a little bit ashamed.

"Turned you up a bit, didn't it? You got through it, though. Thank you, lass."

Still a bit shaky, Chelle shook her head. "Martin, that must have been awful for you. If I was clumsy, I'm sorry."

"You weren't clumsy. You did as well as Jessie could have. Now let's talk of somethin' else. What's goin' on in the village? I haven't had any news since Dr. Halstead was here four days ago." He let out an impatient sigh. "I haven't even had a bloody newspaper for a week. Jessie wouldn't leave me to get one."

Martin stepped past her and took his chair by the hearth. His crankiness made Chelle smile in spite of herself as she returned to the sofa. "I think Jessie's a born mother, even though she's never had a family. She dotes on Greer, too. As for news, Maria Westlake told me it'll be Christmas by the time the insurance money comes through and building materials for the mill can be delivered." She tucked her feet under her, thankful that the tension between them had dissolved for the moment. "I've never been as surprised as I was when she asked me to help with the relief committee. I spoke to her one day a while ago about doing something for Mary Tate's family and she seemed interested, but I hadn't heard from her since. I'd decided she'd just told me what I wanted to hear to get rid of me. Now I'm starting to think she's human after all."

"You've shamed her into it."

Gyp's reedy bark sounded from outside. Martin let him in and settled in his chair again, with the Collie curled up at his feet. Chelle had never seen him in the house before. He must be missing the hours he usually spent with his master up on the fell.

"Perhaps. You know, I feel sorry for Miss Westlake. She's lonely. She told me she's engaged to a young man in London, so I really don't know why she stays here."

"Well, there's a story behind that, or so I've heard. Her mother hasn't spent much time here in years. Phillip Westlake and his wife live separate lives, and John Watson told me she comes and goes with whoever she chooses in town, including other women's husbands. Rather embarrassing for Miss Westlake and her fiancé, if it's true."

"Maybe that's why she seems so unhappy and preoccupied. Last Saturday at the distribution meeting, she looked like she hadn't slept a wink." Maria must be even lonelier than Chelle had imagined. No wonder people thought her proud. "Which reminds me, I haven't thanked you for the produce you sent in."

"I can spare it better than some of the others with big families to feed. Your friend, Kendra—are she and her mother all right?"

"Yes, for now. Kendra's young man has been sending her some money when he can, and it's keeping the wolf from the door. You know, I can't help thinking she hasn't seen the last of her David."

"I've said before you're one as looks for the best in people, Chelle."

She cast a nervous glance out the window. The room was growing dim with the early November twilight. Her father or her aunt had better appear soon, or her reputation would be in tatters. The hired man would be showing up before long to do the evening chores. Would he hold his tongue if he found her here? Not likely.

"I suppose so. I was right about you, wasn't I? Now, I'd better get supper started before Greer wakes up."

## CHAPTER 17

Martin watched while Chelle added dumplings to the pot of beef stew on the range. Then she brought Greer downstairs, wide-awake after her nap. The little one settled on the floor by his chair and petted Gyp, while Chelle returned to the sofa with some sewing. When Greer grabbed a handful of the dog's fur, Martin reached down to stop her.

"Easy, now, don't hurt the old lad." He gritted his teeth and lifted his daughter to his lap. Gyp gave him a grateful look out of dark eyes. Greer tried the old dog's patience at times, but he never lost his temper with her.

Martin grew more and more uncomfortable as the minutes passed. The aroma of good cooking in the air, Greer's chatter, Chelle's bright head bent in concentration as she stitched— he'd never wanted more from life than his farm, his music and the warmth of a family to come home to at day's end, and that was what this felt like, but it was all an illusion.

The day after the fire was a blur in Martin's mind. He'd had a couple of strong doses of poppy to help him over the worst of his pain, but not so much that he didn't remember waking to find Chelle beside him. He wasn't sure what they'd said to each other, but he recalled the feel of her soft lips against his as she kissed him – or was that wishful thinking combined with the effects of the drug? He only knew that she'd haunted his dreams since then.

He heard Gerry Newton's whistle from outside as he arrived to do the milking. Later Martin let Gyp out to get his dish of cream, and froze in the doorway at the sight of the Paxtons' buggy coming up the lane. As they drew closer he saw Hugh's face and knew this wasn't a random call. *Bloody hell.* Martin waited in the doorway until they'd pulled up in the yard and Hugh had helped his wife from the buggy.

"Now then, Hugh, Margaret. What brings you this way today?"

"We drove over to the Binghams' to get some of the fancy molasses they carry," Margaret told him, "and we ran into Jessie Mason. We heard her tell Mrs. Bingham she'd had to come in to her sister's place to help her out, so we thought we'd stop by on our way home to make sure you were all right."

*You mean you wanted to find out who was here with me.* Martin got a firm grip on his temper, stepped back and let them in, bracing himself for their reaction when they saw Chelle.

She had put down her sewing. Composed and quiet, she didn't flinch from Margaret's glare. "Good afternoon, Mrs. Paxton."

"Miss McShannon. I'm surprised to see you here."

"Jessie stopped by to ask Aunt Caroline to come out to stay with Martin, but she wasn't home, so I came instead."

Margaret ignored her reply. "Martin, we need to speak with you. Alone."

"Anything you need to say can be said in front of Miss McShannon."

Hugh crossed the room and stood toe to toe with Martin, his voice dripping ice. "Very well, then. This girl has already shown that she has no respect for propriety, staying here with only you and Jessie Mason in the house. Folk talked for a week about you dancing with her at the Harvest Dance, and no one but her. Martin, you're a young man and it's only natural that you want another wife, even if Eleanor has only been gone a year, but we will not have this thoughtless, brazen creature raising our daughter's child."

Martin's hands balled into fists. It took all his will to modulate his voice. "Hugh, the lass cared for Greer like a mother until I brought her home. She's here today because Jessie couldn't be, Caroline was out and I needed someone. I can't look after the house and Greer, and I can't change these bandages on my own. I won't listen to you or anyone else

179

talkin' ill of Miss McShannon. I fought Drew Markham for doin' it."

Chelle's cheeks bloomed scarlet. Martin silently cursed himself for putting his foot in his mouth. The Paxtons had likely heard about the fight anyway, but mentioning it now would only strengthen their suspicions that he and Chelle were involved in some kind of improper affair. The look on Margaret's face proved him right.

"Very well. You can expect to be summoned to the magistrate's court, then. We'll be suing for custody of Greer."

Martin took a step toward Hugh and felt a rush of satisfaction when the man backed away. "You can try, but you won't succeed. Take me to court and I'll tell the magistrate what kind of parents you were to Eleanor. I don't know that she ever got a word of affection from either of you. I'll also guarantee you'll have nothing to do with Greer until she's grown. Now be off. I won't have her upset by any more of this. You can see yourselves out."

With another venomous look at Chelle, Margaret stiffened her back and marched out. Hugh followed. Martin locked the door behind them. Greer had toddled over to Chelle and been gathered in her arms. He sat next to them on the sofa and laid a hand on Greer's back.

"Christ, what a mess."

The color faded from Chelle's face. Their eyes met over the baby's head.

"It isn't your fault, Martin. It's mine."

"That's daft, lass. You aren't to blame for their beastly minds."

"Perhaps not, but it doesn't matter, does it? I'm a newcomer here, and I haven't done much to give people a high opinion of me. My staying with you when you brought Greer home can be made to look bad to a judge, even though Jessie was here. And I know they saw my bag in the hall just now. If I stay here tonight they'll have plenty of ammunition to use in court, and most judges would agree that a child is better off with two parents."

It occurred to Martin to be grateful that his arms were in bandages. He thought he might have punched Hugh otherwise.

"Two parents! Between them, they didn't make one parent to Eleanor. They don't really want Greer any more than they wanted their own daughter." Gyp barked from the yard, sending Martin to the window. "Who the devil…Oh, it's Colin."

He beckoned through the window. Colin came in, ruddy-faced from his walk. "By the smell of things in here, I've arrived just in time."

Chelle set Greer on her feet and rose to hug him. "You have, Dad. Take off your coat. Supper's ready."

Martin nodded. "Aye, Colin, sit in. Your daughter knows what she's about in the kitchen, I'd say."

They took seats on opposite sides of the table. Chelle put Greer in her high chair and ladled corned beef and cabbage onto plates. Colin smiled in appreciation as he inhaled deeply.

"She does. She had to learn young, with her mother ill. How are you then, Martin? You look like you've had a hard row to hoe."

"It's not comfortable, but that's to be expected. More than anything, I'm tired."

Impatient for her supper, Greer squealed, then pounded the tray on her chair. Colin shook his head. "You've got a little minx there. Tired? I'll never forget what it was like when Chelle and her brother were that age. If one of them wasn't squalling, the other was."

Chelle rolled her eyes and set her father's plate in front of him. "Dad, I'm sure Martin doesn't want to hear baby stories. Martin, here's yours. Eat before it gets cold."

Silence fell as they ate. Martin watched Chelle feed Greer, until he caught Colin watching him with a thoughtful look in his blue eyes. After that, Martin kept his gaze on his plate.

When he'd found Chelle in the byre milking on her last visit, it had set him on edge. Eleanor had enjoyed milking. Seeing Chelle in his wife's place grated on him, but now, watching her with Greer soothed him with a sense of rightness. What would Eleanor think to see another woman caring for her daughter?

After the meal, Colin settled in one of the chairs by the hearth. "I saw Ethan Bowes in the village yesterday, Martin. He's still coughing a bit, but he's doing well."

Chelle lifted Greer from her high chair and Martin took her to sit with him on the rug in front of the fire. "Aye, he was out to see me a couple of days ago. He's feeling pretty cut up and foolish about the whole thing. He never dreamed the fire would spread as quickly as it did. As for that, I probably wouldn't have either."

Colin shook his head. "There aren't many men in Mallonby who could have done what you did, I know that. You're lucky your hands weren't worse burned."

"I made sure of that. I've been playing fiddle so long, it's second nature for me to guard my hands. They're healed now."

His fingers absently ruffled Greer's hair. Colin smiled with more than a hint of triumph.

"The little lass has taken to you. I was right that night she was ill, wasn't I?"

"Aye, you were. This house is a different place with her here."

Chelle joined them and perched on the arm of her father's chair. "She's changed in the last two weeks. She really isn't a baby anymore."

Colin's smile faded. "Martin, Chelle told me you're having some trouble with Eleanor's parents."

"Aye." Martin decided not to mention tonight's episode. If the Paxtons carried out their threats, the whole district would find out soon enough. "They've threatened to sue for custody. The more I think on it, the more I wonder if it isn't because

Chelle here is like Eleanor in a lot of ways. She has a lovely smile, a light step and a big heart, and she has music in her."

Chelle blushed. "I'm flattered, but I'm not musical."

Seeing her reaction, Martin felt his blood start to run fast and light, the way it used to on a night when the dance floor was full and his bow seemed weightless as it flew over the strings. The way he'd felt when he danced with her.

"Yes you are, lass. It shows when you dance. As for Greer, I think she's goin' to be musical too. She likes to hear me play."

Colin leaned back in his chair, making himself at home. "I'd like to hear you play too, Martin, if you'd care to and if it doesn't bother your arms."

"Nay, the doctor said it would be good for them, to keep them from gettin' stiff."

He took the fiddle down, stood beside Greer and began a slow air, one he'd played the last time Chelle had stayed here, the night they'd ended up sitting outside together. He followed it with one of the tunes he'd played at the dance, a lively reel. Colin jumped up and held out his hand.

"Come, lass."

Chelle stepped into his arms. Her father whirled her around the room while Martin played one tune after another. She'd come by her grace on the dance floor honestly, it seemed. Colin was nimble enough on his feet. They danced until Chelle dropped onto the sofa, laughing.

"Dad, I need to catch my breath."

"I'm winded, too. It's been a while." Colin sat beside her. They exchanged a look full of memories before he turned to Martin.

"You haven't forgotten how to play, lad. Sidonie would have enjoyed that."

Chelle smoothed her hair, rose and lifted a sleepy-eyed Greer from the rug by Martin's feet.

"Somebody's ready for bed."

He kissed his daughter's forehead and watched Chelle carry her upstairs. When the bedroom door closed, Colin cleared his throat.

"This row with Eleanor's parents… Do you think they'll actually take you to court?"

A cold chill settled in the pit of Martin's stomach. Whether or not they managed to get the case before the magistrate, the Paxtons would make as much trouble as they could for him and Chelle, that was for sure and certain. He fetched whiskey and glasses, poured two healthy shots and downed half of his own.

"I wouldn't have thought so, but now I think they might. They haven't dealt with losing their daughter, and they think Chelle wants to take her place."

"She could do worse."

Martin just managed not to gape at Chelle's father like an idiot. Did the man have the same touch of foresight his mother was said to have had?

"She might not like you saying that."

Colin swirled his glass, took a thoughtful sip. "The night Greer was ill I told you I wasn't sure I'd done the right thing by bringing Chelle here, but I was talking nonsense. I know my girl, and she's one to be reckoned with when she really wants something. I don't know what happened between her and her young man, but I can make a good guess. His parents wouldn't have welcomed a bride whose father disapproved of the war, and whose brother didn't intend to fight, but if Chelle had really cared for the lad it wouldn't have mattered."

The whiskey seemed to have gone straight to Martin's head. "Colin, I'm all at sea these days. Eleanor's only been gone a year. When I lost her, I thought I'd died too, in every way that matters."

Colin leaned forward, his eyes so like Chelle's when she was troubled. "I remember the day the doctor told me that Sidonie wasn't going to get well. I'd never felt fear like that before, knowing I was going to lose her and there was nothing

I could do to prevent it. And when she passed away, the pain was even worse than I'd feared, but if we're going to live at all, we can't cling to the pain. That's not what Eleanor would have wanted for you and Greer."

Martin's pulse started racing. "No, it isn't. I learned that the night Greer was ill."

Colin glanced at the stairwell again and lowered his voice. "Aye. As for Chelle, I can't read her mind or her heart, and maybe I'm talking out of turn, but I've seen how she reacts when your name is mentioned. The lad she fancied at home was a rich man's son, with generations of blue-blooded Virginians behind him. Chelle is a plain farmer's daughter. I'm not sure she wouldn't be happiest as a plain farmer's wife."

Martin's voice failed him. After the dance he couldn't doubt that Chelle found him attractive, but to have her father see it and give his blessing knocked the breath out of him.

"I don't know what to say."

Colin laughed. "Don't let me rattle you, lad. All I'm saying is life's too short not to take a chance on happiness when it comes around."

Happiness. Martin was still getting used to having Greer at home. That was all the happiness he hoped for, and Chelle had given him that. The possibility of more, of having evenings like this, full of laughter and chaos and the children he and Eleanor had dreamed of, came to life inside him like a lamp being lit, but it carried a price. Risk. Eleanor wasn't the first young woman to die giving birth and she wouldn't be the last.

"I need another drink."

## CHAPTER 18

Chelle woke to the sound of Greer chattering to herself in her crib. It didn't seem strange at all, waking up in this room with the now-leafless branches of the old crabapple tree screening the window. It felt as though it had been only days instead of months since she'd stayed here.

She changed Greer, left the little girl in her crib and went downstairs and out to the privy. Gyp moved from the doorstep to make way for her. Martin had said over supper last night that since his injury, the old dog wouldn't sleep in the barn. He knew something was amiss and insisted on keeping watch over the house.

This promised to be a golden day among the usual lead coinage of late autumn. Over the barn, the Eastern sky was flushed with the pink of sunrise, and a few stars still glowed in the West. A heavy frost coated the cobbles in the yard and climbed the stalks of the brown, wilted perennials in Eleanor's flower bed. The sight gave Chelle a pang of homesickness. Her mother's garden would be lying lonely and dormant now, too, its summer bloom come and gone unappreciated, with no one to put it to bed properly for the winter.

She pushed the thought away and stood on the step, letting the peace of the place settle around her. She missed this, missed the quiet routine of mornings at home, missed seeing the flash of the creek from the kitchen window and hearing the sounds of the animals waking in the barn. She shivered and scolded herself. Gerry would be arriving soon to do the milking and barn chores. She'd better wash and start breakfast instead of standing here waiting to catch her death of cold.

She brought Greer down, put her in her high chair—another family relic Martin had pulled from the attic—and made porridge. Just as it was ready, Chelle heard footsteps on the stairs.

"Morning, Dad," she said without turning around. That quick, light tread couldn't be Martin's. Her father came up behind her and put a hand on her shoulder.

"Morning, lass."

"You look well rested. Did you and Martin sit up late?"

"Nay. We talked for a little while after you went upstairs, and that was all. Does Martin keep coffee on hand?"

"Yes, in the pantry cupboard."

Her father added water to the chipped enamel coffee pot and set it on the stove next to the porridge. He sat at the table, waiting for it to boil and watching Chelle as she fed Greer.

"You do that like you've been doing it for years, Chelle."

It did feel natural, looking after Greer. Thinking back, Chelle realized it always had. "Do I? I guess this one wormed her way into my heart while she was at the forge. I still miss her."

Her father reached for one of the little girl's hands and grinned when she caught his thumb in a sturdy grip. "You'll be a good mother some day, lass. And twins run in families."

Chelle rolled her eyes and grinned back. "Have some porridge, Dad. Martin had better come down soon, before it gets lumpy."

Suddenly looking awkward, her father shifted in his chair. "Martin and I were talking about you last night. Chelle, I'm sure it's no surprise to you that he fancies you."

She felt herself blushing fiercely. Again. She'd guessed that her father had picked up on the attraction between her and Martin, but to have him say so in plain English was another matter.

"I know he does, in a way."

"And how do you feel about him?"

Chelle turned away. "Confused, but that's neither here nor there. Martin isn't ready for a second wife, and I'm not ready to be a wife. I found that out before we left home."

Her father gave her one of his penetrating looks. "What went wrong between you and Rory, lass? Oh, yes, I knew you cared for him. I was prepared to stay in Georgia if he proposed to you, but he didn't."

Chelle gave Greer her last spoonful of porridge and put the bowl aside. Why not tell him? It wasn't a secret worth keeping.

"Yes, I cared for Rory. He did propose, just before we left, but he told me that if we married I'd have to cut all ties with Trey. Rory called him a coward. I couldn't choose between them, so he let me go. Oh, it was for the best, I know that now, but I really thought he loved me. This feeling between me and Martin might not be any different, and there's Greer to consider. Her grandparents despise me, and I'd never forgive myself if they managed to take her."

Her father's gaze turned challenging. "There are never any guarantees, lass. As for the Paxtons, I think they'd likely have objected to any young woman who was friendly with Martin. That's what they're like. And since when have you cared what people think?"

"I care what *I* think."

"Chelle, just remember to be honest with yourself. Martin comes from the same background as you and you seem to understand each other."

The stairs creaked again, louder under Martin's heavier tread. He stepped into the kitchen, tousled and with tired smudges under his eyes. Chelle's heart lurched. Had his burns kept him awake, or was it his conversation with her father?

He was quiet over the meal. Chelle felt the tension in him. Her father must have felt it too, because as soon as he'd finished eating, he stood.

"Gerry's here. I'll help him with the milking."

Martin hadn't quite finished his breakfast, but Chelle needed some distance between them. She put water on to heat for the dishes and busied herself scraping them, keeping her back to the table.

She heard Martin get up and step toward her. She felt his hand on her shoulder and froze, her legs threatening to turn to jelly. When he turned her around, she didn't dare look up, but he tucked his hand under her chin and forced her to meet his gaze. It seared her to the bone.

"Chelle, can you look me in the eye and tell me you don't care for me?"

Her voice faltered. She couldn't think with him looking at her like that.

"No."

Martin drew her closer, rested his bandaged arms at her waist and bent his head. Over the frantic rush of her heart, Chelle heard him sigh. His lips brushed hers, coaxing them apart.

"You're so sweet, lass." His mouth feathered over hers again, then he took her lower lip between his and sucked gently. Aching, tingling pleasure shot through her, melting Chelle's bones and drugging her mind, just as it had the night of the dance. Her arms reached around Martin's neck, her fingers threading into his hair. When he released her lip, her tongue slipped into his mouth to tangle with his. As if from a distance Chelle heard herself make a soft, breathy sound, but it barely registered. There was nothing in her world but Martin, his taste, the solid feel of his body pressed to hers.

When the kiss ended, she stood in his arms, afraid her legs wouldn't hold her if he let her go. "Martin, this is—I have some thinking to do. And I'm going to need time to do it."

"I need time too, Chelle. When I lost Eleanor I didn't think I'd ever feel like this again. And now I've got the Paxtons to deal with." He stepped back and ran a hand through his hair. Greer held out her arms and squealed to be let down from her chair. Chelle lifted her and held one baby hand out to touch Martin's.

"Greer is yours, and you've given her a good home. The magistrate can't be blind enough not to see that she's happy and well cared for. You aren't going to lose her."

\* \* \* \*

189

Jessie got back to the farm shortly before nightfall, looking ruffled. "Charlotte's daughter has finally arrived. I see you folks have managed. I asked four different people if they could come out here, and every one of them had someone sick at home or some other reason why they couldn't leave. Chelle, Colin, I'm grateful to you for stepping in."

Chelle took her coat. "We were glad to, Jessie. There are sausages and potatoes in the oven for supper. They'll be ready in about half an hour. Greer's already eaten, and we changed Martin's bandages this afternoon." For Martin, the most painful part of the process had been seeing how much it hurt Chelle, though she didn't flinch or falter. It felt like a lifetime had passed since she'd done the same thing for him yesterday.

They'd kept their distance through the day, both shying away from the tension that lingered between them, waiting to be sparked by any accidental contact. Martin had buried himself in the farm's accounts, still keenly aware of every sound and movement as Chelle worked her way through small chores and kept her eye on Greer.

He'd dreamed of Greer's birth last night, for the first time in months. Only this time it was Chelle's face he saw lined with pain, Chelle's eyes that lost their light as they looked at him, her hand that slipped from his.

He'd wakened in the dark, shaken, but something had shifted in him the night of the dance, just as it had the night Greer was ill. The dream was only a dream. What he felt when he kissed Chelle, when he danced with her, when he saw her with his daughter, was real.

*Brace up, lad. Colin is right.* He wasn't going to let Chelle go without taking a chance that she could care for him, even if the thought scared the devil out of him.

Chelle and her father stayed for supper. Afterwards, Jessie took Greer up to bed and Martin walked with his guests as far as the lane to see them off. When they reached it Colin went on ahead, while Martin took Chelle's hand to keep her with him. He remembered feeling like this with Eleanor, like they were the only two people in the world. He'd never dreamed it would happen again.

"Somehow, right now the Paxtons don't matter at all."

Chelle turned to him and took both of his hands in hers. "Martin, what did Dad say to you? You really took me by surprise this morning. Not that it wasn't very special."

"Colin said you'd had a young man at home who hurt you. I don't know what happened, Chelle, and I don't need to. I know you well enough for that. I just want you to give me a chance. We have as much time as it takes. I'll be here."

"Like a bad penny," Chelle said softly. "Do you remember saying that to me, the day after the fire?"

The light in her eyes made him desperate to kiss her again, but he'd promised to take this slowly. With an effort of will, Martin pulled his hands from hers.

"No. I don't remember much about that day, but I remember you being there." He ran his knuckles over the softness of her cheek. The contact alerted every nerve. It was time he went in. "I'll see you soon, lass."

Chelle hurried to catch up with her father, who was waiting halfway down the lane. Martin watched them out of sight, then returned to the house and took down his fiddle and bow. He closed his eyes and let his feelings find release through his fingers. The melody they drew from the old fiddle had an undercurrent of sadness, but overall it sounded joyful and young.

Jessie came down as he played the final bars. "Greer's asleep. I haven't heard you play that before."

"I haven't played it before."

Her rather stern mouth resisted grins, but a hint of one tugged at it now. "Chelle told me once that I had an imagination, but I don't need it to see what's happened while I was gone. My own two eyes are enough. I wish you luck, Martin. She's a good lass and a bonny one, and she'll stand no nonsense from you."

"You're getting ahead of yourself, Jessie." With worry settling on him again, Martin hung the fiddle on its peg. "I should tell you the Paxtons were here again today. Of course they found me and Rochelle here alone. They threatened to sue for custody of Greer."

"Did they?" Jessie's face brightened with angry color. "Drat my loose tongue! They were in the store this morning while I was telling Mrs. Bingham what happened to Charlotte. I should have said naught."

Martin dropped into his chair by the fire, stretched out his legs and let himself sink into the time-worn upholstery. "It's not your fault, Jessie. They were bound to make trouble on one excuse or another. I just hate to see Rochelle dragged into this, and she will be."

Jessie vented her feelings by bustling about, getting ready to set bread for tomorrow. "Let's not borrow trouble. The Paxtons may come to their senses, and Chelle's well able to fight back if they don't."

That was for sure and certain. It was one of the things Martin loved about her.

*Love.* He rolled the word around in his mind until he started to get used to it. Yes, he loved Chelle. Loved her warmth, her temper, her way with Greer. Loved her taste, the feel of her in his arms.

*Eleanor, my darling, it's time.*

\* \* \* \*

*November 15, 1861*

*Dear Trey,*

*We're having a regular autumn gale here today. "If Winter comes, can Spring be far behind?" It doesn't seem possible that the year is growing old, that it's been eight months since we left New York.*

*We've been able to keep up with the war news, thanks to the fortunate circumstance that our minister has a cousin in Boston who sends him copies of Harper's Weekly. Reverend Nelson knows you are in the army, so he passes them on to us. At last we're getting something more than the nondescript dispatches they print in the papers here. Dad and I pounce on those out-of-date issues like starving cats on a mouse. The news may not be comforting, but having no real news is ten times worse.*

*From what we read, it seems certain that you will have to fight come spring. As I told Martin yesterday, the Confederacy is fighting for its life with all the force of desperation behind it. Of course, you have no idea who Martin is. He's—*

"Chelle, you have company," Jean called from the foot of the stairs. Chelle put her pen and ink away and hurried down. She'd have to find words later to tell Trey about Martin.

He stepped into the kitchen as she reached it, with a gust of cold wind behind him. Chelle joined him by the stove and took his chilled hands in hers.

"You're half-frozen, lad."

She loved that she'd learned to imitate his broad Yorkshire, while her drawl was completely beyond him. His attempts to mimic her hardly sounded like English at all. He shrugged out of his coat and looked down at her with a light in his green eyes that warmed her from the inside out.

"That wind feels like it's blowing straight down from Greenland." With a gentle tug, Martin brought her a little closer. With his arms just out of bandages he couldn't hold her the way she knew he wanted to, which was just as well, with the whole family sitting at the table except for Jack, who'd gone to the store for the mail.

"There's plenty left of the raisin pudding I made for supper, and it's still warm. It'll stick to your bones for the ride home," Caroline said.

"You don't have to ask me twice, Caroline."

Brian pushed back his chair. "Take my seat, Martin. I fancy the fireside at the Crow tonight, along with a pint of Harry's bitter. Jean, will you come along?"

"Nay, you go on. I've a bit of a headache. I think I'll go upstairs."

Chelle caught herself rolling her eyes. Did they have to be so obvious? Her father stood and put on his cap.

"I'll join you, Brian."

Caroline set a bowl of golden-topped, cinnamon-scented pudding on the table and left the room without bothering to make an excuse. In less than five minutes Chelle and Martin were alone.

In the two weeks since she'd stayed at the farm they'd spent five evenings here in the kitchen. Chelle felt like he belonged in the house as much as she did. She couldn't have dreamed that they'd grow so close so quickly. She walked into his arms for a slow, sweet kiss that left them both wanting more. She couldn't doubt any longer that the attraction between them was real, but was it permanent? She touched his cheek and stepped back.

"Go eat your pudding. Would you like tea?"

Martin took his seat and put on a teasing grin. When he smiled, he didn't look like the same man she'd met on the fell in the spring. Of course, a large part of the change in him was due to Greer, but not all. No, definitely not all.

He started on the pudding, then paused as if considering a weighty question. "I don't know. I rather fancy Brian's idea of summat a bit stronger. Maybe I'll go down to the Crow after I've eaten. I was thinking of it any road, but I knew I'd be fed if I stopped here first. A man needs sustenance when he's out and about on a night like this."

Chelle stepped up behind him and put her hands on his shoulders. "If you eat and run Aunt Caroline won't have so much as a bread crust for you the next time you call, if she lets you in the house at all."

The wind rattled the kitchen window. A picture flashed into Chelle's mind of those gusts shaking the tent where Trey would sleep tonight. Martin noticed the sudden change in her mood and took her hand as she joined him at the table.

"What's troubling you, Chelle?"

With his hand lifted, she caught a glimpse of the web of scars that began on the underside of his wrist and disappeared under his shirt cuffs. Scars he'd accepted without a trace of the bitterness that had once consumed him. Chelle would have loved him for that alone, if she'd been sure she was capable of real love. The love he and Greer deserved.

"I was writing to Trey when you arrived. With winter coming, I worry about him."

"I know, but from what you've said of him, he's well able to take care of himself. Hold on to that." Martin tucked a lock of hair behind her ear and lingered to draw a lazy circle over the sensitive skin there. "If you're going to worry, I'll just have to see if I can distract you."

He proceeded to do just that, with another blindingly sweet kiss laced with the taste and scent of cinnamon. Chelle leaned into him, shutting out the world with Martin's taste, until the sound of Jack closing the yard gate brought them back to reality. He shut the kitchen door behind him, took the two of them in with a glance and cleared his throat.

"Now then, Martin. I see you're havin' some of Caroline's pudding. Chelle, where is everyone?"

Chelle tried for some dignity. "Dad and Brian have gone to the Crow. Jean went upstairs with a headache. I think Aunt's gone upstairs, too."

"Then I may as well join Colin and Brian for a pint. Tell Caroline if you see her. Here's the mail." Jack dropped three or four envelopes on the end of the table, did an about-face and was gone.

Chelle caught a glimpse of her flushed face in the window, her lips still wet from kissing. The sight made her blush even more fiercely.

"He almost caught us."

Martin wore a wicked grin. "But he didn't."

"He wasn't fooled for a second, and you know it." Chelle reached for the mail. A letter for Jean, one for Uncle Jack…her heart jumped when she saw her name on the third envelope in an unfamiliar hand. She wasn't corresponding with anyone but Trey.

When she opened it, all the glow faded from the evening.

"This is from the Paxtons' solicitor. They're suing you for custody of Greer, and they have a court date on December first. I can't believe they have the gall to go through with it."

Martin looked as angry as he had on that summer market day when he'd made Drew back down. "I can, though I've been hoping they'd given up the idea. Of course, someone has told them I've been calling here. They have a real spite against you, Chelle."

And because of her, he stood in danger of losing his daughter. Shame filled her, the deepest shame she'd ever known.

"Martin, I can't bear that I'm the cause of this. I care too much for you and Greer to do this to you. It would be best if you didn't call here anymore. Then you can just tell the magistrate that there's no longer any connection between us. Once Greer has been with you for a year or so, they won't stand a chance with a custody suit."

Martin took the letter, scanned it and tossed it on the table. "I told you before, Chelle, I won't be bullied and I won't have you blaming yourself for this. Damn." He got to his feet, shoulders tight with anger. "I'd better be off home. I've been out most of the day, and Jessie will have picked up the mail this afternoon when she and the little one were in the village. There will have been a solicitor's letter for me, too, I'll warrant. She'll recognize Mr. Slater's name, guess what it's about and worry until I open it." He shrugged into his coat. "I'll see you soon, lass. Goodnight."

He strode out. Major's hooves beat a tattoo on the cobbles. Chelle climbed the stairs and shut herself in her room.

Martin had come so far since he'd taken Greer home. She meant everything to him. He couldn't lose her now.

Chelle's writing case lay on the bed. She opened it, spread her unfinished letter to Trey on the nightstand and retrieved her pen and ink from the drawer.

*Of course, you have no idea who Martin is. He's Mr. Rainnie, Greer's father. I've gotten to know him very well. Trey, I know you left thinking that what happened between me and Rory was your fault, but I know now that our marriage wasn't meant to be.*

Martin had taught her that. Whatever the cost to herself, Chelle couldn't repay him by costing him his daughter.

As he expected, Martin got home to find a letter from Mr. Slater waiting and Jessie outraged. "That's rich, when you think of how they treated their own daughter," she snapped after Martin read the letter. "I'm surprised at the magistrate for even agreeing to hear them."

"So am I when it comes to that, but who knows what the Paxtons told Mr. Slater. Any road, we'll find out at the hearing. Go on up to bed, Jessie. There's naught to be gained by worrying. I'll be going up soon myself."

When Jessie had gone upstairs, Martin poured himself a drink and settled in his chair. He didn't expect to sleep, and he didn't. Through the window, he watched the sky over the byre flush pink with dawn, then went out to do the chores. He came in to breakfast and found Jessie none the wiser that he hadn't gone to bed at all.

The meal was barely cleared away when Hugh Paxton drove into the yard. Martin's foul mood took an immediate turn for the worse. He swore under his breath, reached for his coat and slammed the door behind him.

"Say what you came to say and be off, Hugh. You aren't welcome here."

Hugh climbed down from the seat and stood his ground, though from his expression it wasn't easy. "I take it you've received Mr. Slater's letter. Now you know I meant what I said the last time I was here. I don't want that McShannon girl raising Eleanor's child."

Martin took a deep breath and clamped down on his anger. "I don't believe you and Margaret really care a rap for Greer. This is all about Rochelle."

Hugh swallowed hard, but he didn't back away. "We know you've been keeping company with her. Delia Putnam has been telling all over Carston how you and Miss McShannon behaved at the harvest dance. She's not one of us, to begin with, and she's a brazen little wh—"

The furious rush of Martin's pulse drowned out the rest of the word. He lashed out with both fists and felt them strike flesh, hard. Eleanor's father landed in an unconscious heap on the cobbles.

"Christ." Rage still pumping through him, Martin stood over Hugh. As the rush faded, shock took over. Jessie came running from the house, shivering without a coat.

"Good Lord. What possessed you?" She knelt beside Hugh and chafed his wrist. "Don't just stand there gaping, get him into the house and go for the doctor."

Martin carried Hugh inside to the sofa and left him to Jessie's care. His ride to the village echoed the night Greer was ill, with many of the same thoughts racing through his mind. *Please, God, I can't lose her, too.* He'd never be able to live with himself if this cost him his daughter.

Dr. Halstead happened to be home. He took one look at Martin's face and grabbed his medical bag.

"What are her symptoms this time?"

"It isn't Greer. I just punched the daylights out of Hugh Paxton."

The doctor completely lost his professional demeanor. "The devil you did. Where is he? How bad is he?"

"He's at my place. He was unconscious when I left him. Jessie's with him. Come on, man."

Home again, Martin stopped on the doorstep to prepare himself for the worst. He couldn't fathom his relief when he opened the door and saw Hugh awake, propped up on pillows, holding a bag of ice to his jaw. Dr. Halstead hurried in and began examining him while Martin waited at the table with Jessie.

"He roused about five minutes after you left," she whispered. "He's sore and bruised, and in a rare temper with it, but that's all if you ask me."

Dr. Halstead joined them a few minutes later. "You're lucky, Martin. There doesn't seem to be any serious damage done. You'll be facing a simple assault charge instead of anything worse."

*Assault charge?* Of course. Hugh would have a much better chance of getting custody of his granddaughter with her father cooling his heels in gaol. A sentence of a one or two weeks was all it would take, and the simple facts guaranteed that.

Greer sat by Jessie's feet, playing quietly, a little subdued by the tension in the room. Martin picked her up and held her close while he took a few deep, calming breaths, then he handed her to Jessie and crossed the room to the doctor's seat beside the sofa.

"Hugh, if Eleanor could see us now, she wouldn't be pleased."

Hugh shifted the bag of ice on his face and raised his stone-gray eyes to Martin's. "Don't speak of my daughter to me. You've chosen to replace her with a creature that isn't fit to wipe her boots." He swung his feet to the floor and squared his shoulders. "When I leave here, I'm driving into the village to lay charges against you. Tell Mrs. Mason to get Greer ready. She's coming home with me."

Martin's hands clenched into white-knuckled fists. "No, she is not. Go and send the bailiff for me. That's your right, but as long as I have legal custody of Greer she isn't leaving this house. Now be off. I've already said you aren't welcome here."

Greer started whimpering at the sound of his raised voice. Once Hugh was gone, Martin scooped her into his arms.

"Sssh, lassie, it'll be all right. I swear. There now." He bounced her gently, looking at Jessie over his daughter's head.

"I'll sort out this mess somehow. Take good care of her, Jessie, for however long it takes."

* * * *

The smell of simmering applesauce greeted Chelle as she stepped into the warmth of the Fultons' cottage. Kendra shifted little Davy to one arm and gave the pot a stir.

"Come in and get warm. Would you mind holding him while I get this off the stove?"

Kendra looked a bit flustered today. Chelle took off her cloak and reached for the little boy, who immediately squealed in protest. She gave him to his grandmother, who sat in the rocker by the window.

"Come here, then, lad." Mrs. Fulton put down her knitting and settled Davy on her lap. "Have you been to the store, Chelle?"

"No, I thought I'd call here and get warm first."

Mrs. Fulton exchanged a look with her daughter. Was it just the stove's heat, or was Kendra blushing?

"You likely haven't heard, then. I—I'm sorry. I—"

Chelle's stomach plummeted. "Don't be sorry. Whatever it is, just tell me."

Kendra set the applesauce pot on the table and took a deep breath. "Well, I was in to Bingham's about an hour ago, and there were two Carston girls there. I didn't know them, but one called the other Delia. They were telling Mrs. Bingham that there was a fight at the Rainnie place this morning. Mr. Rainnie's in gaol for assaulting Hugh Paxton. They had plenty to say about you as well. They said you and Mr. Rainnie disappeared together at the harvest dance, and that there's talk going around about what happened at the Wilsons' the night Mrs. Wilson died, that her husband is saying it should be looked into. It's all because of the Paxtons' suit, of course, and I'm sure Mr. Rainnie was provoked, but…" Kendra's voice died away in embarrassment. She knew about Chelle's growing closeness with Martin and had teased her about him often enough.

Chelle's hands turned icy. If Martin had assaulted Mr. Paxton he must have been goaded into it, and Mrs. Wilson's death had been nothing but a natural tragedy, but the facts would be twisted to suit the Paxtons' malice, as would her few minutes alone with Martin at the dance.

"That would be Delia Putnam, and the other girl was likely Win Fuller. I met them at the dance, and it wouldn't break my heart if I never saw them again. They resented my dancing with Martin, and they showed it." She got shakily to her feet. "I'd better get home. I'm sure Jessie will be in to see us. I want to know what really happened with Mr. Paxton. If he was badly hurt—"

"If he had been, likely those two cats would have said so."

Clinging to that hope, Chelle hurried home. She wasn't surprised to find Jessie there with Greer, and the family looking shocked.

"Jessie, I called at the Fultons and they told me Martin was in trouble. What happened?"

Jessie confirmed what Kendra had said. "I don't know what Hugh said, but Martin decked him for it, good and proper. Knocked him out cold."

Colin wore a grim smile. "For a lad who hasn't used them much, Martin has a knack with his fists. Once he's free, he should consider trying his luck in the prize ring."

Caroline glared at him. "Hush your foolishness, Colin. So Martin's been arrested, then, Jessie?"

"Aye. The bailiff came for him about half an hour ago. When you put this together with that fight at the pub, it's likely the assault charge will stick."

"Mr Paxton will see to that, I'm sure." Chelle fought the urge to throw something. Of course, Greer was the one with the least to say and the most to lose in all this. "I'm going to see Martin right now."

\* \* \* \*

The Mallonby lock-up stank of urine and stale beer. Once the door to the cramped corridor closed behind Matthew Grant, Mallonby's aging bailiff, the only light came from the small barred windows high on the walls of the gaol's two cells.

Martin moved into the square patch of dusty sunlight falling on his bunk, grateful for its warmth. The November chill seeped right through the damp stone walls.

The farm would be taken care of. Gerry would come back; he hadn't found other work yet. Martin had sent a message to him when he'd come into the village with the bailiff. As for Rochelle, he'd asked Jessie to take the news to the forge herself. There wasn't much more he could do but wait for his hearing. That wouldn't take place until the next magistrate's court on the first of the month, a week away.

He closed his eyes, tilted his head back and breathed a curse. This would hurt Chelle more than anyone else. He regretted that much more than planting his knuckles in Hugh's face. If it weren't for Chelle and Greer, he'd be glad he'd punched the sanctimonious old goat.

Chelle. She'd put the music back in his life and the life back in his heart, but he wasn't certain she felt the same. He felt her passion with each kiss—she had fire in her, that was for sure and certain—but he sensed uncertainty, too. Why wouldn't a young, radiant lass like her think twice about taking on a widower with a child? With her light feet and that smile, Chelle deserved her share of dances and flirtations before she settled down. He didn't doubt that she'd had the lads on a string at home. And one of them had hurt her.

It would drive him crazy to sit here, helpless, and worry about Greer, so Martin called up an image in his mind of Chelle as she'd looked at the dance, with her smooth shoulders rising above the bodice of her blue gown, damp curls clinging to her forehead, her sapphire eyes glowing. Then he opened his eyes and saw her in the flesh, standing outside his cell with a blanket tucked under one arm, as if he'd conjured her there by magic. He hadn't even heard Matthew let her in.

"Chelle."

She pushed back the hood of her blue cloak and lit up the dingy corridor with her bright hair. "Jessie told us what happened. Are you all right?"

Her concern made Martin feel like even more of a fool. He crossed the cell, took the blanket from her and tossed it on the bunk, then reached the through the bars to take her hands.

"Me? I'm fine. Jessie would have had Greer with her. How did she seem?"

Chelle laced her fingers between his and smiled, a soft, encouraging smile that worked wonders to ease him. "You're cold. Greer is fine. She hasn't had time to miss you."

"I already miss her." With an effort of will, Martin released Chelle's hands. He wanted to hold her as much as he hated having her see him like this. "I'm surprised Matthew let you in here. He shouldn't have."

"He had no choice. You're allowed visitors."

"I'm glad to see you, lass, you know that, but you shouldn't be here. Hugh doesn't need any more ammunition against you than he already has."

She tilted her chin at him. "Don't be silly. I'm already ruined in the Paxtons' eyes. Jessie didn't tell me what Mr. Paxton said to provoke you, but I'm sure he said something. So you really knocked him out."

"Aye." In spite of the whole mess, Martin couldn't keep back a grin. "It was a real satisfaction."

"Oh, Martin." Laughter and regret mingled in Chelle's voice. "Dad says that when you get out of here, you should take up boxing. You don't know your own strength." The laughter faded. "When *are* you going to get out of here?"

"My hearing will be next week, in the same session as the custody suit. I'll probably get another week or two from the magistrate. I only hit Hugh once. He wasn't seriously hurt." Martin looked into Chelle's eyes, wanting to reassure himself as well as her. "Whatever happens, I'm not going to lose Greer. If Hugh wins custody, it won't be for long. I'll do whatever it takes to make sure of that."

Chelle wrapped her arms around herself under her cloak and looked away. "Martin, what did Hugh say to you? Was it something about me?"

"It doesn't matter." He took her chin in his hand and made her meet his gaze. "I'm as determined to keep you as I am to keep Greer. Make no mistake about that, lass."

A shiver ran through her. Was it only his imagination, or did she shrink away from him slightly? The chill seemed to strike Martin's heart, too. "Now go home before you catch your death. I'll be fine. I know Matthew well, and he'll see I don't want for anything. Go on."

Chelle lowered her eyes. "I'll be back tomorrow, Martin. Goodbye." She turned away and didn't look back. The corridor door closed behind her. Martin returned to the bunk and ran his hands over the thick wool of the blanket she'd brought him, thinking of running his hands over the silk of her hair, the satin of her skin.

It couldn't be plainer that Chelle still had doubts. Smart lass. He wouldn't push her for now, but as soon as this mess was straightened away he'd dig in his heels and do whatever it took to put her doubts to rest. Letting her go was not an option.

## CHAPTER 19

Out in the crisp, fresh air again, Chelle took a deep breath. Leaving Martin so coldly was the hardest thing she'd ever done—and the most necessary. If she'd stayed in that dismal hole of a gaol any longer, she doubted she'd have been able to keep her feelings from showing on her face.

When he'd made that comment about doing whatever was necessary to keep his daughter, it had come to her—the only thing she could do to help him. The Paxtons didn't really want Greer. They simply didn't want Chelle in their daughter's place. If she gave them what they wanted, they'd have no reason to follow through with their suit, and they might be persuaded to drop the assault charge as well.

Martin would be hurt, of course, but the wound would be much worse if he lost his daughter. As for Chelle, she'd never forget Martin's touch, his kisses, his music, but she already knew she wasn't the kind of woman who lost her heart completely. Her feelings didn't run that deep. She'd recover, though right now that was very hard to believe.

Her father was waiting for her in the kitchen when she got home. He took her cloak and put his arm around her.

"How is he, then?"

"As well as could be expected. He thinks it'll be two or three weeks before he's free." Weeks spent in a cell meant to hold drunks overnight while they sobered up. For a man used to spending most of his time outdoors, every hour would be hell, and Chelle was going to make it worse. "Martin's more concerned about the hearing next week than he is about himself. This is going to play right into Mr. Paxton's hands. People here might not like that man much, but they respect him." Picturing the light that had flared in Martin's eyes at the sight of her, she fought to hold on to her resolution. "I'm going to call on the Paxtons tomorrow and try to make them see reason."

Her father hung the cloak on its peg and turned back to her with a shrug. "It won't do any good, lass. You can't reason with folk like that."

"I know, but I have to try. It can't make things any worse for Martin, and that's all that matters. The morning's gone. I'd better get the mending done like I promised Aunt Caroline."

Chelle busied herself with chores for the rest of the day. Everyone else in the house was busy, too, so she wasn't pestered with questions. By bed time she'd tired herself enough to fall asleep, in spite of visions of Martin behind bars. If all went as she hoped, tomorrow he'd be free.

Free. Birds soared above her, dark shapes wheeling in a blue summer sky. When one swooped earthward, Chelle's eyes followed its descent. The crow landed on the still form of a soldier, sprawled beneath the merciless summer sun.

The same battlefield. As before, she was driven from one undignified remnant of humanity to the next, until she stopped by a dark-haired man dressed in blood-stained, butternut-colored homespun. The long, lithe form looked only too familiar.

She turned him over. Rory's gray eyes stared up at her, wide and sightless. Reeling, Chelle got to her feet. Her vision blurred. The field became Martin's front room, and it was him she knelt by, his bandaged arms resting on the quilt.

She shouldn't be here. She heard her mother's voice, firm and quiet.

"*Ma petite,* real love doesn't die that easily."

She smelled jasmine. The sunshine dwindled to the glow of the fire that crackled in the front-room fireplace at home, the sound blending with the rustle of the ivy against the window. Then the rustle became the hiss of rain hitting glass, and Chelle woke to the muted light of a wet November morning, her vision blurred with tears.

Was this about Rory, or about Martin?

The image of Rory lying on that field left her sick and shaken. When he'd offered her a choice, she hadn't chosen him. She couldn't risk failing again, not with Martin's heart and Greer's future at stake.

"I know what I have to do, Maman. I just wish it weren't so difficult. I love him—but I thought I loved Rory, too."

By the time breakfast was over, the rain had slowed to a drizzle. Chelle cleared the table, then wrapped up for her walk to Carston. Caroline gave her a quizzical look.

"Where are you off to in this weather?"

"I'm going to Carston to call on the Paxtons. I know," as Caroline's mouth flew open, "I'm wasting my time, but I have to try. I'll stop to see Martin on my way back. Don't wait lunch for me."

If the family had known just what she intended to try, they would never have let her go, that was certain. Chelle left Aunt Caroline staring after her. The five-mile walk to Carston seemed all too short, filled with thoughts of Martin and Greer. How badly was the little one missing him? How miserable had his night been?

Chelle asked the way to the Paxton house from the first person she met in the village. The elderly woman pointed out a cottage set back from the road. She walked down the short lane, gathered her courage and knocked on the door.

Margaret answered it. Chelle stepped inside uninvited to prevent the door being shut in her face.

"Mrs. Paxton, I'm not leaving until I talk to you."

Hugh came out of the sitting room, moving stiffly, his face badly bruised. His mouth set in a grim line.

"What are you doing here?"

Chelle swallowed the choking lump in her throat and found her voice. "I came to make you an offer. If I promise to end all contact with Martin and Greer, will you drop your custody suit and the assault charges?"

207

The Paxtons exchanged a glance, then Margaret wiped her hands on her apron, a quick, nervous gesture.

"How do we know you'll keep your word?"

"You'll hear quickly enough if I don't keep it, won't you?"

Hugh's bony shoulders lifted. "You've done little to keep clear of gossip, my girl. Why are you willing to do this?"

Chelle met his cold gaze and held it. "Because I know you don't really want Greer. What you really want is for me to stay away from Martin, and I care deeply enough for him and Greer to give you that if you'll drop your suit." It was on the tip of her tongue to mention Eleanor, but she thought better of it. "If you sue, you'll have a fair chance of winning, but only a chance. This way, you're assured of getting what you want."

She watched Hugh weigh her words. Was he still too sore and angry to forego making Martin pay for punching him? Margaret seemed willing to leave the decision up to him.

He touched the lump on his jaw and scowled. "Martin owes me for pain and suffering, but whether you choose to believe it or not, Miss, our main concern is our granddaughter. You're right about one thing. We don't want you near her. I daresay Jessie Mason looks after her well enough otherwise. I'm inclined to accept your offer. The child has already been uprooted once, and we don't fancy uprooting her again if it isn't necessary."

He was going to say yes. Chelle's relief mingled with sharp regret. *It can't hurt this much for long.*

"I agree. It would hardly be fair to Greer."

Hugh nodded stiffly. "Very well, then. I'll drive over to Mallonby this afternoon and see to it. But remember this— we'll be watching to be sure you keep your part of the bargain."

"I keep my word, Mr. Paxton. Goodbye." Chelle turned on her heel and left as quickly as she could. Knowing the Paxtons would be watching her from the window, she made herself walk down the lane at an even pace, without looking back. She waited until she was out of sight of the house to stop and give in to the pain overwhelming her.

*It's for the best. He'd be lost without Greer. But how long will I be lost without him?*

\* \* \* \*

Martin slid his empty plate and used cutlery under the cell door, grateful for one thing at least: Matthew's wife Liza was a decent cook. She might not rival Jessie, but he wouldn't go hungry while he was locked up. A small mercy, but not one to be taken lightly.

He returned to the bunk, lay back and fixed his eyes on the patch of hazy blue showing through his window. As he'd done all morning, he let his imagination take him out on the fell, with Chelle walking beside him, the wind whipping color into her cheeks, a smile on her lips. Martin held on to the vision until the corridor door creaked open.

"Visitor for you, Martin." He sat up. Matthew came down the three steps into the corridor, with Chelle behind him. Martin's breath left him with a rush. What was wrong with the lass? Her face was as pale and set as if she were facing the gallows.

Matthew picked up the plate and retreated. Martin came to the bars and reached for Chelle's hands, but she kept them down, fists clenched.

"What's the matter, Chelle? Something's happened. Tell me."

She swallowed, struggling to speak. "Yes, something's happened. I called on the Paxtons this morning. They agreed to drop the custody suit and the assault charge. You'll be free before the day is over."

His relief faded as quickly as it surged. Plainly there was more.

"I don't know how you managed it, but thank you. Thank you isn't enough."

Chelle's eyes brightened with tears, but her voice didn't falter. "You and Greer need each other. I couldn't let you run the risk of losing her. I promised the Paxtons I would stay away from you if they dropped the suit, and they agreed."

"You *what*?" In that instant, all Martin could feel was rage. He would have reached through the bars and shaken her if she hadn't stepped back. "Chelle, you know how I feel about you. I thought—"

"That I felt the same. Martin, I care about you, but since the Paxtons decided to sue I've been thinking about us, and I have to be honest." A tear rolled down the bridge of her nose. She wiped it away, squared her shoulders and looked him in the eye. "I don't care enough to marry you. Not enough for you to risk Greer's future. I'm sorry, but it's for the best."

"You're talking nonsense, lass. Every time I kiss you, it's…it's the same for both of us, I know that. These last few weeks with you… I never thought I could feel like that again."

Her voice dulled with sadness. "I know. I know there's a pull between us, but there has to be more. Martin, the last thing I wanted to do was hurt you."

Martin's anger dulled to the numbness of shock. He'd sensed her doubts, thought he could overcome them, but here she was telling him the plain truth. She didn't care enough to saddle herself with a ready-made family, and she was honest enough to say so. How could he blame her?

She moved a little closer. He reached through the bars and took her hand in both of his.

"You gave me my daughter, Chelle. I'll never be able to thank you enough for that. I'll never forget you."

"And I'll never forget you or Greer. Find a good mother for her, Martin. Goodbye."

She gently pulled her hand from his and walked away. Martin stood there, frozen, and watched her go.

He understood shock. He'd been there before. The pain would come later.

*You'll survive it. You did before, and now you've a daughter to raise. She's the only thing that matters now.*

**\* \* \* \***

Chelle knew she was in for a terrible time with her family when she broke the news. She wasn't mistaken. Surprisingly, Jean took her to task most severely.

"Chelle, how could you?! Martin isn't one of the boys you tormented at home. He really cared for you! There's a time and a place for flirting, but I've no patience with girls who take it too far."

Caroline chimed in. "If I'd had any idea what you had in mind when you went to the Paxtons'—"

"You wouldn't have let me go. That's why I didn't tell you."

Brian left the house in disgust. Uncle Jack said nothing, but his expression said it all. The worst was her father's disappointment.

"Chelle, I thought you were happy with Martin."

*Oh, if you only knew.* "I know, but I just didn't care enough. It's one thing to risk my own happiness, but I couldn't risk Martin's and Greer's. Dad, I think when the war's over and Trey is settled out West, I'll go to him. He'll need help, and if I keep learning from Aunt Caroline I'll be able to work as a midwife. We're a family of movers, like you said. Perhaps I'm not meant for a settled place like Mallonby."

"Perhaps not, but it's hard lines on Martin. But better now than later, I suppose."

"Yes. It isn't as if we'd been courting for a year. He'll survive, and so will I."

December came. The first snow fell, a light dusting that glittered on rooftops and powdered the fell. Mallonby people looked forward to a somber Christmas, with the mill closed and most families living on relief. Chelle threw herself into her work with Miss Westlake and turned a deaf ear to what little criticism reached her. The mill families could hardly cast slurs when she was helping to feed them, and she had little contact with anyone else.

She heard nothing of Martin. That, Chelle told herself, was a good sign. If he'd acted slighted, gossip would have run riot, but he didn't. He and Greer would be fine. She'd done the right thing, though she was still waiting to feel it.

* * * *

Kendra tucked the quilt around her son and crept from the bedroom. The lad was teething, and he'd fussed for the last three nights, but he'd fallen asleep at last. She lit the lamp and sat in the rocker, looking out into the darkness of the winter night. Mam had gone out to call on a friend, but she should be home within an hour.

Kendra hadn't known what to expect from motherhood, but she hadn't thought it would be lonely. Her old friends were lost. Chelle had enough troubles of her own to deal with lately, and it wasn't likely she'd come out in this weather, any road. Kendra felt a familiar spasm of longing for a visit from one of her old girlfriends, or Davy…When would Davy arrive on her doorstep? What would she do when he did?

His letters were friendly, but no more than that. Of course, hers had been the same. The money he sent was keeping the wolf from the door and she owed him for that, but he owed her, too.

The peace in the house felt wonderful. Kendra had stoked the small stove with coal before putting the baby to bed, and now it threw a comforting heat into the room. It was a good night to be counting her blessings.

Little Davy would be weaned soon, giving her more freedom. She'd be able to take in more work, and there were a few families in Mallonby and Carston who didn't care if the woman who did their laundry or sewing had a baby out of wedlock. Then, a few years down the road when the lad was in school, things would be easier. She'd do whatever it took to give him his chance.

The stove's heat made her drowsy. Kendra felt her eyelids droop, blinked and shook her head. She'd better get supper started if she was going to have it ready by the time Mam got home.

She was slicing bread when someone knocked on the door. Chelle, perhaps? Kendra hadn't seen her for a week. A chat before supper would help rub the dullness from a tired day.

She opened the door and stepped back in shock. "Davy! I wasn't expecting you yet."

"Uncle decided he needed me back right after Christmas, so he let me leave a bit early." Davy shifted his feet awkwardly and looked past her into the warm room. "May I come in?"

He looked older, and oh, he hadn't lost his appeal. Work had filled out his chest and arms, and he had more color now than when he'd been at the mill. He'd let his sandy hair grow a bit, and it suited him. The hazel eyes he'd passed on to his son held an uncertain light that threatened to melt her heart again. Kendra nodded and stiffened her spine. She wouldn't turn to mush in front of him.

"Aye, come in out of the cold." Oh, why couldn't he have given her some notice? This wasn't fair. Davy took a seat in the armchair and Kendra returned to the rocker. Silence stretched between them like a taut rope.

"I suppose the little one's asleep."

"Aye. I just put him down. He's teething right now and getting him to sleep isn't easy."

"What's he like?"

"He's a good baby for the most part. He's quick to laugh, and doesn't get out of temper easily." Kendra looked down at her hands. "Davy, thank you for the money you've been sending. I know you aren't earning a lot, and…"

"Kendra, you don't have to thank me. He's my son."

"Aye. I suppose you'd like to see him."

"Can I? Now?"

"Yes, if you're quiet. Come with me."

They walked into Kendra's bedroom. She turned up the lamp a little, then joined Davy by the crib. Looking down at the baby, he let out a deep breath.

"He's real now. That Sunday afternoon up on the fell, we made *him*." Davy reached into the crib, then pulled his hand back and turned to face her. "It was a warm afternoon for autumn, wasn't it? Do you remember, Kendra?"

"Aye, I remember. You can touch him if you want to, Davy. He won't wake. His tooth came through this morning, and he's tired."

He reached into the crib and ran a finger over one of his son's tiny hands. "Kendra, I let my parents send me away and left you here to bear my child alone."

"You offered to marry me, remember?"

"I said the words, yes, but I hadn't a clue what they really meant, and you knew it. I think I have a better idea now." He turned back to her with his lips in a firm line. "I had a long talk with my uncle yesterday before I left. There's a future for me in his business if I work hard. I'll be able to give our son a better chance than he'll have growing up here. Maybe I still don't know much about being a husband, and I know less about being a father, but I'll give it my best. Will you give me a chance?"

A knot formed in Kendra's chest. He hadn't mentioned any feelings for her, but for the baby's sake what choice did she have?

"Aye."

Davy studied her for a moment, then brushed his fingers over her cheek. "You don't look very pleased about it." When she didn't answer, his hand dropped to her shoulder. He pulled her closer, bent his head and brushed his lips over hers. "Are you only agreeing for the baby's sake, Kendra?"

He held her gaze. At her silence, Davy smiled and kissed the corner of her mouth. "We can be good parents, lass. And we can be good together. I've missed you."

He ran his tongue along the seam of her lips while his fingers played in the loose curls at the nape of her neck. Kendra couldn't fight off the hope that surged through her, any more than she could the pleasure of Davy's touch. She opened to him, hesitantly at first, then eagerly, hurt and fear melting away. He hadn't told her in words that he cared, but he was showing her now.

Still, she needed to hear the words. Kendra pulled back and smiled at him, a smile that she felt deep inside.

"Are *you* only doing this for the baby?"

Davy shook his head and laughed. "I do have summat to learn, don't I? I'm sorry. Kendra, I love you. It took me a while to realize it, but I do."

There was no fear in his eyes now. Blinking back tears, Kendra grinned and walked into his arms. "Don't let me go again, Davy. I don't think I could stand it."

Another slow, teasing kiss. "I won't. Now let's go out and wait for your mother. We want to be looking respectable when she gets here."

\* \* \* \*

"Chelle, we're going to be out of onions after I make the stuffing tomorrow. Would you mind running to the store? And pick up a newspaper for your uncle while you're there."

"Yes, Aunt. I may as well go now. I'm not doing much." Chelle dressed for her walk, took some change from Aunt Caroline's jar of butter money and started off, glad to get out of the house. Ever since Kendra had come to see her, brimming with the news that she and Davy were going to be married quietly on Boxing Day and return to York together, Chelle had felt restless and trapped.

She told herself it was just the prospect of losing her friend, but she knew better. Sadness seemed to have seeped into her bones and taken root there. Missing Martin and Greer hadn't gotten any easier with time, and the brooding winter twilight didn't help. The wind off the fell promised snow before morning.

"There you are, and oh, there's mail, too. A letter from your brother, I think." Mrs. Bingham reached under the counter and laid an envelope on top of Uncle Jack's newspaper. "Happy Christmas, Rochelle."

Her mood forgotten, Chelle stuffed the newspaper in her bag with the onions and snatched up the letter. Trey had addressed it to her, so she tore it open and read it as she walked home.

*October 20, 1861*
*Camp Marcy*

*Dear Chelle,*

*By the time you get this it will be winter. Things are more or less the same here. We haven't been told much, but the word is that we will be given our orders when the spring campaign begins.*

*In a way, I'll be glad. Anticipation is worse than reality, and everyone here is growing restless with drill, routine and cramped quarters. We get piecemeal information on the battles that were fought over the summer, but don't know what to believe. I don't doubt you're better informed than we common soldiers.*

*There was an outbreak of measles in camp this month and we lost a few recruits. I never thought I'd be grateful that we had measles when we were eight. I've been well, though if boredom were deadly I'd be six feet under by this time.*

*Now for the difficult part of this letter, Chelle. I can't put it off any longer. There is no easy way to say what I have to say, so I'll do it as briefly as possible.*

*A few days after our birthday in September, a party of high-ranking officers visited Camp Marcy. One of them had a young lieutenant on his staff. I'd been put in charge of looking after the party's horses, and when Lieutenant Carter returned for his, I noticed the knife at his belt. It looked familiar. When I asked him about it, he told me he'd taken it from the body of a dead Confederate cavalryman at Bull Run back in July.*

*I asked him to show it to me. Chelle, it was Rory's knife, the one with his initials engraved on the hilt. I know you've seen it. I'd recognize it anywhere. When I asked Lieutenant Carter to describe the man he'd taken it from, the description fit. According to him, it looked as if Rory had been killed instantly.*

*Chelle, I don't know what to say…*

Chelle stopped in the middle of the street, blinded by tears. A buggy rattled by, so close it brushed her shoulder, but she didn't move. Her heart threatened to burst through her chest, and she couldn't breathe. Then, suddenly, she couldn't stand still. She dashed her arm across her eyes to clear them and started running, out of the village, past the forge and out onto the fell. She came to the sheltered hollow where she and Kendra often stopped on their walks, sank to the ground and fought to catch her breath.

*It isn't true. Trey must be mistaken. It can't be true.*

She saw Rory as she'd seen him in her dream, staring sightlessly at the sky. They'd grown up together, and for nearly a year Chelle had loved him as much as she was capable of loving anyone, but she'd let him go in anger. Now he'd never know how much she'd cared.

She couldn't cry. To cry would make it real. If she started, she was afraid she'd never be able to stop.

Paralyzed with pain, Chelle sat there while the sun disappeared over the horizon. When the first fine sifting of snow began to fall, it didn't register. It began to settle thickly on her cloak, unheeded as she repeated the same three words over and over through chattering teeth.

"It isn't true."

"Get up, Tessa. There's a bait of corn waiting for you, out of this wind. Jump in, Gyp, there's a lad." Martin waited until Gyp was safely settled in the back of the cart, then urged Tessa into a trot. He'd just delivered a load of hay to the sheep. He'd never take his freedom for granted again, whatever the weather, but the cold wind had crept through to his bones and now it was starting to snow as if it meant it. Time for a warm fire and a bowl of Jessie's hot mutton stew.

He shrugged deeper into his coat and thought of Greer to warm away the ache in his chest. This time of day was the worst, just as it had been in the months after Eleanor died. It would take time to root Chelle out of his mind and heart. He hadn't realized just how much she meant to him until he'd lost her. The pain never really left him; the best he could do was to forget it now and then when he was with his daughter.

As the cart started down the slope to the river, Gyp stood and let out a sharp bark. Martin reined the mare to a stop and looked around him. He saw nothing but empty moorland, until his eyes settled on an odd-colored shape in a hollow off to his left. Then the shape moved. He jumped from the cart and walked toward it, Gyp at his heels.

"By all that's holy. Chelle!" He covered the last few yards at a run and knelt beside her. "What's the matter? Has someone hurt you, lass?"

She didn't answer. Martin unbuttoned his coat, pulled her onto his lap and folded the sheepskin around her, holding her against his chest. Shivering, she laid her head against his shoulder.

He saw no blood, no bruises. She didn't seem to be hurt, but she was half-frozen. He held her tighter and pressed his lips to her hair, part of him reveling in her sweetness even through his worry.

"Tell me what's happened, love."

Silence. Questions would have to wait. Martin gathered Chelle up and ran with her to the cart, bundled her onto the seat and climbed up. He took her on his lap again and sent

Tessa along the dark track as fast as he dared. Colin dashed out of the house as the cart rattled into the forge yard.

"Martin, what's happened to her? She should have been home over an hour ago. We thought she'd likely called on the Fultons."

"I don't know what happened. She doesn't seem to be hurt, but she needs warming badly. I found her out on the fell."

The letter fell from the folds of Chelle's skirt as Martin transferred her to Colin's arms. The color drained from her father's face as the paper fluttered to the ground.

"What is it, lass? Is it your brother?"

Chelle looked up. The anguish in her blue eyes stabbed at Martin's heart. God, how long would it be before he'd stop aching for her?

"No, not Trey. Rory."

Colin held her closer. "I'm sorry, love." His eyes met Martin's over Chelle's head. "Thank you from the bottom of my heart, lad. I'd best get her inside."

Martin followed them into the house. Caroline's hand flew to her mouth, then she hurried after Colin as he carried Chelle upstairs. Martin sat on the kitchen sofa and watched, helpless, while Jean scurried around, heating water and blankets. After what felt like an age, Colin came down, looking older than his years.

"She'll be all right. She's asleep. Will you stay for a drink?"

"Nay, Jessie will be waitin' supper for me. I'd best be off home." To stay here and not be able to be with Chelle, watching over her, would be pointless torture. Her family would look after her.

"All right, then. She won't be ready to talk to anyone before morning, any road. Thank God you found her when you did."

"Aye." Whether or not Chelle was part of his life, Martin couldn't imagine his world without her in it. Surely the love he felt for her went with her every day, even if she didn't know it.

It occurred to him that he'd forgotten to ask about the lad whose name Chelle had mentioned. "Was Rory her young man at home? The one she almost married?"

Colin nodded, his face taut. "Yes, he was."

"First her mother, and now this."

"She'll get through it." He put his hand on Martin's shoulder. "Come back tomorrow. She'll want to thank you."

Colin glanced behind him at Jack and Brian sitting at the table, then followed Martin out to the yard and held Tessa while he climbed into the cart.

"Lad, I'm worried about Chelle. She hasn't been herself since she broke off with you. I meant it when I asked you to come and see her."

Martin shut his heart to a rush of longing. She'd told him where she stood in plain English. Why make her tell him again? "I will, but I'm not sure she'll want to see me."

Colin shook his head. "We'll see. If you still care, don't give up on her."

Martin climbed onto his seat and picked up the reins. The smart thing to do would be to leave well enough alone. Pay a brief call, accept Chelle's thanks and get out. He didn't need any more grief. "I'll see you tomorrow." He sent Tessa on and left Colin standing there, watching him.

\* \* \* \*

Chelle woke in the grey winter dawn and sat up in bed. Her stomach rolled with nausea as memory flooded through her.

It was Christmas morning, and all she wanted to do was pull the covers over her head and stay here, nursing her emptiness. Would she ever feel young again?

Someone knocked. When Chelle didn't answer, the bedroom door opened a crack. "Lass, are you awake?"

Chelle swung her legs over the edge of the bed and reached for her robe. She knew well enough that the family wouldn't let her hide.

"Come in, Dad."

Her father crossed the room, sat on the edge of the bed and put his arm around her. "We've naught to hold on to right now but faith, you, your brother and me."

Chelle knocked his arm away and got up to pace the floor. She had to keep moving, stay ahead of the pain.

"Trey didn't know anything for sure. All his information was second-hand."

"Chelle, you know how unlikely it is that anyone else would have Rory's knife if he were still alive. It was marked with his initials."

"He could have been wounded and dropped it. He might have been in hospital and someone else might have been keeping the knife for him until he recovered. That man Trey spoke to might have just assumed Rory was dead, if it was him at all. He could be recovered by now."

"Lass—"

She stopped pacing and folded her arms across her chest, as if she could ward off the truth.

"Dad, I know. I just don't want to believe it." With a sigh, she sat beside him again and rested her head on his shoulder. "Do you remember the time back in the spring when I had that nightmare about a battlefield?"

"Nay, I can't say that I do."

"I'm not surprised. I didn't say much about it. I dreamed that I was looking for Rory, but I found Trey instead. He was badly wounded. I didn't tell you because I remembered what you told me about your mother, and I didn't want to worry you."

Her father stroked her hair. "We know Trey hasn't seen action yet, love."

"But I've had other dreams since, about Rory. He—he'd been killed, and now…"

Her father pulled away to look at her. Chelle saw fear flicker briefly in his eyes.

"Ever since we heard Trey had joined up, you've been afraid for him. So have I. It's only natural that you'd dream of him. Right now, with your brother still in camp, I'm more worried about you." He took her face in his hands. "You frightened us all last night."

"I know. I'm sorry." Chelle smiled for him and stood. "I'll be all right. It's Christmas Day. Let's not ruin it for the family. Go down to breakfast. I won't be long."

That flash of doubt she'd seen in his eyes stayed with her. He wasn't convinced that her dreams meant nothing, but Chelle was through making things harder for her father. She washed her face and put on the new navy wool dress she'd just finished a few days ago, left her hair loose and went down to the kitchen with her head high.

Not long after breakfast, Martin's cart pulled into the yard. Before he could come to the door, Chelle slipped out to meet him. He was the last person she felt like talking to, but she quite possibly owed him her life. She couldn't be a coward now.

Her eyes widened as she glanced around her. A thick blanket of snow lay over the yard and the open country beyond. She'd never seen anything like it. The storm clouds had packed themselves off, leaving everything glittering under a chilly blue sky. A breathtaking winter day, but a harsh one. Chelle found no solace in its beauty.

Martin got down, left the reins trailing in the snow and came toward her. An arm's length away he stopped, his eyes searching hers.

"How are you this morning, lass?"

"I'm better. Martin, I feel so foolish. If you hadn't come along—"

He stepped closer, his brows bent in a puzzled frown. "Foolish? Chelle, you were grieving."

"Yes, I was." Chelle fought the urge to step back. Being near Martin like this brought back every feeling, every memory of each time he'd touched her or kissed her. "You probably saved my life yesterday. What can I say? But nothing's changed." She saw the fresh hurt in his eyes and lowered her own. "Someone's bound to see you leaving here. You'd better go."

His face set, making him look very much as he had the first day she'd met him out on the fell. He climbed back to his seat and gathered the reins.

"Goodbye, Chelle." The words came out flat, with no feeling. Cold to the bone, Chelle went in.

## CHAPTER 20

Drew Markham looked around him with loathing. His father's farm had been the scene of the worst years of his life, but two years of hard labor in the mill had bought him promotion and escape. He'd only returned here twice since leaving, but what he'd heard yesterday had brought him. He'd sweated too much in these fields as a lad to be done out of what was rightfully his.

The farm lay tucked against the side of the fell, near the track leading to Carston. The stone house and byre stood as little altered by the years as the moorland around them, but Drew saw small changes everywhere he looked. The hood over the well needed repair, the gate that filled the gap in the yard's stone wall hung crazily on its hinges, and many of the cobbles in the yard were worn and broken. His father and brother hadn't been doing much of a job of keeping the place up.

He heard voices coming from the byre. Dad and Richard would be nearly finished with the morning chores. Drew turned and walked into the house to wait for them. He was through with milking and swinging a pitchfork.

He added a shovel of coal to the stove and sat at the kitchen table. The room looked as cheerless as it always had in Drew's memory, with the once-white curtains dingy with soot and no rug on the worn floor, which looked like it hadn't been properly scrubbed since the curtains were last washed. Dad wouldn't tolerate dirty dishes or neglected spills, but beyond that he didn't care much. Faded wallpaper curled away from the corner behind the stove, exposing bare plaster. God, how glad he was to be free of this place.

Boots clattered on the front step. Drew's father and brother came in out of the gray winter morning, blowing on their hands. At the sight of Drew, Richard's pale blue eyes turned sullen.

"Now then, Drew. Fancy you dropping by."

Drew's hackles rose, as they always did around his brother. They shared a father, but in no other way were they kin. Richard looked like his mother, black-haired and sharp-faced, while Drew resembled his father. Not that there had ever been much feeling between them, either.

Dad hung his coat on the back of the door and dropped heavily into a chair, while Richard filled the kettle from a bucket on the pantry cupboard. "So what brings you here? You've been scarce enough this past year."

"I heard summat in the village yesterday. Seth Brimsby told me at the pub that you'd said Dad was signin' the farm over to you. Was he tellin' the truth?"

His father gave Drew a hard stare. "Aye, it's the truth. What then? You couldn't get shut of the place fast enough."

*That's for sure and certain. What reason did you ever give me to stay?* "No, I couldn't. Richard can have the place and welcome as far as I'm concerned, but I want to know where my inheritance is going to come from. While I lived at home I worked as hard as either of you. I deserve something."

The contempt Drew remembered so well laced his father's voice. "You turned and walked out without a backward glance, never thinking of aught but yourself, just like your mother. I've naught for you, Drew. You gave up your rights when you left."

*Up yours, old man.* "I know there's some money in the bank in Carston. I see no reason why I shouldn't have a share of that, since Richard's gettin' this place."

"You've got your cheek, comin' here with your hand out after turning your back on us."

His father had always been able to intimidate him with his anger. Drew's throat went dry, but he was through backing down.

"How could I turn my back on you when you turned away from me before I was old enough to go to school? You and Mam couldn't get along, so you visited your spite on me. You've only ever had one son."

225

Before Drew could react, Richard lashed out with a blow to his face. The force of the blow snapped Drew's head back. He tasted blood and got up roaring. "You bloody sodding—"

"Mind your tongue with your father, or there's more where that came from!"

His head ringing, Drew looked at his father and saw no yielding in his eyes. Enough. They could cut him off without a brass farthing, but he was done with them. He'd never set foot on the place again.

"Fine. I didn't really expect any different. The two of you can rot here and be damned. I'm through with you. I won't be back." Drew raised his hand to his throbbing cheek and glared at Richard. "As for this, you'll be sorry, I promise you that. I'm off."

He stood quickly, sending his chair crashing to the floor, and strode out the door. Snow had begun to fall, but it didn't soothe his stinging face or cool his temper.

Panic started to seep through his anger. What if the mill didn't reopen? The payment he'd gotten from Westlake wouldn't go far. He'd been getting his groceries through the relief committee like everyone else, and the house he lived in belonged to the mill.

He'd told himself he wouldn't be greedy, wouldn't push his luck. All he'd wanted was to stick it to Westlake and get enough to compensate him for his lost income. He'd never counted on his family for any help, but now that the words had been spoken, he knew for certain that he was on his own.

He wanted out. He wanted to leave Mallonby and its memories behind, just disappear, and there was one simple way to do that. Get on a ship and go somewhere where an enterprising young man could make something of himself. Australia, or America. America…the Union was welcoming anyone who'd fight for them, but there was a better way. He'd go with enough money to keep himself out of the army and take advantage of the opportunities war offered. All compliments of Phillip Westlake.

\* \* \* \*

Chelle stopped at the top of the Westlakes' drive to brush some of the snow from her hat and cloak. Before Trey's letter had come, she'd promised to bring the records of the relief committee to Miss Westlake for her approval before the New Year. Chelle didn't feel like seeing anyone, but she couldn't go back on her word. All she had to do was deliver the account book and be on her way.

In spite of the snow clinging to the red brick façade and frosting the yew hedge, the Westlake home reminded Chelle of Cedarhill, the Munroe place at home. It had the same imposing feel. A maid with a passing resemblance to Jean answered Chelle's knock. She followed the girl through the familiar front hall. She'd called on Miss Westlake a few times on committee business, but the house never seemed to welcome her.

Inside, it wasn't any more elegant than the Sinclair place, but Chelle couldn't deny it was done up in excellent taste. A wine-colored, fringed oriental rug warmed the hall's parquetry floor. Mahogany furniture upholstered in deep red velvet brightened the dim space, lit only by weak winter sunlight coming through the open doorways of adjoining rooms, which also afforded glimpses of bright curtains as she passed.

Like Cedarhill, this home had dignity, but lacked soul. The Munroes had never mixed much warmth with their civility. She guessed the Westlakes didn't either, but she'd lost her dislike of Maria over the weeks they'd worked together. As conscious of her position as she might be, Maria really did seem to care about her father's employees.

The maid opened the door to a small, cozy room with lace-draped French doors facing the back garden, paper in a muted yellow stripe on the walls and a set of cream-upholstered Heppelwhite furniture grouped around the white marble fireplace. Maria sat at a small oval table, reading. She put down her book and looked up with one of her reserved smiles.

"Happy Christmas, Rochelle. Sit here by the fire. You've had a cold walk."

"Thank you, but I can't stay, Maria. I brought the account book. I've entered everything from the last food distribution meeting."

Maria took the book and turned to the most recent page of entries. "Everything looks to be in order."

"Good. I'll be going, then. Aunt needs my help this afternoon." Maria might think her rude, but Chelle wasn't in a mood to be good company. As for that, Maria looked troubled herself, as she had the last few times Chelle had seen her. "Happy Christmas to you as well, Maria. I'll show myself out."

Maria nodded and picked up her novel. Chelle closed the breakfast room door behind her and walked down the hall. Angry voices stopped her outside the door of Mr. Westlake's study. When she realized she was eavesdropping, she blushed and continued on, but not before she heard Mr. Westlake's words.

"I've no more time to listen to you. As of now, you are no longer in my employ. Get out of here before I have you thrown out."

She didn't hear his companion's reply. Not wanting to run into an angry discharged servant when she'd obviously been listening, Chelle hurried out. She walked through the village and past the Fulton's cottage, lightless and cold-looking under the grey sky. Mrs. Fulton had gone to York with Kendra for a few days to help her and David find a place to live.

Chelle had gone to Kendra's wedding and seen her off with all the good wishes she could muster, without saying anything about Trey's letter. She'd asked the family not to mention it to anyone, as she didn't want to be questioned or condoled with.

*Rory and Martin and Greer. Maman, I never thought life could hurt like this.*

\* \* \* \*

Drew slammed Mr. Westlake's office door behind him. His face burned with anger, while panic made his gut clench. He'd been so sure he'd be able to get more out of the man. Now he was out of a job whether the mill reopened or not, with barely enough money to pay for a steerage berth and keep him for two or three weeks when he arrived overseas. He'd have to take whatever work he could find, or else join the army. Drew had no intention of dying in a foreign war, and it enraged him to think that his slavery in the mill here had been in vain. Everything he'd worked so hard for was lost.

One thing was certain – before he left, he'd make sure everyone in Mallonby knew the truth about the fire. When he confirmed what many already suspected, they'd find a way to make Westlake pay, and Drew could sit back and watch it happen.

A flash of blue, disappearing around the bend in the road on the way to the village, caught Drew's eye. He knew that cloak. He'd seen it on the McShannon girl often enough to remember it. What was she doing out here? Past the Westlakes', there wasn't another house for two miles.

Drew looked down and saw the marks of a woman's boot heels in the snow on the doorstep. Tracks made by the same boots led down the drive toward the road. So she'd been here. What truck would a common girl like her have with the Westlakes? Oh, yes, she was on the relief committee. She must have called to see Miss Westlake.

Drew recalled hearing someone in the hall just as Westlake was telling him to leave. He'd assumed it was one of the servants, but now…It didn't matter. She hadn't seen him, and anything she might say would be lost in the general outcry about the fire. Drew dismissed the McShannon girl from his mind and headed into the village. The Split Crow was the place to begin getting his revenge.

Warm air enveloped him as he stepped inside. The pub was full of mill hands making the best of a less than cheerful holiday season. Martin Rainnie sat at the bar, a mug of ale in front of him. The sight of him spurred Drew's anger to another level. He took a breath, unclenched his fists and reminded himself that he was here for a reason.

He found a seat at the opposite end of the bar from Martin. "Bitter, please, Harry." The pub owner picked up Drew's coins and brought his drink without comment. Drew's eyes flickered to Martin.

*I'll see you again, Rainnie, before I put this place behind me.* He took a swallow of his ale and looked around the room.

"Right good crowd, Harry. Miss Westlake was generous with her handouts for the season."

"It's been slow enough." Harry shrugged and ran a rag over the bar. Drew raised his voice so that the people around him could hear.

"Aye, and who's to blame for that? Our own Father Christmas, Phillip Westlake. Well, I've got aught to say about him. If those insurance investigators had done their jobs, the man would be in prison right now. He set that fire with his own two hands. I was on my way back from the dance that night and I saw him standing at his window, watching our livelihood go up in smoke."

Harry dropped his rag. "I'd have thought you too sharp to bite the hand that feeds you, Drew. You'd best not be talking like that without proof."

"What I saw is all the proof I need, and Westlake doesn't feed me, not anymore. I quit today, though of course he'll say he fired me. I won't work for a man who nearly cost three people their lives."

The noise in the pub faded as heads turned Drew's way. The man next to him, Ben Thompson, a long-time mill hand, turned on his stool.

"You saw him watchin'?"

"Aye, plain as day. The fire was just startin' to catch. When I got to the village, Ethan had given the alarm and folk were already comin' out. I went along to the mill with them. You all saw me there."

Drew took a breath, waiting for indignation to spread through the crowd as quickly as the fire had spread through the warehouse. In the pause, Martin rose from his stool and took two slow, deliberate steps toward him.

"So you saw Westlake standin' in the window watchin' the fire, and you waited until now to say so? Why?"

Drew raked him with a look. "Do you think the investigators would have believed me? There was no evidence for anyone to see, and I had my job to protect. But I couldn't live with myself, so I went to see Westlake today and told him I was through."

A sullen, angry buzz swelled in the room. Martin's voice cut across it, dry and sharp.

"If you're telling the truth, you're no better than Westlake. If you'd come forward after the fire, perhaps he could have been charged. The investigators might have looked harder for evidence. I don't believe for a minute that you were afraid for your job. You decided to see what you could get out of him for yourself, didn't you?"

"It's easy for you to talk, Rainnie. You didn't lose your livelihood in that fire."

Martin rose, took two quick steps and grabbed the front of Drew's shirt, spinning him around. "No, but I came within a hair's breadth of losing my life. So did John and Ethan, but all you cared about was lining your pockets."

Ben Thompson looked Drew up and down in disgust. "I daresay Martin's right. You're no better than Westlake. All you care about is yourself." Ben turned his back on Drew and faced the rest of the room. "Lads, I think we need to have a talk with Mr. Westlake. Who's comin' with me?"

Martin released Drew with a push that bent him back over the bar and stalked out. Nobody commented. The other mill hands in the room gathered around Ben, shutting Drew out. He'd turned them against Westlake, but thanks to Martin, they'd turned against Drew at the same time. In one afternoon, he'd lost his family, his job and what standing he'd had in the village. There'd be no turning back now.

# CHAPTER 21

Martin covered the distance from the pub to the forge in less than five minutes. If he'd read the mood at the pub aright, he hadn't any time to waste wheedling his way into a meeting with Phillip Westlake, but his daughter would probably see Chelle without hesitation if she said it was urgent.

If Chelle would go to the Westlake place with him.

The thought of seeing her made his pulse race. Would he ever really get her out of his blood? In spite of his best efforts to prepare himself, he lost his breath when she opened the door. Chelle's hand tightened on the door jamb and her pupils dilated at the sight of him.

"Martin, what are you doing here?"

"Just listen to me for a minute, lass. There's going to be trouble at the Westlakes' and I need you to go with me to warn them. I'll waste too much time getting in the door if I go alone. I'll explain on the way."

He understood now why Chelle's father was worried about her. She was a little thinner and paler than she'd been in the fall, but more than that, the remote expression on her sweet face frightened him. He'd seen her sad, he'd seen her angry, but he'd never seen her look like that.

"The Paxtons—"

"Bugger the Paxtons. Chelle, Miss Westlake and her father could be in danger. Will you come with me or not?"

She lowered her gaze. "Yes, I'll come with you."

They took the path by the river to avoid being seen in the village. Martin suspected it would take half an hour or so for the crowd at the pub to work themselves up to forming a mob. It would take nearly twenty minutes to reach the Westlake place. As they hurried along, Martin told Chelle what he'd seen and heard at the pub.

"Drew never did have much good sense, for all his cleverness. He thought folk would hail him as a hero instead of tarring him with the same brush as Westlake."

Chelle shivered. "There's something in Drew that frightens me. He's more than just a fool and a boor. He's got meanness in him. Kendra felt the same."

They hurried on with no breath to spare for talk. When they reached the house, Louden answered the door and gave Martin a doubtful look.

"Is Mr. Westlake expecting you?"

Chelle answered. "I've come to see Miss Westlake. It's urgent and important. She and her father may be in danger. Is she home?"

"Yes, Miss. You and Mr. Rainnie may wait here."

They settled in two of the armchairs in the hall. Martin felt as if his might break under his weight. He shifted uncomfortably and glanced around him. Seeing the inside of this place would do nothing to ease the anger of Mr. Westlake's employees if they showed up here.

"I've never seen the like of this. Have you?"

Chelle gave him a half-smile, the first real response he'd seen from her. "Yes. When my brother was a small boy, he made friends with the son of the largest planter in our county. As we got older, Justin drew Trey and me into his social circle. That's how I met Rory. His home wasn't all that different from this."

Martin didn't answer. How could he ever have thought Chelle might consider making a life with him, when she might have had a home like this? Why would she trade servants and silk for chores and calico? She might be a plain farmer's daughter, as Colin said, but she had the grace and courage to hold her own anywhere.

His bleak thoughts scattered when Maria Westlake came down the staircase at the end of the hall. A pretty lass, it couldn't be denied, but to Martin's eyes Chelle looked just as much the lady.

"Rochelle, Mr. Rainnie, Louden said something about Father and me being in danger. What's this about?"

Chelle glanced at Martin, then drew a breath. "Maria, there's been some unpleasantness in the village today. Word is being spread that your father started the fire at the mill, and people are upset. Mr. Rainnie told me. We both thought you should know, so I came with him to tell you."

One look at Miss Westlake's face convinced Martin she knew the truth. He couldn't help pitying her, but there wasn't time.

"Miss Westlake, we need to speak to your father. Now. The two of you would be wise to leave Mallonby as quickly as possible."

Without a word, Maria turned and disappeared up the stairs. She came back with her father behind her, shrugging into his jacket. Martin felt a grim satisfaction as he saw the fear under Westlake's flimsy mask of annoyance.

"Mr. Rainnie. I'm glad of the chance to thank you personally as I have publicly."

"I don't want your thanks, just your attention. I was in the pub this afternoon, and Drew Markham came in. I'll warrant you've seen more than enough of him lately. Any road, he convinced the crowd that you set the fire at the mill yourself. They were getting to be in an ugly mood, and I thought you should know."

"Again, I owe you—"

Martin cut him off sharply. He was in no mood for civility. "You owe me naught. I know Drew told the truth. You don't give a tinker's damn about the people here and never have. Personally I'd enjoy seeing them deal with you, but you aren't worth going to prison for. I'm only here because your daughter doesn't deserve to pay for what you've done. Get her packed and off to London, and if you have any sense, go with her. I wouldn't see folk here suffer any more on your account."

Mr. Westlake flushed. "I'll prosecute anyone who threatens me or my daughter. That troublemaker Markham is simply spreading rumors."

"Then why did you pay him off?"

The color drained from Phillip's face as quickly as it had spread. Martin chuckled, a dry bitter sound that didn't relieve the anger pressing on him.

"Don't bother lying. You aren't good at it. Just pack and get out of here. There's no evidence to charge you, but you'll pay regardless." He glanced at Maria's stricken face. "Every day, for the rest of your life, I'll warrant."

Phillip's shoulders slumped. "Maria, tell Louden to see to my packing and send for the carriage. As quickly as possible. Then get Susan to pack for you." He turned to Chelle. "You've been a friend to Maria. Thank you for that. Now you and Mr. Rainnie had better go."

Martin answered. "No. We'll stay for a while. If that lot from the pub comes out, I want to be here to meet them."

Maria's face was pale with humiliation. "Rochelle, I'm sorry."

Chelle shook her head. "None of this is your fault, Maria. I wish you all the best in your marriage."

Mr. Westlake didn't protest Martin's plan to stay. In a few minutes, Maria and her father were ready to leave. Martin and Chelle stood beside Louden, watching the carriage rattle down the drive.

"I never guessed. As true as you live, I never had an idea. I can't think why. I've worked for him for ten years."

Martin shrugged. "Some folk you never really know. Let's get in out of the cold and wait. I don't expect it'll be too long."

They kept watch from the hall windows. Within fifteen minutes, a group of men appeared on the road. Martin shrugged into his coat. "Louden, it'll be best if you stay here with Miss Rochelle. The sight of you won't calm them any."

Louden nodded. Martin shot Chelle a stern look when she threw her cloak over her shoulders.

"You're staying here, lass."

"No. Don't bother arguing with me, Martin, there isn't time. They'll be less likely to forget themselves in front of a woman. Let's go."

Short of getting Louden to restrain her, there was nothing Martin could do, and she knew it. He stalked out the door with Chelle at his heels. They met the group of nineteen or twenty mill hands at the end of the drive.

Ben Thompson, the man who'd spoken at the pub, faced them with his feet planted in the snow, fists clenched. Martin held his gaze.

"Go home, Ben. You've come out here for nothing. Westlake and his daughter are gone. They're in their carriage, and they've got a head start on you."

"You warned them!"

"Aye, I did. Westlake's caused enough misery here already. I wouldn't see him be the cause of any more."

"Damn you, Martin, he's got it comin'!"

"True enough, but at what price? Do you want to go to prison or hang because of him?"

"That's fine for you to say. You've got your farm. He hasn't harmed…" Ben's voice trailed off as he remembered. Martin nodded.

"I'm scarred for life on his account, and I still say he's not worth it. Now that the truth's out, Westlake will likely sell the mill quickly. I have a feeling Miss Westlake will still want to help in the meantime."

"She will," Chelle put in. "Her father doesn't deserve any sympathy from you, but she does. Any harm you do here tonight will hurt her as much as Mr. Westlake."

Ben flashed Chelle a scornful look. Mary Tate's father stepped up beside him.

"It's easy for you to talk forgiveness. My daughter died of the hurt she got in that sod's mill. Why should his daughter get away scot-free?"

Martin shook his head. "You've never seen the day you'd harm a lass, Ephraim, and you know it. And if you could, is that what Mary would want?"

The mood of the crowd was changing. Martin looked at each man in turn as he spoke.

"I'm the last person to blame you for being angry. I'd like to give Phillip Westlake a taste of my fists as well as you would, but that won't bring your jobs back. I think that when Westlake's business associates in London find out about this, he'll suffer enough. Now, I'd prefer the fireside at the Crow to standing out here in the cold. If anyone cares to join me after I see Miss McShannon home, I'll treat."

Ben glanced at the Westlakes' home, then turned away with a shrug. "We'll do naught but hurt ourselves here, Martin, you're right about that. I'm going home. Maybe I'll see you at the Crow later."

In twos and threes the mill hands turned back toward town, leaving Martin and Chelle standing in the snow, surrounded by an awkward silence. Chelle's eyes were downcast, her hands wrapped in her cloak, her shoulders tense. Martin lifted a hand to take her arm, then halted the motion half-way.

"Come, lass, let's get you home."

After telling Louden the danger was past, they set out. Twilight had faded to a clear, moonlit winter night. Chelle fell into step with Martin as they started down the road.

"What do you think will happen now?"

"I suppose Mr. Westlake will spend a few days in London, waiting to see what happens here. Ben and the others will probably get around to asking for some legal advice. There are barristers who will take on cases like this for little or no payment. I heard of a couple in London while I was there. I expect the magistrate will give them some help."

"But there's no evidence. It's only Drew's word against Mr. Westlake's."

"Aye, but any road, Drew can be charged with blackmail. If he is, Westlake will have to testify, and that could lead to charges against him. He'll be shamed, if nothing worse. He won't want to come back here permanently, I'll warrant."

"I wonder what Maria's fiancé will think of this."

"Who knows? Depends on whether or not he really cares for her." Martin turned and looked at Chelle's face in the cold moonlight. She was too young, too bright and vital to look like that, so sad and defiant at the same time. Words tumbled out before he could check them.

"Like I care for you. Chelle, I can't tell you how much it hurts me to see you so unhappy."

Chelle met his gaze, her eyes wide and dark. She started to step back, but Martin had reached his limit. He gripped her arms through her cloak to hold her still. A shiver ran through her and into him.

"Martin, please, don't do this."

"Chelle, the Paxtons can go hang. This isn't about them. It's about you and me. Looking at you now, I think you lied to me the day you made that bloody fool agreement, and I was just as big a fool to believe you. I think you care for me as much as I do for you."

Color flamed in her cheeks and Martin knew he was right. Chelle spoke in a choked whisper.

"I told you I cared for you, Martin. I cared for Rory, too, but it wasn't enough. Now he's gone. You and Greer deserve someone who can give you more than I can."

Temper flaring, Martin gave her a sharp shake. "Chelle, I don't know what you're afraid of. It isn't the Paxtons, that's for sure and certain. I would have told them to do their worst if you'd given me the chance. Tell me."

Chelle jerked herself free. "Martin, I was completely honest with you that day at the gaol. If you can't accept that, I don't know what else to say. Now, please, for Greer's sake, leave me alone."

She ran from him, disappearing from view along the riverside path. Bloody hell. All he'd managed to do was make a fool of himself and risk trouble with the Paxtons again.

*You've lost her for good and all this time, lad. When will you learn to let well enough alone?*

# CHAPTER 22

Drew finished packing his duffle bag and looked around the cold, sparsely furnished main room of his cottage. He'd never bothered to make it comfortable. He hadn't grown up with comfort and didn't miss it. A good thing, as he had a harsh new beginning in a foreign country ahead of him.

It wasn't the prospect of toil that filled him with rage. He'd never been afraid of hard work. It was the injustice of it. When he recalled the look he'd seen last on Westlake's face, when he thought of the contempt his former workmates had shown him when he told the truth about the fire, he longed to hit someone—anyone.

No, not just anyone. Martin Rainnie. Drew had one last call to make before he left Mallonby behind. He intended to repay Martin for turning the crowd at the pub against him, and for his blows back in the summer. And this time, he was prepared. He felt in the pocket of his coat for the brass knuckles he'd bought a few years ago on a trip to York, and smiled as his fingers closed around them. Time to get a bit of his own back.

Drew shut the door behind him and walked through the village, still quiet in the dim winter morning. He'd find Martin at chores and deal with him away from the house. He'd stop short of killing the man, but not too far short.

As he neared the forge, Drew caught a glimpse of movement in the fenced yard. A flash of blue. Rochelle stood at the well, turning the windlass. She filled a bucket, set it on the step, then picked up a basket and disappeared around the side of the small stable.

Call him a small man, would she? Now was his chance to teach her a lesson. He knew Rainnie cared for her. They'd created enough of a stir in the village with their doings at the harvest dance. This would make Drew's revenge all the sweeter.

With an eye on the house, Drew stepped inside the gate. She'd gather the eggs and feed the chickens. He had fifteen or twenty minutes before anyone would think about looking for her. More than enough time. The snow muffled his footsteps, and if the girl heard anything, she'd assume it was someone from the house. He reached the side of the stable in four quick strides and moved along the wall. No need for brass knuckles here. He was going to enjoy this.

\* \* \* \*

Chelle had just finished gathering the eggs and turned to latch the door to the chicken coop when an arm snaked around her waist and a rough hand clamped over her mouth. A man's voice hissed in her ear.

"Make a sound and I'll kill you."

Chelle bit him, but before she could scream a heavy blow to the jaw sent her reeling into the snow. Then Drew was on top of her, slamming his fists into her body, forcing the air from her lungs. Chelle couldn't fight him. Her head swam with pain and lack of oxygen. Then another blow connected with her jaw, and she blacked out.

Martin looked up from his milking at the sound of Gyp's sharp bark. He saw no one in the yard, but something must have set the dog off. He left his bucket of milk in the aisle and walked to the door, with Gyp at his heels.

Drew Markham stepped into the doorway, smiling. Before Martin could get set, cold metal slammed him in the belly. He toppled backwards into the aisle as Gyp shied back into a stall. Drew followed Martin down, punching with both fists.

He saw stars as his head struck the barn floor, but he managed to roll away from Drew's next blow. The third struck Martin's ribs, but his surprise had worn off. He caught Drew's wrist and jerked it to the side, hoping to snap it, but Drew rolled with the motion and broke free. Martin realized he was facing a much more experienced fighter. Drew swung his metal-clad fist again and opened a cut on Marin's cheek.

"You'll look as pretty as the McShannon girl when I'm finished with you. I gave her a taste of the same on my way here. I wanted to give you both something to remember me by."

Martin had never felt such rage, but he didn't launch the flurry of punches Drew clearly expected. Instead, he scrambled to his feet, took a step back and smiled. "Is that a fact? I'm going to enjoy making you wish you'd never been born."

Breathing heavily, Drew got up. Martin sensed doubt in him like a predator smelling blood. The initial assault hadn't worked, and he outweighed Drew by at least twenty pounds.

*Keep your eye on his right.* Martin began circling his opponent, buying time while he caught his breath and his head cleared. When Drew feinted with his left and swung a right, Martin ducked and drove his head into the man's belly. As Drew fell, Martin caught his right wrist and twisted it. He felt the bones snap, heard Drew scream, and sailed in with both fists, battering his face and body until he flopped like a rag doll with each blow.

*Enough.* Martin drew a bucket of cold well water and bathed his face and hands. He felt like he'd been trodden down by a horse, but the rush of the fight kept him moving. When Gyp came whimpering out of his hiding place, Martin picked him up and held him close.

"It's all over, old lad. Come on, we'd better get this bit of filth to town." He carried Gyp out to the cart and set him on the seat, then lifted Drew and tumbled him into the back. He didn't know if he'd fatally injured the man or not, and he didn't care. The bastard had hurt Chelle. Martin hitched Major to the cart and drove to the forge as fast as the cob could move.

Colin met him in the yard, his face a mask of worry. With his heart thudding against his sore ribs, Martin jumped to the ground.

"How badly is she hurt?"

"We don't know. She's still unconscious. Brian's gone for the doctor. Christ, Martin, look at you. Has the world gone mad?"

"No, only Drew Markham. He'll be needing the doctor, too. I might have done the bastard mortal harm, I don't know. He came out to my place and jumped me. He told me he worked Chelle over. How long ago did you send for Dr. Halstead?"

"Only half an hour ago. Come in and sit down, you're about to keel over. Leave the garbage in the cart." Colin's troubled face lightened a bit as he looked over Martin's shoulder. "There they are now."

The doctor hurried upstairs with Caroline. Jack and Brian brought Drew in and laid him on the kitchen sofa. When he started to stir, Colin leaned over him and grabbed him by the throat.

"Lie still and keep your mouth shut, you son of a bitch, or I'll put a knife between your ribs and call it good riddance." Drew obeyed. Martin tended to the cut on his face, then joined the McShannons at the table.

"What's taking Dr. Halstead so bloody long?"

Colin tried to look reassuring. "Patience, lad. While we're waiting, why don't you tell us exactly what happened the other night out at Westlake's? Chelle wouldn't say much for all my badgering, and every person we talk to has a different story."

Martin briefly gave them the facts. "When it was all over, I tried to talk to Chelle again about us, but—" He broke off as Dr. Halstead appeared at the top of the stairs.

"She regained consciousness while I was working on her. She has a broken rib and another that's likely cracked, her kidneys are bruised and a few of her teeth have been loosened. I gave her a healthy dose of poppy. She's in for a miserable time, but her injuries will heal. We'll have to watch her for pneumonia. That's my main concern. Now for this one."

The doctor made no effort to be gentle as he set Drew's wrist and stitched a cut on his jaw. Martin smiled grimly at the news that Drew had broken ribs as well. If he died of pneumonia, it would be what he deserved. At the very least, Chelle wouldn't suffer alone.

After patching him up, the doctor volunteered to drive Drew to the gaol. When they'd gone, Martin faced Colin.

"I need to see her."

Chelle's father held his gaze for a moment. An unspoken message passed between them. They would get Chelle through this together.

"Aye, come along."

Caroline and Jean came out of the bedroom as Martin and Colin got to the top of the stairs. Martin wouldn't have thought shy, quiet Jean could look so angry. Then he stepped into the bedroom with Colin.

Rage swept all thought of his own hurts from Martin's mind. He wouldn't have known her. Chelle's face was bruised and swollen, her breathing shallow and ragged. He wanted to run down to the gaol and choke the life out of Drew, as slowly and painfully as possible.

Deep in a laudanum-induced sleep, she didn't respond when Martin touched her hair, spun silk between his fingers. Its scent wafted up to him, cool and subtle. God, he loved her. He would gladly have taken her pain on himself if only he could.

"Rest well, lass. Drew's paid for this." He lifted Chelle's hand to his lips. "You came to me when I was hurt. I'm going to stand by you whether you want me to or not." He sat on the edge of the bed and looked up at her father. "I know she cares for me, Colin. I'll stay by her for as long as it takes to make her see it."

Colin joined him and rested a hand on Chelle's shoulder. "I thought you'd feel that way. She's a luckier lass than she knows, Martin."

* * * *

She was in the playhouse at home, building mud pies with Cathy Sinclair and Clara Hughes. She heard her mother's voice reading. "O Wild West Wind, thou breath of Autumn's being." The rest of the poem flowed from her memory, Maman's favorite work by Shelley. But Greer was crying and Chelle couldn't listen any longer.

No, Martin would take care of the little one. He was right here beside her, holding her hand, his touch warm and comforting.

Dreams blended seamlessly with reality until Chelle surfaced in the muted light of a snowy morning, the lamp burning low on the nightstand. Pain knifed her in the side with every breath, her head throbbed and her mouth tasted abominable. The bedroom door opened and her father stepped in. He sat in the chair by the bed and touched her cheek.

"You're awake. How do you feel, lass?"

"Awful." What was the matter with her voice? She didn't sound like herself at all. "Dad, what happened?"

"You were badly beaten, Chelle."

It made no sense. Her mind felt too thick and sluggish to follow him.

"Beaten? When?"

"Three days ago. We've been giving you laudanum for pain. You've a broken rib and your kidneys are badly bruised. Do you remember anything of it?"

"No. Who would—"

"Drew Markham. He decided to take out his spite on Martin before leaving town, but he came across you first. There's one consolation, though. He looks a lot worse than you do. Martin beat him within an inch of his miserable life.

Drew's in the village lock-up, still punch-drunk and with a broken wrist and ribs. Martin took a couple of blows himself, but he's healing. He's been here most of the time."

"He has?"

Her father took her hand and leaned close. "Yes, he has. Chelle, if it's escaped your notice, Martin loves you."

What had Dad said? Something told her it was important, but she couldn't stay awake to puzzle it out. Something about Martin. He'd been here. That hadn't been a dream. Would he come again?

She fell asleep waiting for him.

Two days later, early in the white and rosy winter afternoon, Chelle sat up in bed worrying down some of Aunt Caroline's chicken soup. The doctor had decreased her dose of laudanum, leaving her sleepy but coherent. She'd just finished eating when Jean knocked on the bedroom door.

"You have a visitor, Chelle."

"Who?"

"It's Mr. Rainnie."

"Send him in."

Chelle steeled herself against a tumult of feelings as Martin came in. He wore a collarless grey linen shirt that set off his strong neck and the breadth of his shoulders, the stormy color of his eyes and the fire of his hair. Her heart beat painfully against her strapped ribs, responding to his presence, his voice.

"You look better today, lass."

"I look a fright, and you know it." Her gaze fixed on the healing cut on his cheek, the bruising on his jaw. Could anything be dearer than his face?

"You look a little the worse for wear yourself."

"Aye, well, you've seen me like this before." He smiled, and her heart did another painful flip.

"Yes, and on my account. I seem to keep giving you occasions to come to my defense, and you seem to keep stepping in to defend me."

He hitched his chair closer to the bed and brushed her hair back from her forehead, his eyes full of anger and regret. "I didn't defend you this time, Chelle. Drew got to you first. When he told me he'd hurt you...I've never wanted to kill a man before, but I honestly wouldn't have cared if I had."

His look suddenly made Chelle very conscious that she was in her nightgown. She pulled the quilt up to her shoulders and tried to fight off the blush rising to her cheeks.

"Martin, I don't remember much of the last few days, but I know you've been here. And I remember what you said to me that day at the Westlakes'." She'd thought of little else since waking this morning. Dreams, memories, fears. Now, with Martin beside her, they vanished, leaving only a calm certainty. An ocean away from the white farmhouse her father had built out of Georgia pine, her heart had come home.

"You asked me what I was afraid of. I want to tell you what happened between Rory and me."

Martin took her hand. "I told you before, I don't need to know."

"Yes, you do. Rory asked me to marry him, but he had conditions. He wanted me to cut all ties with my brother."

"That's a hell of a thing to ask."

Shock flared in Martin's eyes. Chelle squeezed his fingers. "I know, but he asked it. I thought I loved him, but I couldn't do it."

Martin let out an exasperated sigh. "How can you be so dear and so daft at the same time? So you've been blaming yourself and thinking that I'd want more than you could give, too."

"You and Greer. I love both of you so much. Every time I've needed you, you've been there. No matter how many times I pushed you away."

"I took a fair amount of convincing myself." Martin bent and touched his lips to hers, a slow, tender kiss that told her everything she needed to know. "I was determined to turn my back on Greer and on you. Rory will always be your first love, just as Eleanor was mine. But I don't care about being your first love, Chelle. I just want to be your last."

# CHAPTER 23

The rough spring wind greeted Chelle as she stepped out of the forge yard. She tucked her braid into her cloak and pulled up the hood as she followed the cart track onto the fell. In the past few days the grass in the pastures had turned green, and the air smelled of new growth. It would soon be a year since she'd arrived in Mallonby.

It felt like a miracle to be able to move freely again. She'd healed slowly after Drew's attack. He'd been charged and sentenced for blackmail and assault. Mr. Westlake had escaped charges, but only due to lack of evidence. Maria had written to Chelle, saying that her father was selling his business holdings and retiring, in much-reduced circumstances. He'd sold the mill soon after leaving Mallonby, and the new owner had wasted no time in getting it back into production. A friend of Maria's fiancé, Mr. Stratton was quickly gaining a name as a fair, if strict employer.

Chelle walked quickly to warm herself, past Martin's lane and across the river, until she came to the side path that led to his pasture. As she drew closer, she heard the bleating of new lambs and Gyp's familiar bark. Martin was here, as she'd expected.

She crested the low hill between them and watched as Gyp, working with his new partner, Carlo, cut a ewe with newborn twin lambs from the flock. Wearing the same coat he'd worn the first time they'd met, the raw wind ruffling his hair, Martin strode down and caught one of the lambs.

A warm, tingling sensation spread from Chelle's heart through her body. Hope. It had come back to her almost imperceptibly, like the green stealing over the drab brown of the fell. It quickened her step as she started down the path toward Martin.

Still unaware of her presence, he gave the lamb in his arms a quick inspection, then caught its twin. When he released it and called off the dogs, they ran to meet Chelle. A slow smile spreading across his face, Martin followed them.

"Mornin', lass. I wasn't expecting to see you out here."

"It's a fine morning for a walk, so I thought I'd surprise you. How is Carlo shaping up?" Chelle had given the young dog to Martin for his birthday in February. It looked as if they'd already become a team.

"First rate. I think Gyp appreciates the help. I meant to drop by the forge this afternoon. Tessa and Neely need shoeing. Will you be home?"

A different kind of warmth spread through Chelle in response to the light in Martin's eyes. All winter, while she healed, he'd been there for her, dropping by almost every evening, bringing Greer for visits. He'd gone to the Paxtons and told them to bring their custody suit forward again if they chose, but they'd better be prepared to explain to the magistrate why they'd withdrawn it the first time if they thought him an unfit parent. Chelle's bargain had actually worked in Martin's favor. She knew it was a foregone conclusion in the village that they would marry once she was fully recovered, but they had both been content to take each day as it came while their love blossomed and grew.

"Yes, I'll be home. Are you finished here?"

"Aye. Five lambings overnight, and all right as rain." They fell into step on the path, with the dogs chasing each other around them. Chelle recalled the day she and Martin had met, the anger and pain she'd seen in his eyes. She knew now what he'd been feeling. She'd felt it all for Rory over the past weeks, until grief had shrunk to a small, patient ache that would always be with her. An ache that would deepen joy, rather than destroy it.

There was something different about this morning. Perhaps it was just the spring. Chelle hadn't been out for a long walk since her injury, and the simple freedom of it stirred her blood. Martin seemed to feel it, too. The air between them crackled with the old tension.

Walking beside Martin, Chelle stole a glance at him. What she saw in his eyes made her breath catch. Then he reached for her hand.

"Winter's over, Chelle."

She swallowed the lump in her throat and nodded. "Yes. It's been a long one."

"Long enough. Come here, love." Martin drew her into his arms. His mouth claimed hers in a passionate kiss. Chelle slid her fingers into his hair and kissed him back with everything in her. When they finally had to stop, he ran his thumb over her lips and smiled again, a smile that made her heart flip and her legs turn to jelly. She rested her head on his shoulder, relishing his warmth, while her heart sang a melody as wild and sweet as any Martin could coax from his fiddle. At Christmas, she'd thought she'd never feel like this again.

No. She'd never felt like this before. She hadn't been capable of this kind of joy before she left home. She'd had to learn what heartbreak was first.

Martin pressed his lips to her hair, then stepped back and tucked a finger under her chin. "Chelle, I'm going to speak to your father this afternoon."

Chelle blinked back sudden tears. Rory would always be hers to remember, always young, a part of her memories of home. But this was home now, and she couldn't imagine a better future than loving Martin and Greer. She met his gaze and mustered a stern look.

"Don't you think you should speak to me first?"

A smug grin. "Why? You just gave me your answer. You're mine, lass, just as I'm yours. We settled that months ago."

She tilted her chin at him, crossed her arms and narrowed her eyes. "You're pushing your luck, Mr. Rainnie." But she couldn't pull away when Martin drew her back into his embrace.

"Am I wrong?" His lips brushed hers in a feather-light caress. Hers parted of their own accord, inviting him in. Martin pressed a teasing kiss to the corner of her mouth, then another, until she couldn't hold back a frustrated moan. He chuckled in triumph, then bent to nip at her lower lip. "I'm not, am I? Marry me, Chelle. Today. Tomorrow."

Chelle struggled to speak. With Martin's mouth teasing hers, her breath just wouldn't cooperate.

"Tomorrow! Aunt Caroline would never forgive me. Give me a month to get a dress made."

"A month. I was ready to wait six." Martin ran his tongue across the seam of her lips, then gave her the deep, satisfying kiss she wanted. "You aren't much of a bargainer, love."

Chelle wrapped her arms around him, laughed and kissed him again. "I'm not trying to be. I'm as impatient to be together as you are. Let's go. We'll talk to Dad together."

* * * *

They were married on a bright May morning in the old Mallonby church, with only Jessie and the McShannons in attendance. Martin had sent for a dozen white roses for the altar, but otherwise the only decoration was the spring sunlight streaming through the stained-glass windows. Tears glistened in Chelle's father's eyes as they left the vestry to begin their walk down the aisle. Greer marched ahead of them, stiff with importance, looking over her shoulder every few steps. Colin took a deep breath, paused and tucked Chelle's hand more firmly under his arm.

"Be happy, love."

Chelle kissed his cheek. "I will be, Dad. I just wish Mother and Trey could be here."

She glanced down at her pale blue organdy with its daintily embroidered bodice, ribbon-trimmed sleeves and skirt that draped simply but gracefully over her hoops. She'd sewn every stitch of the dress herself, always thinking how her mother would have enjoyed helping her. She closed her eyes on a sharp pang of sadness, but it eased as quickly as it had come. Her mother *had* helped her. Chelle had learned every stitch by watching her. Maman and Trey were here in her heart. Then she and her father reached the doors opening onto the aisle and she saw Martin waiting for her by the altar, saw love and pride blossom on his face, and she had no room in her thoughts for anyone but him.

He looked utterly out of place in his best suit and starched white collar. He took Chelle's hand and mouthed "You're beautiful. I love you." She mouthed back, "I love you, too." Greer sat in the front pew beside Jean and watched, wide-eyed, while they said their vows and put their hearts in each other's keeping. Then, when Martin took his wife in his arms for a heartfelt kiss, Greer escaped Jean's grasp, slid from her seat and tugged on Chelle's skirt to be picked up.

She lifted the little girl and handed her to Martin. Under Reverend Nelson's indulgent gaze, he enveloped his family in a hug. Then it was back to the forge for a wedding breakfast. While the family laughed and teased and ate, Martin's eyes kept meeting Chelle's, every glance making her more eager to be alone with him. Finally he stood and drew her up beside them.

"Time to take my wife home. Jessie, come to visit often. I'll miss you, and so will Greer."

Jessie had found a new position on a comfortable farm near Carston, but she'd made it clear that she didn't intend to let Greer slip out of her ken. Her dry answer made everyone smile.

"Aye, I daresay the little lass will miss me."

Chelle turned to the high chair beside her, untied the apron that did service as a bib and lifted Greer into her arms. Dressed in white muslin with a broad green ribbon sash for her walk down the aisle as flower girl, she beamed at everyone. She'd loved being the focus of attention at the church.

"She certainly will." Chelle would miss Jessie, too, but at present all she wanted was to go home with Martin and shut the door on the world.

Martin slipped out and brought Major to the door. Chelle gave Greer to Jean. "Be good, sweetheart. We'll see you after church tomorrow."

Jean grinned and gave Chelle a little push. "Go on now, and stop fussing. You'll only be three miles away. I looked after her when she was a wean, remember?"

"I know. I'm being silly. I'll see you tomorrow." After another hug, Chelle tied her cloak and stepped out with her father behind her. He helped her into the pony trap, then shook Martin's hand.

"Be good to her, lad, but I know I don't need to say that."

"No, Colin, you don't. We'll see you tomorrow." Then they were on their way home.

When they reached the farm, Martin lifted Chelle from the trap and carried her over the threshold. The house smelled of lemon, beeswax, and the pickle-jar full of wildflowers Jessie had left on the table. From the way the place shone, she must have scoured it from top to bottom. When Martin put her down, Chelle slipped her arm around him and looked about her with a full heart.

"Home. Martin, I loved this house the first time I set foot in it."

"That's because you belong here." He took her hands in his. "Now come here. If I don't kiss you, I think I'll lose my reason."

One heartfelt kiss led to another, and another. Lips strayed, hands roamed, until Martin scooped Chelle into his arms and carried her upstairs, mouths still clinging. More flowers waited on the dresser in his room. Jessie had made up the bed with a bright blue and white quilt and new, crisp linen sheets. Chelle turned them back while Martin shed his suit jacket and tie. Then they came together again in a warm embrace.

"Love, you have too many clothes on." His hand slid over her breast, his thumb teasing her nipple through the soft fabric of her gown. Chelle shivered and ran her fingers across his broad shoulders.

"So do you."

Between slow, tender kisses, Martin began working the buttons on her bodice. He undressed her slowly, giving her time to get used to the intimacy of it, though she hadn't asked for time. She ached for him to love her, burned to feel his hands on her. When she stood in just her shift, he ran his eyes over her with a mixture of desire and pure reverence.

"Chelle, love, can you possibly want me as much as I want you?"

"Oh, yes." Ready to melt with want for him, Chelle freed Martin's shirt from the waistband of his trousers and began undoing the buttons. Excitement made her clumsy, but finally she pushed the garment off his shoulders and pressed a kiss to the side of his neck. She felt the wild thrumming of his heart as she explored him lightly with lips and fingertips. Touching him was as arousing as the feel of his hands on her.

She loved the taste of his skin, his unique flavor. Her hands strayed, discovering the planes and angles of Martin's big body, undoing his trouser buttons, while he pulled pins from Chelle's hair and let it tumble around her shoulders. She dotted his chest with soft kisses while his fingers stroked through her curls. Then he stepped out of his trousers, lifted her shift over her head and gathered her close.

"You're lovely, lass. So beautiful."

"So are you." Chelle ran a finger down the ridged skin on one of Martin's forearms. His scars only made him dearer to her, reminding her how easily she could have lost him. She loved everything about him—the rusty curls that clustered on his chest and around his rigid eager sex, his flat, dark nipples, the silky warmth of his skin over layers of hard muscle. "You're perfect. I can't wait for you to love me."

He did, with a passion that left Chelle astonished and trembling, awash in waves of pleasure. She came back from the clouds with Martin lying in her arms, his back damp with sweat under her fingers, his tousled head on her breast. She held him close, trying to fathom how much she loved him. Heart, soul and body.

"Martin...I had no idea..."

"God, Chelle, you're glorious." With a deep sigh, he rolled her onto his chest. "I...It's been a long time. If I was rough, I'm sorry."

Rough? Chelle's body felt so loose and languid he could have pounded her to jelly and she wouldn't have cared.

"If you were, I didn't notice." She looked up and saw an absolutely sinful grin on Martin's face, propped herself on an elbow and tweaked his ear. "You're looking pleased with yourself."

His grin widened. "Why not? I haven't gone to bed at noon with a beautiful woman often enough to make it common."

Chelle trailed her fingers across his chest to tease one flat nipple. "Do you intend to keep me here all day?"

Martin chuckled, a deep, warm sound, and kissed her nose. "Don't tempt me, you wicked little slip."

They did stay in bed until twilight fell and their stomachs began to protest. Brian had come, done the evening chores and discreetly gone home. Chelle slipped into her shift, lit the stove and put the ham and scalloped potatoes Jessie had left for them in the oven to heat, while Martin, wearing only a pair of work pants, kindled a peat fire in the old fireplace and lit the lamps.

They ate by the hearth, sharing kisses in between bites. Afterwards, Martin took down his fiddle. Chelle settled beside him on the sofa. As he played, she heard lovers' voices, children's laughter, all the happiness that the years would hold.

"That's us, isn't it, Martin?"

"Aye, Chelle, that's us."

## *EPILOGUE*

November 1865

Chelle drew the curtains against the cold, rainy November night and turned back to the crib where her son slept, now that he'd outgrown the old Rainnie cradle. Traces of tears glistened on his soft baby cheeks in the lamplight. He hadn't wanted to be put down before Martin got home from his weekly music session at the pub. At eighteen months, Trey James Rainnie already had a definite mind of his own. With Greer in constant mischief and another little one due in three months' time, Chelle rarely had a moment's peace.

She tucked the quilt more closely around her son and ran a hand over his fine curls. With his dark hair and near-black eyes, he was so like her mother and her twin. As it always did, the thought brought mingled joy and sadness.

Trey had been badly wounded at Antietam in the autumn of '62. Chelle's dreams of him and Rory had proven eerily true. She'd never recall those battlefield visions without a shiver. She'd wanted to name her son James after Martin's father, but he'd insisted on calling the boy Trey.

"For luck. He'll meet the lad one day."

Trey's last letter had been written over a year ago, in the summer of '64. He'd sounded weary and, Chelle's instinct told her, very troubled, in spite of his assertion that he was well. And then…silence. Even with mail disrupted by the chaos of the war's ending, she'd expected to hear from him by now if he were all right. Slowly, inevitably, she'd begun to think of her brother in the past tense, along with her mother and Rory, part of another place and time.

She heard the front door open and close, shook off her mood and hurried downstairs to meet Martin. He hung up his fiddle case and shrugged out of his oilskin coat, smiling in spite of sopping hair and the cold water that had run down his back.

"Love, you're soaked. Who was at the Crow tonight?"

"It's a plain sort of night, that's for sure and certain. There were ten of us there, in spite of the weather. Jason came, and Malcolm Blake was back. He's over his bronchitis and able to sing again." He gathered Chelle close with one arm and laid his other hand over her swelling belly. "Are the little ones asleep?"

"Yes, finally." Chelle looked up into Martin's sea-colored eyes, saw a teasing glint there. "You look like the cat that stole the cream."

Martin chuckled and held her tighter, the scent of him warm and familiar. Behind them, the stove sent waves of grateful heat through the room. Chelle stood on tiptoe for a slow, lingering kiss, relishing the taste and feel of the man she loved more with each passing day. Then she stepped away.

"Out with it. I can tell you're hiding something."

"Clever lass." Grinning, Martin pulled an envelope from his pocket. Chelle caught a glimpse of the American postmark before he held it up out of reach. Her pulse started to race.

"That's from Trey!"

"What'll you give me for it?"

Without bothering to answer, she started tickling him. Martin couldn't fend her off and keep the letter out of reach at the same time. She finally snatched it from him, hurried to the table and turned up the lamp.

*Colorado Territory.* So Trey had survived the war's end and made the journey West safely. Chelle dropped into a chair, her fingers so clumsy with anticipation she could hardly tear the envelope open.

*Dear Chelle,*

*I'm sitting here by my fire, listening to a coyote calling down by the river about a mile away. It's a fine, still summer evening, one of those nights when I can't seem to believe that the noise I lived with for the last four years was real.*

*I'm now the proud possessor of a hundred and eighty acres of Colorado grassland, a hundred head of cattle and half a barn. And*

*Cloud. He made it through all the fighting with me, and I rewarded him by making him pull a wagon all the way out here. He hasn't forgiven me yet.*

*I still feel out of place here. Sometimes when I wake in the morning, I think for a few seconds that I'm at home, that the war was only a vivid nightmare. At other times, it seems as if this place is the dream and the war is reality, and I'm still in the middle of it. Still, I think, with time I'll learn to love this land.*

*I've got my hands full with work. I have five years to prove up on my claim, and I might need every day of it, but if I'm going to have a place of my own, this is my chance. I'm taking each day as it comes and trying not to look back.*

*The home place is gone. I found out through Army channels that it survived the war – only three places were burned in Morgan County – and I sold it to a man from New York. I think he plans to live there, if the Sinclairs, McAfees and Munroes will let him.*

Tears blurred Chelle's vision, tears of happiness and sadness mingled. It hurt to think of home belonging to strangers, but Trey had survived. He was safe, or at least he had been when he wrote, and if fate was kind she'd see him again.

She felt Martin's hands on her shoulders as he leaned over her. "Trey's all right, then?"

"Yes, he's all right. He's found a place to settle." Chelle laid a hand over one of Martin's as she read on. Trey didn't offer any explanation or apology as to why he hadn't written in so long, but he said enough for her to read between the lines. He hadn't written because he couldn't bear to until now.

*There's blood on my hands, Chelle. I need to feel earth on them again. Time will tell if any good will come out of the last four years. I don't know anymore.*

"He's physically well I think, but he's troubled, and he's alone."

Martin's lips brushed Chelle's hair. "He hasn't had time to come back to himself, love. What he's been through would have to shake him, but he comes of strong, stubborn stock. He'll get through it. You'll see."

Chelle folded the letter, stood and leaned into Martin again. With his arms warm and strong around her, she felt hope rising like a spring in March. Like the baby growing inside her. She'd found out where she belonged, and Trey would, too.

*You'll have your place, Trey. I know you well enough to know that. And when the time is right, you'll have so much more. Just like I do.*

# ABOUT THE AUTHOR

Jennie Marsland is a teacher, an amateur musician and watercolor artist and, for over thirty years, a writer. She fell in love with words at a very early age and the affair has been life-long. She enjoys writing children's fiction, poetry and lyrics as well as romance.

With a background in Animal Science and molecular biology, Jennie has been a lab technician and a science teacher at different times in her life. She is now pursuing her love of language as an ESL teacher, meeting people from all over the world and helping them learn to communicate in English. She finds it as rewarding in its own way as penning novels.

Jennie has always loved books that take her back to an earlier time. Glimpses of the past spark her imagination. Perhaps there's an archaeologist buried in her somewhere. Everyone has a story, and it's the stories of ordinary people that affect her the most.

Jennie developed a soft spot for Westerns by reading her father's collection of Louis L'Amour and Zane Grey novels as she grew up. She thinks they contain everything a girl – or a woman –could want...handsome, rugged heroes, spirited heroines and horses, but she's planning on trying her hand at other genres as well. So many stories, so little time.

She finds her inspiration in family stories passed down from her parents and grandparents, and in the beauty of Nova Scotia's landscape. When she's not writing or working she gardens, plays guitar and spends time with her husband, two cantankerous elderly cats and the most spoiled dog on earth.

Lightning Source UK Ltd.
Milton Keynes UK
176605UK00001B/43/P